"If we were characters in one of your books, what would be happening to us at this point in your story?" Carter asked.

Looking at her strawberry rather than at Carter, Khela answered his question. "I suppose what was supposed to happen would have happened already. My heroine would have slipped into the shower with the hero for hot, urgent 'first sex' in the tight, steamy confines of the shower stall."

Carter inhaled deeply through his nose, his eyebrows rising with the expansion of his chest.

Khela ran her knuckles along her thigh, unmindful of the way Carter's eyes followed their path. "The showerhead is on a flexible cord, so they would have had all kinds of fun with that. They would have spent at least fifteen-hundred words learning each other's taste, textures, and responses," she went on, "and then he would have surprised her by putting her pleasure first. And he'd know very creative ways to please her . . ."

—ༀ—

MR. FIX-IT

CRYSTAL HUBBARD

Genesis Press, Inc.

INDIGO LOVE SPECTRUM

An imprint of Genesis Press, Inc.
Publishing Company

Genesis Press, Inc.
P.O. Box 101
Columbus, MS 39703

Copyright © 2008 by Crystal Hubbard

ISBN: 13 DIGIT : 978-1-58571-326-4
ISBN: 10 DIGIT : 1-58571-326-0
Manufactured in the United States of America

First Edition

Visit us at www.genesis-press.com
or call at 1-888-Indigo-1-4-0

DEDICATION

This book is dedicated to Lucas Black, one of Alabama's best exports, and to Mike Taylor, in whom I found the heart, breath, mind and soul of my hero. And a robust knot . . .

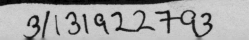

ACKNOWLEDGMENTS

Many thanks go out to the late Dr. Eugene Bell, whose Commonwealth Avenue property led me to fall in love with Boston's Back Bay, and to Beverly Jenkins, Brenda Jackson, Francis Ray, Rochelle Alers, and Donna Hill—goddesses all. A special thanks goes out to my readers, who constantly encourage me to keep spinning tales.

I also owe an incredible debt of gratitude to Sidney Rickman, who edited so much of my work, and to Doris Innis, who undertook the daunting task of editing Mr. Fix-It. I would not have been able to rebuild without her expertise.

While the cover of this book bears my name, by no means was it a solo endeavor. Deborah Schumaker and Valerie Dodson helped this book get into your hands and I thank them for their love, generosity, compassion, understanding, patience, and professionalism in the midst of some of my darkest days.

PROLOGUE

"What are you eating?"

"Nuh um."

"It doesn't sound like 'nuh um.' As a matter of fact, it sounds like suh um. Suh um cream-filled. A Hostess product?"

"What are you, their in-house police?"

"You're self-medicating with food and it's got to stop, or you won't fit into your dress tonight. Who're you mad at?"

"I'm not mad at anyone."

"Something's bothering you. I can hear you opening another package of HoHos."

"I'm hungry. I'm allowed to eat when I'm hungry."

"How many HoHos have you eaten today?"

"How did you know they're HoHos?"

"Because I know you. How many?"

"Eleven."

"Eleven individual HoHos or eleven *packages* of HoHos?"

"Packages."

"Thirty-three, huh? Who should I call first, Guinness or a cardiologist?"

"Ugh. Now I think I'm sick."

"What you are is stressed out. Is it the convention?"

"What convention?"

"The East Coast Writing Association Convention."

"Oh . . . that. I, uh, forgot all about it."

"Yeah, right. It's in seven hours. You're getting the Torchbearer Award tonight, you're the keynote speaker at tomorrow's luncheon, and you expect me to believe that you forgot about it?"

"I have to cancel. I feel hot and I've got a weird rash on my forearm. It wouldn't be right to expose all those conventioneers to my very contagious and possibly fatal skin condition. I think it's necrotizing fasciitis."

"Necro what?"

"Flesh-eating bacteria."

"Necro, please. You're not contagious, dammit, and you are going to this convention! Do you know what I had to do to get my date to agree to wear a tux tonight? I practically dislocated my jaw. It's a wonder I can even yell at you right now."

"Daphne—"

"You have to stop doing this to yourself, Khela. This isn't the first time you've been asked to attend one of these things. Why are you going mental?"

"This one is different."

"Because of the award?"

"No—Yes . . . I don't know!"

"Stop scratching."

"I'm not scratching!"

"Then you must be marching through cornflakes, because I can hear your raggedy fingernails raking across your ashy forearm."

"Look, if the only reason you called was to heave abuse at me, I don't have time for—"

"Khela . . . you don't have a date, do you? Is that what's bothering you?"

"No. To both questions."

"I thought you were going to ask the concert pianist who lives beneath you."

"He's too close."

"What about the fella you met in New York at Cameo's holiday party?"

"He's too far."

"Ask Todd, the babe from Calareso's."

"Emphasis on 'babe.' That kid's all of twenty-two years old."

"Ask that super super of yours."

"You want me to take a country-fried Schneider to a black-tie affair . . ."

"He may be a maintenance man, but he's no Schneider. That's one plumber butt I'd *pay* to see."

"I'm not taking my super."

"Ask Jay."

"I'm hanging up."

"Don't, I'm sorry I suggested him. It was a stupid joke."

"Yeah, on me. Jay and the parade of Jays that came after him are the reason I am, and forever shall remain, a dried-up old divorcée."

"Don't say that, Khela. True love is your stock and trade. Fate won't deny you one of your own. The only reason you haven't found it is because you've stopped looking for it."

"Then I'll never have it because I don't have the energy for the pursuit or the heart for more disappointment."

"Oh, you'll have it, all right."

"You sound so sure, Daphne."

"I'm sure that true love will find you now that you aren't looking for it. That's how it always works. Come on, who else can you invite to the convention? I know . . . ask Rocco."

"My boxing coach?"

"Sure. Why not?"

"He's too grunty. And he would spend the whole night asking people to punch him in the stomach so he can show off his abs."

"Well, I'm all out of suggestions, except for one. Who says you need a date, anyway? Go stag."

"Right . . . who needs a date . . ."

CHAPTER 1

*"She fastened her fondest hopes and most heartfelt desires
upon the kindness of a familiar stranger . . ."*
—*from* Practically Perfect *by Khela Halliday*

"I need a date." Khela smashed home the bone-white receiver of her classic rotary phone. Pacing a tight circle in her bright white kitchen, she chewed her right thumbnail. "I need a date and the pickin' is slim, especially this close to the convention."

One of Daphne's suggestions bounced around in Khela's head like a hyperactive child.

"It wouldn't hurt to ask him," she reasoned aloud. "He's definitely got the right look." And by "right," Khela meant hot. "Super" was as much a description as it was a job title when it came to her friendly neighborhood handyman. He was tall, solid and sculpted without being bulky with muscle. His hair, the color of sun-burnished wheat, always looked rakishly perfect, and every time his mischievous, brandy eyes danced her way, her leg bones turned to jelly. He was well-spoken, his pronounced Southern accent setting his speech apart from every other man she knew in Boston. He was well-mannered, but perhaps most important, he smelled good.

The day she moved into the building, she had caught a lungful of him. The combination of his own manly scent, his sandalwood aftershave and the pine banister polish he'd been working with had hit her like a shot of medical-grade narcotics. The initial sensory high she had enjoyed upon their first meeting had never completely waned, and she had never planned to act on it.

"We're friends," she told herself, further seeking to rationalize her decision. "Well, we're friendly, at least. I mean, what's the real harm? It's a one-time deal and the worst he can do is say no."

She returned to a small table in a corner of the kitchen and picked up the phone. Using her index finger, she searched the list of important phone numbers taped to the tabletop and located his number. Without realizing she was doing so, she held her breath as she dialed the string of digits. Pressing the receiver to her ear with her shoulder, she counted off the rings and clawed at a new crop of hives along her inner forearm. *One . . . two . . . three . . .*

"Hello?" answered a distinctly male, distinctly familiar voice.

"I need you," Khela blurted. She slapped her forehead. "I mean, I need you to fix something for me, Mr. Carter."

"Okay," he exhaled. "Let's see . . . I have a tile problem in C at one. I can come to your place after that. Will you be in?"

She closed her eyes and clutched the phone to her ear with both hands. He had said nothing provocative, nothing remotely interesting, yet, shaped by his Deep South drawl and spoken directly into her ear, his words gave Khela pleasant goosebumps.

"I'll be here until about six." She gnawed the inside corner of her lower lip. "Could you come around five, or do you have plans for this evening?"

"My tenants are my first priority, Miss Halliday. What's the nature of your problem?"

I need to get my pipes pumped, she thought, recalling what Daphne had said to him the last time she had summoned the super to Khela's unit.

"Miss Halliday?" he prompted.

She snapped back to attention. "Yes. Um . . . just bring your tool."

"Pardon me?" he replied, working around a cough or a chuckle. Khela couldn't tell which.

"Tools!" she quickly amended. "Your hammer. And your drill. All of your tools, not just . . . I'll show you what's broken when you get here."

A beat of silence, then "You're a very strange woman, Miss Halliday."

She sighed heavily. "You have no idea, Mr. Carter."

"If that's all, Miss Halliday . . ."

She dredged up the courage to spit out her last request. "Actually, there's one more thing I'd like you to bring with you. If you could."

"Yes?"

She squeezed her eyes tight. "A tux."

<hr />

Curiosity got the better of him, which was why he now stood at the door to unit A with his toolbox in one hand and a tuxedo in a plastic drycleaner's bag in the other. For three years, Khela Halliday had resided in the penthouse unit of the Commonwealth Avenue brownstone, and for the past few months, the unit, it would seem, was falling apart around her.

Her maintenance calls had become more frequent, as often as once a week since he repaired a dripping faucet on Valentine's Day, and only during visits from her friend Daphne. Of the two, Daphne was the most sociable, always opting to stay and talk to him while he fixed the ice dispenser or changed a light bulb while Khela retreated to the solitude of her loft.

Daphne's abundant strawberry spirals and playful, feline-green eyes certainly were appealing, but his preference for Khela's sultry, coffee-dark eyes and thick, cinnamon brown hair meant that his interest in Daphne would develop no further than a friendly flirtation.

Khela was the one who had made him stutter on their first meeting—the day she moved into the building.

He'd been in the foyer polishing the brass banisters. Because of their intricate design, it had been a tedious, meticulous task. The brownstone was built in 1889, but the brass banisters, glass chandelier, gilded mirrors and mahogany entry doors had been added as part of a Beaux Arts-inspired renovation in 1919. He took great pride in the appearance of his building and enjoyed taking care of it, but his love for the property paled somewhat the instant Khela Halliday walked into the enormous foyer carrying a Perrier-Jouët box packed with printer cartridges, sloppily stuffed manila folders, a miniature Easter Island head and a dusty lamp with a ceramic base made of unevenly stacked books.

Her shoulder-length hair pulled into two uneven ponytails and her face screwed into a determined grimace, Khela had lugged the box toward one of the brass-front elevators, a 1994 upgrade. "Let me get that for you," he'd offered, intercepting her halfway.

She'd gladly turned over her burden, and he'd easily hefted it onto one shoulder. Blowing an errant lock of hair from her face, she'd stood facing him, her hands lightly resting on her hips, and he'd had his first full look at her.

She was shorter than he, her head even with his shoulder. The rosy undertones of her burnished-peach complexion and her low-slung blue jeans gave her a youthfulness that made it impossible to tell if she was sixteen or twenty-six. Her dark, shining eyes had swept over him, and he'd fought the urge to check out his reflection in the glass door to make sure there were no sweat stains on his T-shirt or rips in his jeans. When she'd taken the corner of her full lower lip into her mouth, he'd caught himself staring and wondering how soft her mouth would be against his.

"Y-You're the new penthouse tenant, right?" he'd managed.

"Khela Halliday," she'd answered in a low, slightly raspy voice that did to his ears what her face had done to his eyes. Then she'd offered her hand. "Unit A, as of today. Good to meet you."

He'd shaken her hand, and in retrospect, he realized he probably had held it for too long. "I'm Carter Radcliffe. This is one of my buildings."

Her eyes had darted from the tool belt at his waist to his abandoned brass polish before she said, "So you're the man to call when my pipes get clogged?"

"Not exactly," he'd started, but before he could finish, sound and fury in the shape of a petite, firebrand redhead had stormed into the lobby.

"Khela!" Daphne had practically hollered, "you need to get out there and bust some chops. I need your television unpacked and plugged in by the time *Days* comes on. You promised that I could watch *Days* if I helped you move. Today's the day we're going to find out if Hope is really Hope or if she's an impostor hired by Stefano. I can't miss it!"

"Uh, would you mind just setting that box in the elevator, Mr. Carter?" Khela had asked. "I really do have to get back to the moving van before my friend Daphne chases off my heavy lifters." And with that, she had finished moving in and moved on.

In the years following, he'd never disabused her of the notion that he was the man to call when she needed help, even though the management service that ran the building had a maintenance team to handle repairs. And he had not bothered to correct her and Daphne's use of his first name as a surname. Since last Thanksgiving, they had begun to move past the cordial but dispassionate hi-and-bye exchange whenever they crossed paths and had actually engaged in meaningful conversation.

There was the cold November morning when she'd bumped into him standing in line for coffee at Dunkin' Donuts, and she'd asked him how the Patriots had fared against the Bills. Then there was the time in January when she had trouble hailing a cab, and he'd gotten one for her, but not before she'd told him that she'd spent her New Year's Eve reading a romance anthology about four couples that meet at a New Year's Eve ball. He couldn't remember a thing about the plots of the stories she had summarized, but he vividly recalled her regret at not having had a date for the night.

And now, three months later, as he waited for her to answer her door, he found himself eager to find out why she so urgently needed his tool.

Oh, yeah . . . and his tux.

Khela was one of the building's most intriguing tenants. He knew that she worked from home and that she wrote books, but he had never bothered to check one out. He assumed that she was successful. Once a 10,000-square-foot single family home, the five-story, limestone brownstone had been converted into four condominiums. At 3,400 square feet, Khela's was the largest.

The lower floor of her penthouse was wholly residential, with living, dining and sitting rooms, two bedrooms, two and a half bathrooms, the kitchen and a private terrace overlooking Storrow Drive, the Esplanade and the Charles River. The one place that had always been off limits to him was the loft overlooking the living room, and it was there that, during his maintenance visits, she retreated. Beyond Daphne's amusing chatter, he would listen to the faint click of rapid-fire notes from a computer keyboard in the loft, where Khela wrote whatever it was that enabled her to afford the pricey penthouse and fill it with top-of-the-line furnishings, not to mention an original Basquiat.

When she opened the door and ushered him into the living room, he glanced up at the loft, hoping to see more than the black tubular legs of a desk and the long white blades of a ceiling fan.

"This looks really good," Khela said, examining the tux through its plastic. "I'm impressed."

"You sound surprised." Carter draped the tux over the back of the butternut leather sofa.

Khela began unwrapping the tux. "I'm surprised that you were able to get one at such short notice."

"Hey, I go the extra mile to please my favorite tenant."

Her head swiveled to face him, the effect of his innocent words causing her cheeks to blaze. His cocky half smile and twinkling eyes gave her reason to suspect that nothing he said or did was entirely innocent.

His green T-shirt, with its white BOBCATS lettering, stretched across his broad chest and complemented his eyes; his faded, relaxed jeans fit him in all the right places. Khela spent a long moment studying the long muscles and corded veins standing out in the arm ending with his heavy toolbox. Before she got carried away imagining what it would feel like to trace his bicep with her tongue, she shifted her gaze back to his face.

"Whoever gave you this tux has excellent taste." She ran her fingertips over the finely woven wool. "I've seen designer tuxes that aren't this nice."

"It's Calvin Klein."

"Who did you get it from? The concert pianist in unit C?"

"Got it at a yard sale." He wryly smiled as he moved a step or two past her, farther into the living room. "So tell me what's broken and how I'm supposed to use a tux to repair it."

The picture of girlish innocence, she tucked a fingernail between her teeth and started for the darkened kitchen. Carter followed her, enjoying the view every step of the way.

Khela was cuter than hell in a sleeveless white tank, denim shorts and white Keds with white anklet pompom socks. Carter's thick eyebrows shot upward. He hadn't seen anklet pom-pom socks since he used to watch the girls' tennis team practice in high school. It was nice to see that they still made them, and that pretty girls with sexy legs still wore them.

Not that Khela Halliday was a girl. Falling into step behind her, he had no trouble seeing that she was most definitely a woman, confirmed by her supple curves and gentle swells in all the right places.

"You're staring at me," she said, not turning around.

"You're scratching," he observed, setting his toolbox on the spotless counter of the center prep isle.

She clenched both hands into fists, forcing herself to quit raking her nails along her inner forearms. "I have a condition," she said uneasily, inwardly cursing herself. "Half the time, I don't even know that I'm scratching."

He took her right arm and examined it, lightly stroking his fingers along the red weals her scratching had produced. Khela's skin responded, adding a fresh crop of goosebumps to the angry stripes joining her wrist to the crook of her elbow. "What is it?" he asked.

"The Ebola virus," she deadpanned. "I'll be dead by morning."

He snatched his hand away before logic kicked in. She'd be a bag of skin filled with liquefying organs if she had the Ebola virus. She would not be standing before him as flushed and pretty as a figure in an Impressionist painting. "Is something bothering you?"

"Why do you ask?"

"A lot of people get hives when they're stressed out," he explained.

"How 'bout you get to fixing my busted hotbox and leave my ugly welts to a dermatologist?" She pointed to the light fixture centered in her ceiling fan. "The lights went out for no reason."

"Yes, ma'am," he said, his expression and tone frosty as he went to the light switch and flipped it.

Khela took a deep breath to settle her nerves. She hadn't meant to snap at him, and she wished she could take her obnoxious remark back. He had come, so far so good, and he had a great tux, double good. Now all she had to do was ask him. "Mr. Carter?"

He raised an eyebrow as he went to the utility closet built into the wall next to the stove. "Yes, ma'am?"

"Stop calling me 'ma'am'," she complained irritably. "I'm younger than you are."

He opened the closet and unlatched the tiny steel door concealing the circuit breaker. "You don't know how old I am."

"You're thirty-two."

"Guess my weight, I'll give you a prize," he teased. "How did you know my age?"

"Daphne." Everything she knew about him came secondhand from Daphne, who would perch on a counter or lean against the wall and chitchat with him while he made his repairs.

Daphne was the reason unit A required so many little tweaks and adjustments lately. Breaking things was more fun than simply calling Carter and inviting him over for coffee and conversation like a normal person. Not that Khela should be throwing stones at that particular glass house. A normal person would be able to speak to Carter as easily at home as she did out on the street.

Even though she had lived in the brownstone he maintained for so long, she hadn't had cause to run into him often. She worked from her loft bedroom, which doubled as her office, and she could go for days without leaving her unit. Only since Christmas, when Daphne had been visiting and seen Carter shoveling the sidewalk, had Carter become a more frequent presence in her apartment.

There was something about him that rendered her guarded when he was in her home. He seemed too comfortable, as though he owned all he surveyed. When he turned his lovely, disquieting eyes on her, she felt as though she were his property. She should have been offended, but she wasn't. That fact alone was enough to send her into hiding whenever Daphne schemed to get him to unit A.

Khela shook off her feelings of anxiety to watch Carter work. She guiltily stared at the smoky-gray glass floor tiles as Carter surveyed the circuit board. He immediately zeroed in on the problem. The switch powering the kitchen was in the OFF position. He flipped it to ON, and the instantaneous reaction launched his testicles into his neck.

Every appliance lined up on Khela's long black granite counter was zapped to life: the blender, toaster, mini flat-screen television, radio, electric can opener, food processor and sturdy Kitchen Aid mixer whizzed, blared, screeched, whirred, grated and clanged in a cacophony of ear pollution that had Khela and Carter dashing around the room, hitting switches and buttons and snatching plugs from outlets.

When the only noise left was the whir of the ceiling fan, which spun in a blur at its fastest speed, Carter grabbed Khela's wrist and pulled her to the circuit breaker. "The next time you want to get me up here, don't turn on every dang appliance in the place. Just flip any one of these switches. You could have shorted out my whole building with this little stunt."

He released her wrist, gently brushed her aside and closed the door to the circuit board. He had his toolbox in hand and was heading for the door when Khela overtook him and blocked his way.

"Your accent becomes stronger when you're angry," she blurted. "Alabama, right? Decatur?"

Too late, he tried to hide the fact that he was impressed with her guess. "I was born in Decatur but I grew up in Speake."

"I've got family down South," she explained. "You learn not to confuse the Decatur speech with that of Tuscaloosa or Mobile."

"You got a good ear, Khela." He tried to nudge past her. "Are you holding me hostage, or . . ."

"I'm sorry I snapped at you," she awkwardly apologized. "Earlier. When you asked about my hives."

"Not a problem." He tried to step around her, but she glided into his path, holding her hands up.

"Mr. Carter, please. I'd like to speak to you for a minute." His forward momentum carried him right into her waiting palms, and the heat of her delicate hands through his T-shirt stopped him clean. "I do have something on my mind," she admitted. She abruptly dropped her hands, sticking them deep in her pockets as though punishing them for enjoying the feel of the hard muscle under his shirt.

"Does that something have anything to do with my tux?"

She nodded. Her ponytail danced and Carter wondered what that hair would feel like tickling his bare chest.

"I have an event to go to tonight," she explained. "It's formal, and it's business-related. I'm expected to maintain a certain image, and I can't show up without—"

"A date," he finished for her.

"Right." She swallowed nervously.

"So you're asking me on a date."

"Yes," she smiled. "No!" she quickly corrected, gesticulating madly. "No, this isn't a date. It's a favor. A great big-ass favor that I don't know how I'll ever repay you for if you agree to do this for me."

He turned a shoulder toward his tux to hide a sly smile. "Why do you want me?"

Because you're so frickin' hot! was her first response, which she suppressed only by biting the corner of her lip. She also couldn't tell him that the sight of him in his worn jeans made the backs of her knees sweat, or that the offhand, casual smiles that came so easily to his sensuous mouth made her thighs quiver. If he only knew that his scent was the one she recalled on particularly lonely nights when she sought a moment or two—or three—of battery-assisted tension release. "You have the right look," she said lightly. She scratched the back of her right hand and started pacing the living room.

"Miss Halliday?"

She stopped pacing, stopped scratching. "You can call me Khela."

"What time should I pick you up, Khela?"

She dazzled him with a smile of relief and gratitude. "The event organizers are sending a car for me at seven."

"That really doesn't give me much time to get home and slap on that tux."

"Where do you live?" she asked.

"Didn't Daphne tell you?"

"She said you lived nearby," Khela recalled, although nearby could be any number of towns—Somerville, Mattapan, Roxbury, Hyde Park, Jamaica Plain. Boston was one of the smallest big cities on the east coast.

"I live across the street," Carter said. "In the white limestone with the dark green awning."

"That explains how you get here so fast when Daphne calls," Khela reasoned. "Do you take care of that building, too?"

"Sure do," he said.

"That's a nice trade-off," Khela said, assuming that he lived in a Commonwealth Avenue townhouse for free as part of his compensation for his superintendent services.

"I'd better get a move on it," he said. "I've got a quick repair in another unit before I wrap myself in this tux."

The apples of Khela's cheeks deepened in color, and Carter had the feeling that her blush did not bode well for him. "Actually," she said, slanting her gaze away from his, "if we're going to do this right, you'll need a little more than just a tux . . ."

"How much more?" he asked warily.

"Do you have a suitcase?"

—∼∾∼—

Carter slung his weekender into the trunk of the limousine blocking one of the two lanes of westbound traffic on Commonwealth Avenue. Typical Boston, the inconvenienced drivers forced to pass in the one remaining lane communicated both displeasure and interest through loud, sustained honking.

Inside the limo, Khela sat with one leg elegantly crossed over the other, her hands neatly resting on the clasp purse balanced on her knee. She leaned forward and wrapped her knuckles smartly on the tinted window to speed the driver along. "How long can it take to stow a duffel bag?" she muttered irritably.

Looking more carefully out the window, she saw that the limo driver was laughing and talking to her date.

She pressed her lips together to hold back a smile. *I have a date, I have date!* she sang in her head. He was her super, but no one at the convention would know that. She was tempted to knock on the window to signal him to get into the car. The drive to the Harborfront Regency Hotel was short, but Boston traffic was unpredictable, and Khela didn't want to risk being late.

The driver slid into his seat and Carter entered the cabin. He positioned himself on the long bench seat, his back to the driver and facing Khela. They had agreed to meet at the car, so Khela was getting her first good look at him. And damn, did he ever look good.

She'd intended to school him on some of the authors he would meet, but her intentions evaporated in her contemplation of him. As good as the tux had looked lying across the back of her sofa in its drycleaner's bag, it looked a thousand times better on the man in front of her. He sat with the masculine elegance of James Bond, one leg hung lazily over the other, his right elbow propped on the armrest. Above his warm brown eyes, his hair had been combed off his face, the left-side part executed with almost surgical precision. His cuff links—surely imitation platinum, and the best she'd ever seen—glittered in the glow from the track of pale amber lights circling the roof of the cabin.

When he opened his mouth, Khela half expected him to offer her a medium-dry martini—shaken, not stirred. Instead, he offered an apology.

"I'm sorry I dawdled back there," he said as the driver smoothly eased the limousine into traffic. "Jerry makes a lot of runs to and from the brownstone, so I see him fairly often."

"Was he surprised to see that you were a passenger this time?" Khela uncrossed her legs and, after carefully rearranging the long skirt of her diaphanous gown, brought her feet up to the seat and made herself more comfortable. To Carter, she looked like a contemporary Aphrodite in repose upon the dark aniline leather.

He cast an amused glance at the privacy screen between them and Jerry. "Nothing much surprises Jerry."

Carter was thankful she had heard none of Jerry's snickered speculations as to why it had taken Carter so long to "bag" Khela, or his lascivious suggestions as to what activities they would engage in during the course of their "lovers' getaway."

Without disabusing Jerry of his pornographic notions, Carter had responded to his comments with good-natured chuckling. He was spending the weekend with Khela, but she'd made it perfectly clear that this was a legitimate business trip, not a monkey-business trip.

Not that Carter would mind a little monkeying around.

The pale apricot of Khela's gown imparted a warm honey glow to her bare arms and shoulders. The dusky-peach blooms in her cheeks came from nature rather than from a makeup counter; Carter knew that because they intensified in color the longer he stared at her. When she dipped her head, dangling diamond baubles at her ears glittered, and graceful tendrils of her upswept hairdo caressed her long neck.

He shook his head ruefully. From ingénue to starlit goddess . . . this possibly could be the longest weekend of his life.

"Exactly what kind of convention is this?" he asked, eager to think of something other than the way the subtle spice of her perfume made his heart jog faster.

"Ro—" she started, catching herself mid-word and finishing with "iting."

"Ro-iting?" Carter repeated with a James Bond-worthy lift of an eyebrow. "Never heard of it."

"I'm a writer, Mr. Carter, and we're going to a big writing thing." A rapidly spreading blush softened her prim delivery. "It's the East Coast Writing Association Convention."

"Hmm," he grunted quietly.

"What's that supposed to mean?" Khela was suddenly second-guessing her decision to bring him with her. To her own ears, the East Coast Writing Association Convention sounded like a gathering of authors wandering from vendor to vendor collecting pens, bookmarks and other promotional schwag from industry folk. There was that aspect to it, but there was the other side— the reason Association members turned out almost in full every year: the writers.

Every year, fiction and nonfiction authors in every genre arrived en masse in the host city to reconnect with distant friends, attend workshops devoted to their craft and career, celebrate their successes, and bemoan their failures, all in the company of their fellow artists. The pens, notepads, tote bags, T-shirts and complimentary books just happened to be dandy fringe benefits.

"It doesn't mean anything," he said. "I knew you were a writer, but I didn't know that you were so big."

Stung, Khela stared at him. She'd been amazed and gratified that he had accepted her invitation, but now a stab of regret made her head slightly achy. It wasn't her style to flaunt her career or her success, but for reasons unknown even to herself, she wanted him to be impressed. She would have settled for interested. Or at the very least, she'd hoped that he would have asked her about her work.

But in all fairness, they didn't know each other, not at all. He had come to her apartment fairly regularly lately grateful for her flirty friend. Khela smiled to herself, imagining Daphne's reaction when she saw her favorite super transformed into super sexy.

CHAPTER 2

"Men are the weaklings, the cowards, the frauds!
Women don't need to be rescued, it's that
men need to be heroes!"
—from Secrets and Sins *by Khela Halliday*

Daphne's pop-eyed, wide-mouthed reaction to the sight of Carter in his formalwear was nothing compared to Khela's increasing amazement—and alarm—at his performance as the evening progressed. From the moment he helped her from the limo and onto the red carpet in front of the Harborfront Regency, he had been gracious, charming, and had displayed the manners of a royal consort. He was the first man under the age of sixty that had ever pulled out her chair to seat her for dinner.

He was too good to be true.

He was also one of only two men seated at the head table, and the only one of her ten tablemates who wasn't a romance author.

Garland Kenny, who wrote lavish medieval historicals for Warrington House under the name Margaux LaPierre, was almost two feet shorter and a hundred pounds heavier than Carter. Garland seemed just as captivated by him as the eight women were.

"All this industry talk must seem terribly boring to you, Mr. . . . ?" Garland ventured halfway through the first course—an endive salad with caramelized onions, apples, spiced pecans, goat cheese and sherry-walnut vinaigrette. "I'm sorry, but Khela neglected to give us your name," he smiled, revealing two rows of ultra bright capped teeth.

"Forgive me, Garland." Khela leaned over her untouched salad. "This is—"

"Carter Radcliffe," Carter interrupted smoothly, with a devilish grin at Khela. Her expression of mortification and the reappearance of another ferocious blush made him take one of her hands in both of his and pat it as he undertook an explanation. "When Khela and I first met, she thought Carter was my last name. She called me 'Mr. Carter' for years before she realized that Radcliffe is my family name. She still calls me Mr. Carter from time to time. But only when she's feeling particularly fond of me."

Khela quietly cleared her throat and then introduced her other tablemates even as she wondered why Carter had yet to release her hand.

"Tell me, Carter," said Martine Kendall, one of Cameo Publishing's best-selling Regency authors, "are you a writer, too?"

He chanced a glance at Khela, who was staring resolutely into her salad plate. "No," he said simply. The rest of the table waited in vain for him to elaborate. He took a bite of his salad instead.

Khela looked at him, pleased at how relaxed he seemed with nine pairs of expectant eyes boring into him.

At fifty-five, Martine was handsome in a dated Alexis Carrington from *Dynasty* kind of way. Early in her career she had flourished as a mystery writer, and Khela knew that Carter's unembellished "No" would not keep her at bay.

"Carter is a jack of all trades," Khela hurriedly explained. "When people have, uh, problems, they come to him. And he fixes them," she finished lightly.

His hand tightened around hers as he rested it on her thigh. "Actually, I handle the operation of—"

"You're a troubleshooter!" Garland chimed in gleefully. "A genuine corporate runabout. I should have guessed." He pointed his fork at Carter. "The cut of the suit never lies. You're corporate, not creative like the rest of us here!"

Garland's guffaws drowned out the polite laughter of the women. Khela was glad to see that Garland's interruption derailed Martine—so glad, her hand relaxed within Carter's.

"Let's talk about something other than work," Martine said with a roll of her heavily lined eyes.

"I had contemplated slipping out for an update on the Red Sox–Yankees game," Carter said, sitting back and hanging his hand over the back of Khela's chair. When his thumb brushed softly over the skin between her shoulder blades, her ever-present blush began to burn. "But honestly, Ms. Kendall, I'm enjoying all the shop talk. It's surprisingly stimulating."

His thumb continued to ignite sparks of heat that traveled beyond Khela's cheeks. He splayed his fingers, drawing his fingertips lightly over her bare shoulder blades until the warmth of his hand came to rest on her right shoulder, close to her neck. Khela turned her face slightly to the right, and his index finger whispered along her jaw. A pleasant shiver moved through her.

"You're a man," Carmen Almeida said to Carter. Carmen wrote multicultural romances under the pen name of Carrie Fiore for Cameo's Sizzler line. "I need a man's opinion." She cast a disdainful glance at Garland, who was using the flat surface of his knife as a mirror to tidily twist one end of his Snidely Whiplash moustache. "I'm working on a novel about a woman who isn't sure which of two men fathered the child she's carrying."

"Why darlin', that hardly sounds romantic," offered Kitty Kincaid, a sixty-something author from Georgia who cultivated the same Southern belle image she assigned to the heroines of her lengthy, Savannah-based historicals. She pressed the diamond-laden fingers of her left hand coquettishly to the base of her throat. "But I suppose anything goes in those hot-blooded contemporaries you churn out by the dozens, Carmen. I myself would never create a leading lady of such questionable morals."

Carmen's long blue-black hair was arranged in fetching layers of curls atop her head. Elegant tendrils of her hairdo quivered with subdued anger, which sent color rushing to her terra cotta skin.

Writers rarely criticized each other's styles and genres, at least to their faces, but the tension had begun brewing between Carmen and Kitty at the start of the evening, from the moment Carmen's *A Hard Man Is Good to Find* and Kitty's *The Cutlass and the Corset* were listed as nominees for the much-coveted Romance Reader's Choice award . . . the engraved crystal teardrop now sitting at Carmen's right elbow.

"Kitty," Carmen began sweetly, "you stick to your thirty-year-old antebellum virgins and I'll keep peddling realistic characters modern women can identify with."

Black-clad waiters glided in to replace their salad plates with the second course, and the table was spared Kitty's response. Carmen, who had selected the grilled Maine lobster tails with orange chipotle vinaigrette, returned her attention to Carter.

"If you were one of the men in the situation I described, what could the woman say or do to make you sympathetic to, rather than disgusted by, her predicament?"

January Rose—her actual name—injected her thoughts on the subject. "I know your work, Carmen, and I know you." She gave Carmen an approving wink, and the heavy laugh lines about her dark eyes deepened. "There's no way you have your heroine knocking boots with two men." With a sly look at Carmen, she added, "Unless they were identical twins."

Carmen's brow lifted. "Very perceptive, Rose," she grinned. "In my manuscript, my heroine—unbeknownst to her, of course—is drugged at a party, and has sex. She's sure it was with the man she's been dating, until she turns up knocked up, and the man's twin claims that he was the one who was with her around the time the baby was conceived. Even worse, he claims that *she* was the one who seduced *him* at the party."

"Clever," Garland said as he piled cucumber, dill and champagne compote atop a sizeable bite of the salmon he'd chosen for his entrée. "Clear-cut villain at work."

"Carter?" Carmen prompted. "How would you react to being told that your twin brother could possibly be the father of a baby you desperately want to be yours?"

He finished chewing a bite of his grilled chicken and touched his napkin to his lips. "I suppose my gut reaction would be to distance myself from both my brother and the woman. But loving both, I'd have to find a way to forgive and accept the situation. A brother is blood. That's an unbreakable bond. And if I loved this woman . . ." His awareness of Khela suddenly became keen and he felt her gaze on him. "If I loved her, I know I wouldn't let her go. No matter what."

He met Khela's eyes then, and he didn't notice the way his response left the table spellbound.

"What are your thoughts on the subject, Khela?" Kitty asked.

"I—I . . ." she stammered. Thoughts? She had none. To produce thoughts, one had to be capable of thinking, and with the soft golden light from the chandeliers sparkling in Carter's eyes, Khela's brain relinquished control to parts of her body residing well below her brain. "I . . ."

"Khela?" Carter stroked the backs of his fingers along her cheek. "Are you okay?"

Another pleasant shiver coursed through her before she could snatch her gaze free of his. "I-was-just-thinking-about-the-exploding-genitalia-of-the-drone-honeybee," she said in a rush, her hand trembling as she raised her water goblet to her mouth and took long, noisy gulps.

"I beg your pardon, honey?" Kitty drawled.

"That certainly bears explaining," Garland chuckled.

"Nature has interesting ways of ensuring parentage." Once again, embarrassment set Khela's face on fire from the inside out. "There are thousands of male honey-bees—drones—in a hive, but only one female. Competition for the queen is fierce, so to make sure that her babies have only one daddy, nature devised a bomb." The table, Carter especially, was intrigued, so Khela went into greater detail. "When the drone mates with the female, he sticks his palp—"

"Now it's my turn to beg your pardon," Carmen deadpanned. "What's a palp?"

"His reproductive organ?" January guessed, peering at Khela over the top of her purple-rimmed half-glasses.

"Right," Khela said. "When he consummates the deal with the queen, the process eviscerates him. The drone dies at the moment of climax."

"What a way to go," Garland said under his breath, winking at Carter, who almost spat out a mouthful of grilled asparagus.

"No other male can mate with the queen because the dead drone's palp blocks entry," Khela said. "Nature found a foolproof way to ensure parentage."

January whistled. "Suicide. The ultimate proof of paternity."

"The Argentine Blue-Bill has a spiny penis with a bristled tip," Khela went on, "kind of like a bottle brush. These ducks are pretty promiscuous, and scientists theorize that the tips evolved as a way to remove the sperm of previous ducks when an Argentine Blue-Bill male mates with a female."

"Ew," Carmen chuckled.

"My dear Khela," Kitty gushed, "you never fail to entertain and educate, and when I look at you here with this handsome, adoring man stuck to you like hair on a biscuit, I am persuaded that you truly are a torchbearer for romance."

The Torchbearer Award would be presented after dessert, and with two courses remaining, Khela felt her time was running out. She had no appetite, and now that Kitty had actually mentioned the award, Khela literally felt as though she were suffocating. She plucked the napkin from her lap and dropped it atop her chicken. "Would you please excuse me?" She sprang from her chair and was halfway to the exit before Carter and Garland could even stand.

"I like your friends."

Khela inched closer to the narrow strip of flat stone separating a pair of the two-story windows forming the harbor side wall of the banquet hall. With Boston's skyline puzzled together in glittering lights before her and hundreds of guests enjoying raspberry sorbet enrobed in

Belgian chocolate behind her, Khela was ready to gnaw her own leg off to escape the upcoming award ceremony.

Carter's appearance at her side calmed her—a little.

"You didn't have to follow me." Her fingers dug into the flesh of her upper arms, and she shivered. "I just needed some air." Of course, if she'd known that the April night would be so chilly, she would have run to the lobby instead.

"Ms. Kincaid seems to think she offended you in some way," Carter explained.

"Go in and tell her I got the vapors. She'll appreciate that."

Carter peeled off his jacket and draped it over her shoulders. His proximity, his clean woodsy scent in the jacket and the weight of it covering her in warmth down to her knees almost made her turn and bury herself in his embrace. Even though she remained still, he must have sensed her need because he rested his hands on her shoulders and gave them a comforting squeeze.

"Are you still cold?" His breath caressed her left ear.

"No." The breeze carried away the quiet syllable.

"But you're shivering." His hands moved to her upper arms, raising goosebumps under the jacket to prickle her skin.

"I'm nervous," she lied, before truthfully adding, "I'm really not looking forward to standing before all those people at the luncheon tomorrow. Tonight's different. I don't have to make a speech. All I have to do is stand there and look pretty and grateful."

"I have a feeling that you'll be fine."

Khela turned then, her gaze met his, and before he could cloak his expression with indifference or merriment, she translated the look in his eyes: she had managed the pretty part. She gripped the lapels of his jacket, pulling it closer about her shoulders.

"Uh . . ." Wishing that he still had his jacket to hide the evidence of his reaching attraction to Khela, Carter shifted his eyes toward the banquet room. The lights had dimmed and three soft beams from overhead illuminated the podium set on a stage lining one wall. "I think you're on soon."

He discreetly opened one of the glass doors just enough to hear the matronly president of the national Romance Authors of America Organization finish up her spiel.

"Once every ten years, the romance writing arm of the ECWA nominates five authors to whom we are indebted, for without their brilliant stories, hard work and dedication, the genre of romantic fiction would cease to hold its own against those who refuse to acknowledge it as a legitimate form of literature. Most of you know who you are."

A soft rumble of chuckling traveled through the darkness. Khela almost applauded the president's words. Many of the writers in the room, specifically those published by university presses, had a tendency to openly joke about romance.

"Khela Halliday's debut novel, *Satin Whispers*, was a Cameo Publishing Private Collection release ten years ago, when she was a twenty-one-year-old senior at

Fieldcrest College in St. Louis, Missouri. That book landed on the *New York Times* and *USA Today* bestseller lists and led to an unprecedented seven-book deal with Cameo Publishing. The rest, as they say, is history. Ten years and eighteen books later—fourteen of them best-sellers—Khela has written for Cameo's Private Collection, Treasury, Whisper, Sizzler and Unlaced lines, and next year, her first young adult series will debut with Cameo Sass books."

The president paused for a round of polite applause. "Khela has made us laugh, cry, think and wonder, but most importantly, she has made us believe in the power and possibility of true love," she continued. "Tonight, we honor one of the best among us. Without further ado," the president said proudly, "I'd like to present our guest of honor, Ms. Khela Halliday, with the Torchbearer Award for Excellence in Romance Fiction. Congrat-ulations, Khela!"

The banquet hall exploded with applause, startling Khela into Carter's arms. Her ears ringing and on fire, she allowed Carter to escort her back into the room and up to the stage.

The moment took on a dream-like quality, as though she'd been swept into a fairy tale, or worse, one of her own over-the-top romances. The skirt of her diaphanous gown tickled her ankles as she climbed the three short steps, assisted by Carter, who handed her off to the ECWA pres-ident. The gilded chandeliers, the marbled floor, the women in jewels and ball gowns, the men in dapper tuxedos and cutaway coats—it was too awesome to be imagined.

At a table in the middle of the room, Daphne led a standing ovation. Her fiery mane of waist-length curls lashed her tablemates as she waved her arms and beat her hands together like a trained seal.

Her date, a bonafide Latin stud named Russ, Rex or Raphael, loitered at the open bar, flirting with an unimpressed blonde barmaid. Daphne had a knack for finding men who were completely wrong for her. But at least she found guys. Unlike Khela, the fraud. The night was a lie, right down to Carter, the handsome prince who slowly backed away from the stage, softly applauding, the golden stage light giving his eyes warmth and depth that Khela could have basked in all night.

Carter was the biggest lie of all.

Tears burned Khela's eyes as she crossed the stage. She cast a last look at her last-resort date, and he blew her a kiss with the debonair ease of a modern Cary Grant. Applause erupted anew, and, as she accepted a handshake, a kiss on the cheek, and the heavy Torchbearer statue from the association president, Khela burst into tears. She forced a smile, and it hurt her face so much that her tears intensified. She struck them away, and again found Carter. With his pinkies hooked in the corners of his mouth, he let loose a stadium whistle that made the table of black-clad mystery writers next to him clap their hands to their ears.

Instead of being glad that he was finally impressed, Khela fought the urge to upchuck. She was no champion of romance. She was a big fat liar, and as she stood on stage, her back bowing under the weight of the

Torchbearer teardrop, she felt as though guilt would roast her alive from the inside out.

Carter's smile faded as he studied her face. Her table-mates were clapping, but each of them—save January Rose—had a lean, hungry look aimed not at Khela but at the award clutched in her arms.

Carter suddenly realized that there wasn't a romance author in the room who wouldn't trade places with Khela right there on the spot, and he wasn't fooled by her empty smile, or her tears.

Those aren't tears of humble joy or happiness, he thought. *They're tears of misery.*

He caught her eye once more, and wrinkling his brow, he mutely conveyed his curiosity and concern.

Khela looked right into the blinding stage light, hoping that he hadn't read the horrible thought stuck on a continuous loop in her mind: *I'm a phony, and you're nothing more than a prop.*

Khela's eyes still stung from the tears she'd shed onstage as she walked through her complimentary suite. Someone at the East Coast Writing Association had either a diabolical sense of humor or a complete misunderstanding of what romance writers were really like.

I'm here for business, she grumbled to herself, scanning the room, *not a honeymoon.*

Champagne chilled in silver buckets propped on one end of the full bar in the living room and an ornamental stand next to the dining table. Plump, fresh strawberries heaped around a tiny gold chafing dish full of glossy dark chocolate formed a centerpiece on the cocktail table between two long sofas set before the dazzling view of Boston Harbor.

Khela walked through the office section of the suite and into the master bedroom to change, where she was assaulted by the sight of a beautiful Chippendale four-poster abundantly sprinkled with blood-red rose petals.

She grabbed her suitcase in both hands and hauled it onto the bed, crushing rose petals and releasing their delicious fragrance. She tried to ignore it as she selected pale-grey yoga pants, white cotton bikini briefs and a matching camisole, and then slammed the suitcase shut.

She went into the bathroom and found that her presumptuous hosts had also corrupted that room by drawing a pearly milk bath decorated with fresh violets and lilac spray roses, the water kept warm by temperature controls set to a comfy 88 degrees. Khela scowled at yet another bottle of chilled Dom Perignon and the two champagne flutes accompanying it. She plunged her arm into the bath and flipped the drain lever, and with satisfaction, she spent a moment watching the water start its journey to the Atlantic.

She quickly changed, leaving her ball gown in a heap on the floor, and brushed her hair into a ponytail before stomping barefoot into the living room. She drew up short when she spotted Carter, still in his tux, idly standing at the window with a half-full tumbler in his hand.

CHAPTER 3

"Men like him should come with a warning label."
—*from* Hazardous to Your Heart *by Khela Halliday*

She'd forgotten that he had his own cardkey to the suite, so she certainly hadn't expected to find him standing at the windowed wall, framed by the harbor nightscape. The rugged, rough-edged maintenance stud she'd invited to the convention was so convincing in his costume that, for a moment, she believed him to be what she'd wanted him to be: the perfect romance hero sprung from the pages of one of her books.

Resenting his flawless performance, Khela scowled at him. "Didn't you have enough to drink downstairs?" She plopped herself on the sofa and reached past the strawberries and chocolate for the slender black remote control. With one press of a button, the doors of a tall entertainment center slid open, revealing a big flat-screen television and sound system. Khela rested her feet near the strawberries and tuned in to her favorite home-shopping channel. Her least favorite segment was on.

"Nice," she muttered with a roll of her eyes. "If you buy the thirty-inch machete, you can get a set of six steak knives." She turned to Carter. "What the hell does anyone need with a 65-piece knife set that includes a machete?"

He looked at her, his brow furrowed, swirling the liquid in his glass. "For the record, boss, this is water, not booze. What's going on here, Khela?"

Uncomfortable under his scrutiny, she fixed her eyes on the knife show.

Carter took a seat across from her, on the opposite sofa. "All night I've been trying to piece things together, and the only thing that doesn't make sense is you."

She stared at the television, but paid little attention to the new item up for sale—twin samurai swords with acid-etched blades.

"You lost me," she mumbled.

"I didn't know you were a hotshot romance novelist."

"I like to keep my business my business." She stubbornly crossed her arms over her chest. "More people should try it. It's fun."

"Those people down there really respect and admire you and your work. I never knew that romance was so big. Kitty Kincaid said that almost half of all paperbacks sold in the United States are romance fiction. Garland Kenny told me that romance fiction is a billion-dollar industry here in the U.S. alone."

"Yep," she snapped. "That's all romance is. Just one big ol' industry."

Carter drew a five by eight-inch program from his inner breast pocket. He opened it and read: "The Torchbearer Award is given once every ten years to the author whose books best honor and promote the spirit of true romance." He slid the program onto the table. It stopped near Khela's feet. "Martine Kendall said that you're the first author ever to win it in her first year of eligibility and that writers, readers, editors and booksellers voted for you in a landslide. She also said you were the first African-American author to take home a Torchbearer."

Khela finally turned to face him. "Oh. You're still talking."

He tipped his chin toward the door of the suite. "Why is your Torchbearer Award buried in a canvas tote bag full of bookmarks, ballpoint pens, nameplates and promotional copies of new Cameo releases?"

"Why do you care?"

He braced his elbows on his knees and laced his fingers together. "Call me interested."

She gave him a toothy, artificial smile. "Hello, Interested. I'm Minding My Own Business. Pleased to meet you." She crossed one leg over the other and turned one shoulder into the back of the sofa to fully face the television.

Carter skirted around the cocktail table to join her on her sofa and fill her view. "I think it's odd that a woman who's written a string of best-selling romance novels doesn't seem to have one romantic twitch in her entire body."

Khela screwed her mouth into a tight pout before she attacked. "You're supposed to be scenery, not a commentator. My books, my twitches and my body don't have a doggone thing to do with *you*."

She grudgingly admired the way he sat there, taking the force of her temper without shrinking back, but she was a bit taken aback when he calmly set his tumbler on the cocktail table and stood. "I think I'll shower and change now."

He crossed the room, going past the bar area to the second bedroom. Khela watched him disappear, her heart sinking with each step he took. He left the door open, and beneath the carnival barking of the knife show host, she heard the zipper of Carter's duffel bag, the opening of another door, and then a muffled blast of water.

Sighing heavily, she ran her fingers through her ponytail. He hadn't sounded angry and he had spoken without rancor. He had a point, which is what had infuriated her so. Listening to the water, she paced the living room, impatient for him to finish.

After ten minutes, her patience had completely run out. "How dirty can he be?" she wondered aloud as she entered his bedroom.

She noticed how ordinary the room looked with its double bed, television console, nightstand and phone. The only flowers in the room were the ones printed on the duvet. Clearly, her ECWA handlers had thought the room would go unused. Making a mental note to make up the bed and remove all evidence of Carter from the room before housekeeping arrived the next morning, Khela barged into the bathroom.

Like the bedroom, his bathroom was much smaller than hers, the shower stall little wider than a standard closet. Carter had managed to fog the glass door completely, revealing little more than a bit of bicep, a section of chest and a glimpse of a hip.

Khela began to itch. It wasn't her usual uncomfortable, nagging itch. This was a yearning variety that required deeper, more physical relief. She cleared her throat.

Startled, Carter shook water from his eyes and spat a stream of water from his lips.

"Why do you take such long showers?" she asked.

"I have to clear my bathing schedule with you this weekend, too?" She was the reason he'd decided to take a shower. She might have chosen her outfit based on comfort, but all he'd seen was the way her breathable cottons had clung to the long, elegant lines of her thighs and defined the perfect shape of her bosom. Her camisole wasn't quite transparent, but it was certainly sheer enough to reveal the darkness of her breasts and the darker caps tipping them.

The initial blast of cold water had done what it was supposed to, but with Khela standing on the other side of the glass, the fine hairs framing her face curling and her camisole becoming more sheer in the steamy humidity, Carter's flesh sprang painfully to life.

"Your body is so simple." Khela crossed her arms over her chest, to Carter's disappointment. "You don't have to shave anything, you don't have to condition your hair. Get wet, soap up, rinse off and get out. Five minutes is the longest you need to be in here."

"There's another bathroom, Khela, and I'm sure the hotel has plenty of hot water. What do you care how long I shower?"

"I don't." Her eyes were drawn to his chest, where the water beat upon his defined pectorals as he smoothed his hands over them, rinsing away the last of the woodsy-scented soap he was using. "I was waiting for you to come out so I could apologize for what I said out there. About that scenery crack."

"Don't apologize. I'm flattered." He flexed his biceps, then his triceps, exaggerating the poses until Khela gave him a reluctant smile. "I've never been the pretty thing on a successful professional's arm."

Khela tried to wish away the condensation hiding him from her as she leaned against the sink counter and bowed her head. "I have an image to maintain, Carter. I couldn't walk into that banquet alone or with an ordinary man."

"I'm ordinary." He turned off the water and beckoned for a towel.

"There's nothing ordinary about the way you look, Carter." Khela took a step toward the shelf above the toilet and drew forth one of the fluffy white bath towels. She tossed it over the stall door. "If Brad Pitt and Chris Cuomo were in a sauna on Mercury, they still wouldn't be as hot as you. You're a damn stud. You can't not know how handsome you are."

Unsure how to respond to her unabashed compliment, he wrapped the towel around his hips and exited the shower. Nothing but the towel stood between Khela and his dripping nakedness in the tiny bathroom. "Thank you," he finally said.

Khela watched droplets of water trace paths through the dark hair on his chest. If it were possible for a man to have perfect chest hair, Carter's was. It wasn't too sparse, as though the hair was nothing more than a hormonal afterthought, and it wasn't dense as though he were part Sasquatch. It was just right, and so inviting that she wanted to lean forward and rub her cheek against it.

"My fans expect me to live the romance I write about," she explained, transfixed by the movement of his chest and arm muscles as he began drying himself with one end of the big towel. "They expect me to be my work. My sales would plummet if readers found out that I'm a complete fraud."

"You make it sound like you're stealing from them." Carter had dried the same spot on his shoulder for so long, he had to check to make sure he hadn't rubbed the skin off. Khela stood within arm's reach, and it took every ounce of willpower he possessed not to lasso her in with the damp towel and draw her closer.

"At least that would be more direct. What I do is worse." She tipped her head back when he took a half step forward. He was so close now she could feel the heat of his damp skin.

"What is it that you do?" He stopped drying and held the ends of the towel together at his hip.

Khela's eyes darted downward to steal a look at the bulge below his waist before returning her gaze to his face. "I deceive them. I make them believe in something that doesn't exist."

Sharing his air was making her lightheaded, so she sidestepped away from him to stand at the end of the counter, near the door.

"What's that?" He tucked the ends of the towel in to keep it in place, and then took a toothbrush and a tiny tube of mint toothpaste from the shaving kit near the basin. He ran his fingers through his hair, slicking it from his face before he began scrubbing his teeth.

"Happy endings. Romance. Love."

Carter worked up a good lather, spat and rinsed. "How are you any worse than the guys who wrote *Cinderella* or *Romeo and Juliet?* You're spinning tales. That's why it's called fiction. Your readers know it isn't real." He turned sideways to move past her and into the bedroom.

"Most of them do, but a lot of them don't." She followed him, going to the single window while he went to the bed, where a pair of blue sweatpants lay. "I get hundreds of letters every year from women who tell me that they gave their boyfriends a second chance, or that they finally called the man they've been lusting after, or that they got married, all because of something I wrote. My books are fiction, but the words still have pow . . . *wow* . . ."

She'd turned from the window just in time to catch a glimpse of Carter's bare backside as he pulled his sweatpants on.

"They have what?" Carter asked calmly. His baggy pants hung low his hips, revealing the full stack of his abdominal muscles. When he turned to rifle through his duffel bag, Khela touched her index finger to her mouth to make sure she wasn't drooling.

"Power," she finished. "Words have power. Apparently I quite convincingly write about things in which I don't have a twitch of faith."

"Maybe you just haven't found the right man." Carter withdrew a faded, threadbare Atlanta Braves T-shirt and pulled it on. "It's man, right?"

"No, my first choice for a date this weekend was Gabrielle Union, but her tuxedo was at the cleaners."

"Oh, yeah? Then you and I have the same taste in women." Carter padded out of the bedroom barefooted, but not before Khela caught his impish smile.

She dashed into the bathroom to gather his shaving kit and used towel. She plopped the items on top of his duffel bag then quickly scanned the room, to make sure Carter hadn't left anything else in it. Satisfied that she had everything, she lugged the heavy duffel into the living room area.

"Kicking me out already?" Carter asked.

"If another writer or someone from RAAO comes by, I don't want them to know that we're not sharing a bedroom. It wouldn't look right."

"To who?"

"To me."

"What do you care what other people think about—"

"When you buy something a celebrity recommends, you assume that they know the product, that they wouldn't promote it if it wasn't something they could stand behind. Right?"

"Yeah," he said. "I suppose."

"Well, the commodity I sell is romance. You're part of the marketing of that commodity."

"So to sell your product, you have to create the illusion that we're—"

"Having lots and lots of sex," she finished.

With a small shake of his head, Carter settled on the sofa with the remote in one hand and a strawberry in the other. "I didn't mean anything by that man crack I made back there," he called as he dunked the strawberry in the pool of chocolate. "I didn't want to assume anything. And that could have been the reason you haven't been happy with men."

"Why do you assume that the problem lies with me?" she sniped, scurrying past him and stopping at the door to the master bedroom to heave the duffel bag in. "Men are the ones that make relationships so hard. Men are self-centered, inattentive, and worst of all, they take women for granted." She sauntered toward the sofa, her arms held wide. "You know that *we'll* call and *we'll* choose the restaurant or movie, and *we'll* be responsible for our own orgasms. Men think that the only thing they have to do is show up close to on time and change their underwear on a semi-regular basis."

Carter grimaced. "Ew. What kind of men do you date?"

She sat down heavily on the sofa and tucked her legs under her. "The only kind out there—the wrong kind. Women love my heroes, and here's why: I pick a man, any man that I know, and write down everything that he's not. I end up with perfect romance heroes. They may be flawed, but they're capable of learning and relating to a woman and loving her so much that they're willing to—"

"Change?" Carter suggested before biting into the big strawberry. "Women always want to change a man."

"I was going to say adapt."

"Adapt is a high-rent version of change."

"Change is when a woman wants a man to stop scratching his ass every night after he slumps into bed with her. Adapting is when a man scratches his ass while he's brushing his teeth in the bathroom, where she doesn't have to hear or see it."

Called to defend his gender, Carter used the remote to mute the television. "Okay, you make a really good point, but—"

"I make an excellent point." She took the remote, and though she wasn't the least bit interested in the Elizabethan Bedding Show, she turned the volume back up.

"Inviting me here isn't going to help you, you know."

Inexplicably wounded by his offhand remark, she tried to force some interest in the luxurious, 20-piece quilted gold bedding ensemble. "I don't need help. I needed a favor, and that's what I got."

Carter pulled the dish of strawberries and chocolate closer. He grasped the long green stem of a strawberry and transferred the heavy fruit to the still pool of chocolate. Khela's tummy grumbled its envy when Carter brought the sweet treat to his mouth. Other parts of her body responded with jealousy when he used the tip of his tongue to collect a drop of chocolate from the plump round of the strawberry.

"What you need is a man," he said before chomping into the chocolate-drenched fruit.

Khela's mouth dropped open.

"I'm not talking about the chumps you've been with, who've clearly soured you on relationships," Carter went on. "You need a real man."

She daintily cleared her throat. "I have one. You. And on Sunday night, you turn back into a pumpkin."

His movements casual but deliberate, Carter retrieved the bottle of Dom Perignon from the end of the bar. Room service had already stripped the foil and untwisted the wire cage, and as he returned to the sofa, Carter used his thumbs to work at the cork.

"Heads up, doll," he said, bracing the butt of the bottle against his right hip.

Twisting the bottle rather than the cork like a professional sommelier, Carter freed the cork with an understated pop. A wisp of champagne fog escaped the bottle, but there was no cartoonish overflow as he brought the bottle to Khela. He sat facing her, their knees touching.

"Nice work," she said, taking the bottle in both hands. "Not a drop wasted."

"Sloppiness is for show. For amateurs."

"Cheers." She raised the bottle in a quick toast before taking a hearty swig from it. Champagne wasn't her favorite libation by any means, but there was something delightfully decadent about drinking complimentary Dom Perignon from the bottle.

She passed the bottle back to Carter, who took a long swallow from it before propping it on his knee.

"I'm white, you know," he said matter-of-factly.

"I prefer to think of you as melanin-compromised," she said, rolling her eyes.

"I would have thought it might be a disadvantage for you."

"I don't understand."

"Well, you said you needed a certain kind of man to accompany you this weekend. Wouldn't it be more convincing if you were here with a black guy?"

"You're the best I could get on such short notice," Khela said.

"You're a real sweet talker, you know that?"

"What I mean is that I needed someone handsome. That's all. Someone who fit the mold of the heroes I create. My heroes are all races. You love who you love, plain and simple."

"That's profound, from someone who doesn't believe in love."

She continued as though he hadn't spoken. "I've dated black men, white men, Latin men, Jewish men. My ex-husband is—"

Carter abruptly sat up. "You have an ex-husband?"

"Don't look so surprised. It comes with the territory."

"Are a lot of you writers divorced?"

Khela stared at the vaulted ceiling as she gave him an accounting. "Martine is on her third husband. Kitty is still with her second. Garland—"

"He's straight?"

"—is on his sixth or seventh longtime companion," Khela finished. "January Rose was married for twenty-eight years. Her husband died last year. Heart attack. Rose is the only person I know, author or civilian, who found true love. Then her husband ups and dies on her."

"I'm sure, given a choice, he wouldn't have upped *or* died."

"It just frustrates me." Khela stared at her feet. "Even the people who find real love don't get to keep it."

"They had twenty-eight years," Carter pointed out.

Khela whipped her head around to face him. "Would that be enough for you, if you managed to find the one person in the world who made every day worth living?"

Her gaze locked onto his, the yearning in her eyes almost palpable. Too late, Carter looked away, self-conscious at having perhaps revealed too much of his own longing.

"January Rose is a genuine sorceress," Khela said softly, looking away. "Her romances are so good because she has lived what she writes."

"What about Carmen?" Carter passed her the champagne.

"What about her?" Khela remarked sharply.

"Is she divorced?"

Prickled, Khela snapped, "What if she is?"

The left side of Carter's mouth rose in a telling smile. "You're jealous."

"Of what?" she scoffed.

"My interest in Carmen."

"No, I'm not," she lied to his face. A spiky ball of acid green jealousy rolled around in her stomach, surprising her with its potency. "Are you really interested in her?"

He sat back, holding the bottle to the chandelier light to gauge the amount of champagne remaining before he answered her. "She's really beautiful."

The jealousy ball expanded exponentially.

"She seems very smart, too," Carter went on.

Khela's champagne hissed and fizzed in her belly and started to come back on her.

"But she's not my type," Carter grinned.

"You suck," Khela snarled around a reluctant smile. She relaxed into the sofa and snatched the champagne from him. After her stomach settled, she gulped another swig. "But since you brought it up, what kind of woman *is* your type?"

Carter picked up two more strawberries and toyed with them in one hand. "Do you want to know my ideal, or what I'd settle for?"

"Both."

"My ideal is easy." He cleared his throat. "I want someone smart. Attractive. Unpredictable." He glanced at her. "Unpredictable in a fun way, not a let's-carry-vials-of-each-other's-blood way." He found it easier to confess his desires to his strawberries, so he kept his gaze on them. "I want someone who'll look at me and see what really matters. And want me, anyway."

"What about money?" Khela's mouth went dry.

"What?"

"You want your dream woman to be smart, pretty and a barrel of monkeys. Don't you want her to have a well-paying job, too?"

Confused, Carter shook his head. "I'd rather she had a job that made her happy."

She thrust her chin at him. "But money would be a nice perk, wouldn't it?"

"Why do you have your tail up all of a sudden?"

"I'm not . . ." She stopped when she heard the hostility in her voice. She softened and said, "I don't mean to. It's just that men seem to be more attracted to my bank account than to me."

Carter snickered. "You're no better."

Khela almost punched him. "What the hell does that mean?"

"You invited me tonight because of the way I look. That's just as bad as someone wanting to date you because of your income."

She stifled her initial reaction to his insult, which was to cuss him out, when she noticed his somber expression. He was right, not that she'd ever admit it to him.

"You sound like you've got experience in being used," she said quietly.

"I was engaged to a woman who wanted to marry me because she liked my genes," he sighed.

"I don't know if I blame her," Khela admitted. "You do look pretty good in your Levis."

Carter reached over and gave the end of her nose a light thunk. "G-E-N-E genes, scribbler, not J-E-A-N-S. I overheard her and her parents debating our future the night before the wedding. It was at the Cypress Ridge Golf and Tennis Club in Decatur. Her parents were paying for everything, since my people didn't have a pot to piss in. Savannah—"

"You were engaged to a woman named Savannah?" Khela chuckled.

49

"Do you wanna hear my tale of tragedy and woe or not? 'Cause I can just go on to bed, if—"

"Go on," Khela urged. The champagne loosened his tongue, intensifying the slow, sleepy, undiluted 'Bama drawl that Khela could listen to all day. "I'm sorry." She giggled softly. *Savannah . . .* "I'll bet she was a pageant girl, wasn't she?"

He chuckled. "The name gave it away?"

"Yep. So what was she? Miss Chilton County Peach Blossom? Miss Elkmont Soybean?"

"She began her career at three when she won Grand Supreme at the Southern Baby Belles and it ended nineteen years later, when she came up third runner-up for Miss Alabama. That's when she decided it would be best to get hitched, start makin' babies, and force her husband into her daddy's cattle business."

"At least she told you her plans up front."

"Uh uh." He slowly shook his head. "I didn't know the master plan until I overheard it at the wedding rehearsal dinner. She and her parents were talking to some of their kin, and I heard them say that Savannah's people had enough brains and money to take care of us, but that I had good genes to contribute. Our children would be tall, strong and good-looking, and in another generation, you'd never know that 'lesser' stock had been a part of their evolution."

"That's gross," Khela said.

"I was just a human version of Secretariat to them. Someone to sire good foals. Savannah and I had words about it. She admitted that love wasn't her motivating factor in accepting my proposal. I called off the wedding, left Alabama before her daddy could load his rifle and I haven't been back for more than two days at a time since."

"So we're both walking wounded," she replied.

"I guess so," he muttered.

They sat, silent, watching the bright lights break over the harbor.

"I'm sorry I used you," she said softly.

"I'm sorry I'm so handsome."

His remark was just the right thing to break the tension, and they spent the next moment laughing. Carter scooted closer to Khela, putting his feet up on the cocktail table so that his ankle touched hers.

"If we were characters in one of your books, what would be happening to us at this point in the story?" he asked.

She shrugged. Looking at her strawberry rather than at Carter, she answered his question. "I suppose what was supposed to happen would have happened already. My heroine would have slipped into the shower with the hero for hot, urgent 'first sex' in the tight, steamy confines of the shower stall."

Carter inhaled deeply through his nose, his eyebrows rising with the expansion of his chest.

Khela ran her knuckles along her thighs, unmindful of the way Carter's eyes followed their path. "The showerhead is on a flexible cord, so they would have had all kinds of fun with that. They would have spent at least fifteen-hundred words learning each other's tastes, textures and responses," she went on, "and then he would have surprised her by putting her pleasure first. And he'd know very creative ways to please her. She would respond in kind, of course, probably trying techniques and positions she'd only heard of or read about."

Her voice softened, and now she spoke more to herself than to him. "The way he stared at her would almost be enough to bring her to orgasm. She might touch herself while he watched, partly to tease him, partly to let his reaction thrill her even more. When she was ready, she would pull him to her, and their bodies would fit together as though they had been made for each other. She would have found carnal freedom and expression the likes of which she hadn't before thought herself capable."

She shook herself from her reverie and looked up to see Carter staring at her, his forehead creased in rapt attention. "She would make love to this man with her whole self. Without guilt, without regret . . . without expectation."

After a moment of silence in which he was aware of nothing but the contact between his ankle and Khela's, Carter rattled his words loose. "Would your hero ask permission before he kissed the heroine?"

Pensive, Khela stared at the chafing dish. Seduction in a bowl. That's what the warm chocolate represented as she toyed with the giant berry in her hand. Everything about chocolate was designed to seduce—its scent, color and certainly its creamy, sinful taste. But the pool of melted chocolate before her held no temptation, not compared to Carter.

His eyes fluctuated between honey and cinnamon as they delved into hers, and Khela longed to run her fingers through his dark hair. He smelled so fresh, masculine and clean. So much better than chocolate.

"No," she replied. "He wouldn't need to."

Her strawberry fell to the carpet and rolled under the cocktail table as she pitched herself onto Carter. His strong hands caught her ribcage in time to keep her mouth from crashing violently into his. She kissed him, and he let her, opening his legs to cradle her between them. Her heavy, eager breaths mingled with his as she tasted each of his lips and his chin before deeply kissing him once more. Awkwardly, she maneuvered her hands under his T-shirt and raised it, exposing his chest. Tiny nips here and there sent his blood rushing south, and Khela settled more comfortably upon the hard bulge pressing into her lower abdomen.

He palmed her backside as she cupped him and caught his lower lip between her teeth. Carter shifted, rolling her onto her back to lie half atop her. He covered her throat and chest with kisses, savoring her softness. She took his face and brought his mouth back to hers, amazing him all over again at how well she kissed.

If her writing was only half as good, it was no wonder she'd had so many bestsellers. Carter grinned against her lips, wondering what else she did with such skill.

He slipped one strap of her camisole from her shoulder, kissing its path to the cap of her shoulder. His lips traveled lower, over the thin cotton jersey, until they closed over the taut tip protruding from it. Khela drew in a shivery breath, her spine arching toward Carter. The warm, languid melting sensations she wrote about began to flow through her as Carter spoiled her flesh. When he slipped a hand under the waistband of her pants, she thrust her fingers into his hair and guided his head to her neglected breast. His fingers delved deeper, his longest coming to rest along her moist cleft. Slowly, wonderfully, beautifully, he began to stroke her, his touch light and knowing.

Khela shamelessly moaned into his kiss, gripping his wrist and thrusting her hips against his hand. His finger slid inside her in time to feel her tight constrictions, and he kissed the graceful arch of her neck as she closed her eyes, surrendering to the pleasure of release.

"Khela?" he whispered between calming kisses applied to her face and neck. "Why did you throw my bag into your room earlier?"

Still panting, she choked back a laugh. "I didn't want housekeeping to come in tomorrow and see that we were sleeping in separate bedrooms. Word spreads fast in a hotel."

He nuzzled her neck and took one of her hands. She smiled lazily when he directed it to the rigidness distending the front of his sweatpants. "Are we sleeping in the same bedroom?"

She chewed a corner of her lip. "Would we actually do any sleeping?" she chuckled. "I still can't feel my toes."

Carter hooked his fingers into her waistband and peeled her pants from her body. He took his time running his hands along her smooth legs. "Is that a line from one of your books?"

Sensation returned to Khela's extremities in the form of indignant fury. She scrambled to sit up and yanked her pants from Carter's grasp.

"Uh oh," he mumbled, sitting up and adjusting his pants.

"Let's get one thing straight, Carter. I'm a writer, but I'm not what I write, okay? In my day-to-day life, I don't work from a manuscript. If I say something, it comes from *me*, from in here." She gave her heart two hard jabs. "It doesn't come from some made-up story!"

He scrubbed his hands over his face. "I'm sorry. I didn't mean to insult you."

Khela knew that she was overreacting, but she was committed to her rant because it was a fine distraction from the hunger Carter had started raging inside her.

"Maybe I should have just gotten separate rooms." She angrily thrust her legs into her pants. "We're not fooling anyone. No one's going to believe that we're red-hot lovers."

"You convinced me, for a minute there." He rested one arm along the back of the sofa. "Now the writer is writing me off."

"You certainly have a way with words, Carter." And with his hands, and lips, and fingers . . .

"Maybe I should write a book," he said. "A mystery. It would try to explain why a love-starved woman would initiate a kiss with a man she's enlisted to be a hot prop, only to turn him away after a harmless slip of the tongue."

She narrowed her eyes at him. Had she imagined the emphasis he placed on his last few words? They had a very real effect on her pulse, which throbbed hard in unusual places. "I'm going to bed now." She crossed her arms over her chest and stiffly walked toward the master bedroom.

"Khela, don't." He stood and followed her. "Don't just walk away without giving this a chance."

She paused at the door to her room. "There's no 'this.' You and I aren't a 'this!' We're a weekend of make-believe, and I lost sight of that for a minute. Once we get through the luncheon tomorrow, you and I can go right back to being what we were before."

"Tell me what you think we were, Khela. I'm curious."

His challenge cooled her blood, transforming her lust into needles of humiliation at having thrown herself at him. "We were just another couple of single thirtysome-things in the Back Bay," she said. "Look, you don't have to come to the luncheon. There's really no point in car-rying on with this charade. I apologize for dragging you here."

"Khela," he said, starting after her when she disap-peared into the master bedroom. She closed the door, nearly snapping his nose off. He rested one hand lightly on the door and debated his next move.

He was still working out what to say when she reemerged to set his duffel bag at his feet. He was at a loss for words, but Khela wasn't. "Goodnight, Carter," she said softly, and retreated once more behind the closed door.

CHAPTER 4

"How shall you know Temptation? Not by its taste, scent, touch, appearance or voice, but by its persistence . . ."
—*from* An Angel's Prayer *by Khela Halliday*

An ocean of faces, most of them female, swam before Khela. She blinked rapidly to clear her vision, to better focus on individuals. Her left hand gripped the edge of the podium centered on the dais while her right flirted with a glass of ice water sitting at the upper-right corner of her prepared remarks. ECWA romance writers and RAAO members comprised her audience, so she recognized quite a few of the people staring expectantly at her. Unpublished members outnumbered the "pubs" twenty to one. Khela couldn't decide which group frightened her more—the unpubs, with hope and hunger shining in their eyes, or the pubs, most of whom barely managed to conceal their boredom.

What was another keynote address to women who had been in her position before, some of them four or five times a year?

Merrie Bollinger sat at a table smack in front of the dais, her benign smile doing little to ease Khela's nerves. To the uninformed observer, Merrie looked as if she should be wearing a gingham apron and baking oatmeal cookies for her eleven grandchildren.

But Merrie was a seasoned veteran, the author of eighty-seven historical romances for RayderThorne Publishing Corporation. She spoke at RAAO chapter conferences several times a year, which frequently had Khela wondering how the sweet-faced Merrie could write so many books.

But then Khela had read a few of Merrie's books, and she'd discovered her secret. It was easy to write dozens and dozens of books when you were recycling the same story over and over.

Khela swallowed back her catty deduction, and scanned the crowd. She had no right to criticize Merrie's work, or anyone else's. There was a time, not too long ago, when she had attended her first romance writers' conference, and she had been captivated, listening to a seasoned author who had taken time out of her life to impart wisdom and encouragement to a roomful of writers.

She and Daphne, her roommate of three years, had been juniors at Fieldcrest. Back then, Daphne had the largest personal library Khela had ever seen, and it was built solely of Cameo romances. While Khela had been an able student, double majoring in biology and western civilization, Daphne had been working on a creative writing degree, with the ultimate goal of becoming a Cameo author.

Khela majored in fields that would prepare her for employment that would grant her financial security, but she honored her love of storytelling through a minor in

English. And she continued to scribble her stories in spiral-bound notebooks, which she never showed to anyone, not even Daphne.

Daphne had done all the right things—according to Daphne. She'd joined RAAO and one of its Missouri chapters; she had attended meetings, annual conferences and the national convention. She belonged to critique circles and book-discussion groups, and she maintained the strictest discipline, faithfully writing from 10 P.M. to midnight five nights a week.

When Daphne invited her to the Chicago RAAO chapter's fall conference, Khela had gone primarily out of curiosity and to enjoy a weekend with her roommate in the Windy City. Daphne had registered for a one-on-one appointment with one of the major-league editors attending the conference. Her fearlessness hadn't fully matured yet, so she dragged Khela with her to the five-minute, make-or-break meeting. Tongue-tied, Daphne had barely managed to babble the pitch she'd practiced for two weeks prior to the conference, and afterward, she'd rushed off to the ladies' room to barf up the bleu cheese and artichoke soufflé she'd had at lunch.

Assuming that Khela was next on her appointment list, the editor had beckoned her into Daphne's vacated seat. Khela had pitched a story idea that she made up on the fly, splicing together everything she'd ever learned from Daphne about romance novels with one of her favorite pieces of classic literature.

"My hero is a stormy, husky, brawling man with big shoulders," she had said, wildly improvising. "And my heroine is a painted woman with a reputation for luring one too many farm boys. My book is the story of how these two disparate souls use their cunning, strength and tenacity to defy expectations and overcome the burden of destiny to find love on their own terms."

Cameo editor Fawn Ellman had then asked Khela the one question that almost tripped her up. "What's the title?"

And without thinking, Khela had responded with the first thing that popped into her head. "*Satin Whispers.*"

The name of the moisturizing body lotion in the hospitality basket at her hotel.

Fawn had requested the full manuscript, and Khela had spent the next two months working furiously on a book that hadn't existed, not even in her imagination, before her sit-down with the editor. She found out about Fawn's acceptance of the manuscript the hard way— through a phone message relayed to her by Daphne, whose conference experience hadn't been so fortuitous.

Daphne had spent one week in a sulky, sullen mood, but then she had read Khela's first few chapters. Enraptured, she had congratulated Khela and had become her staunchest supporter, even helping her with some of her class work so that she could devote more time to her manuscript. *Satin Whispers* was released a year later, on Daphne's twenty-first birthday.

Khela's gift to her was the dedication: *To Daphne Carr and Carl Sandburg, for obvious reasons.*

A few months later, after graduating with honors, Khela moved to Boston to take an assistant researcher position at a small bioengineering firm. She'd enjoyed the work—few recent college grads had the chance to develop cutting-edge biologic matrix products right out of the gate.

But when Fawn offered a multibook deal with Cameo, Khela veered from a career path that had once seemed perfect.

The polarized windows of the banquet hall softened the intensity of the sunlight reflecting off the placid surface of the harbor. Unlike the night before, when she'd accepted the Torchbearer Award, she now easily saw clear to the back of the room, where people stood two rows deep to hear her keynote address.

More than ever, Khela truly appreciated how damned lucky she'd been all those years ago. There were better writers and better storytellers, Daphne foremost among them, sitting attentively at the ivory linen-draped tables dotting the enormous room. The next Beverly Jenkins, the next Theresa Medeiros—hell, the next Khela Halliday—was probably right there in front of her, sipping a slightly chilled Boyden chardonnay, or picking the bitter radicchio from her mesclun salad.

What can I say to give that woman what I clumsily stumbled upon? Khela wondered, misery clawing at her insides. *How can I inspire these women to pursue their dreams of romance when I don't believe in love myself?*

"Miss Halliday? Are you all right?"

A light touch of a hand on her shoulder shook Khela free of her reverie. The woman who had presented her with the Torchbearer now stared at her, a moue of concern behind her pleasant smile.

Tears boiled behind Khela's eyes as she nodded. She offered a weak smile that seemed to do little to convince the RAAO president, who nonetheless, backed away and left Khela alone on the dais.

She cleared her throat, and glanced down at her note cards. Then her head snapped back in a double take.

The silent crowd in the back parted to admit another guest—Carter, dressed in a crisp white button-down and freshly pressed khakis. He hunkered down, as if it were possible to make himself any less noticeable as he murmured "Excuse mes" and "Sorrys" in the preternatural quiet. Even though he bumped knees, shoulders and displaced a guest or two, his polite words were met with openly adoring looks from every woman he passed.

His hands briefly lighted on the back of Rose Gracen's chair. The petite Inspirational-romance novelist's cheeks flamed as her pert nostrils flared to inhale the air he had just moved through.

Venus Black, the star author of Throb Books, actually licked her cherry-red lips and ran three red-taloned fingers along her décolletage when his backside swept past her face.

Daphne glanced away from him long enough to give Khela a hearty thumbs up, but Khela looked at him only after he had removed her pink Prada croc clutch from the one empty chair at the head table. After seating himself in the chair, he plopped the clutch onto his lap. His expression unreadable, he stared at her.

She swallowed hard, but the hard lump in her gullet remained. Her super-looking super had the attention of every woman in the room, and every one of them probably believed him to be every bit as educated, wealthy and sexy as one of the heroes in her books.

With a gnawing, burning sensation growing in her belly, she imagined what they would say if they knew that the Prada clutch resting on Carter's lap probably cost more than he earned in a year keeping up her brownstone.

The handbag was as much a part of her charade as Carter. Daphne had "loaned" it to her, along with the two-carat diamond studs glinting in her earlobes. Khela's idea of accessorizing was typically limited to a pair of simple white-gold hoops and nothing more. Daphne had convinced her to purchase the clutch and diamonds in celebration of her liberation, meaning her divorce almost four years ago from a man who'd forced her to pinch pennies while he secretly spent her royalty checks as fast as they came in.

The clutch and the earrings were pretty, but not thousands of dollars pretty, and they spent more time at Daphne's than they did at Khela's, as they were two of Daphne's favorite items to borrow.

Khela eyed Daphne fanning herself with her hand as she whispered to her nearest tablemates, each of whom seemed to nod in agreement as they stared at the back of Carter's head.

Right then and there, Khela knew that Carter wasn't to be shared. Prop or no prop, he was hers for the weekend. She caught Carter's eye, and without changing his flat expression, he winked at her.

The playful gesture sent a sense of ease through her, starting at her mouth, which finally formed a tiny smile. He had been gone when she awakened that morning, and with all the workshops, readings and meet and greets she'd had before lunch, she'd had no time to dwell on his absence.

But he was here. Clean-shaven, with his short hair neatly combed off his face, he was the picture of casual masculine coolness, even with her girlie clutch on his lap. Despite her attitude malfunctions of the day before, he hadn't fled. Her relief was so great it washed out the shame she might have felt at having behaved so badly toward him.

His presence was a comfort, which Khela attributed to one fact: with every woman's eyes on Carter, they were no longer on her. She cleared her throat once more, and began her speech.

" 'All women, as authors, are feeble and tiresome. I wish they were forbidden to write, on pain of having their faces deeply scarified with an oyster shell,' " Khela read, grinning broadly at the horror on Kitty Kincaid's face. "Those are the words of Nathaniel Hawthorne. I keep them posted on my office wall, above my computer monitor. My first novel, and every novel I've written since, was written in defiance of Hawthorne's words."

Applause erupted, and Khela lowered her eyes. They landed on Carter, who sat up straighter as he stared at her. She began anew once the clapping died down. "As a genre, romance fiction is as wildly popular as it is disrespected. What we do, as storytellers, might not cure disease or reduce the national deficit, but it makes those things easier to bear. We entertain. We offer an escape. W-We . . ."

Her throat tightened and her words stalled. A tiny sip of water loosened her pipes enough for her to say, "We practice a very specific form of witchcraft."

Soft laughter rippled through the room. Khela only wanted to cry.

She started her wrap-up. "I'm supposed to provide guidance, but you already know how this game is played. You know that publishing moves on geological time. You know that each 'no' is one step closer to a 'yes.' The only advice I can give you is the same advice I was given ten years ago by one of our genre's best, January Rose, when I was the one sitting on the other side of a podium like this one: 'Write the story of your heart. If you can write it, you can sell it, and people will read it, and they will believe in it.' Those words, too, are posted on the wall above my computer monitor—above Hawthorne's. My first novel, and every novel I've written since, was written in honor of those words. And now . . ."

She found January Rose in the crowd, and the older lady kissed her fingertips and sent Khela a silent thank you. Khela's next words remained stuck in her throat. It was impossible to make herself finish with what she had planned. She couldn't, not here, not with Daphne, January Rose, Kitty Kincaid, Carter and dozens of other people looking at her with pride, affection or envy. She took a deep breath and said, "I wish you all the best in your careers."

The banquet hall exploded in applause, with Carter, her clutch tucked under one arm, on his feet banging his big hands together hardest of all. When he turned and slightly flapped his arms, spurring the audience on, the noise rose at least twenty decibels. The applause and cheers continued as Khela made her way to the head table, where Carter offered her his vacated seat. An observant waiter swooped in with another chair for Carter.

"That was awesome," he whispered, his lips and his breath caressing her ear. "You were great."

Smiling sickly, Khela wondered if anyone would notice if she ducked under the table and vomited into her purse.

———&⁓———

Carter paused in the archway between the banquet hall and another larger room, where long tables formed a giant "U." There, the authors signed books for the general public. Stacks of books were at each author's elbow, with a placard bearing the author's name and head shot propped in front of them. Before this weekend, Carter had been completely ignorant of the many sub-genres of romance. From erotic fiction that read more like hardcore pornography to Christian fiction that placed love of God above love of any creature born on Earth, Carter saw something for every connoisseur of romance.

"See anything you like?"

"Hey," Carter said, returning Daphne's greeting. "Looks like you did." With a nod he indicated her navy-

and-white ECWA tote bag, which was stuffed with books. "Did you leave any books for the riffraff?"

"There's plenty," she chuckled. "Most of these are promotional copies from all the publishers represented at the convention, not just the romance factories."

She selected a hardbound book with a glossy dust jacket. The image of a blond, blue-eyed man shown straight on and partly eclipsed by the profile of a pretty brown-skinned woman dominated the front cover. The book's title, *Soul Surrender,* stretched across the top of the cover, with KHELA HALLIDAY embossed in gigantic letters across the bottom.

"This is one of Khela's latest," Daphne said, displaying the book for Carter. "It won't be released until next month, and it's already on two bestseller lists."

"How's that possible?" Carter asked.

"Pre-orders," Daphne said. "Khela's got quite a following."

Carter looked around, awed all over again at the number of people waiting for signed books from Khela and her colleagues. "Does she do this every year?"

Daphne forced the book back into the overstuffed tote. "Does who do what?"

"Khela."

"She usually comes to this convention and the Romance Authors of America Organization's national convention." Daphne repositioned the heavy tote to prevent the strap from gouging her shoulder. "Khela's idea of being a writer is to sit at home in her loft, working at her laptop for hours and hours."

Carter tried to spy Khela through the throng, but the romance fans refused to accommodate him. Daphne's version of Khela's heaven sounded painfully dull. But Carter had a hard time imagining anything about her being dull.

The time he'd spent with her so far had proven something that he had only suspected in the course of his many casual dealings with her—that she was the most exciting woman he had ever met.

"What are you guys doing after the signing?" Daphne asked him.

"I'm not sure. We haven't had much time to talk today."

"I can't wait to see your costumes tonight. Khela—"

"Hold on," Carter cut in, holding up his hands. "Costumes? For what?"

"The ball." Daphne's green eyes widened. "She didn't tell you?"

"Do I look like she told me?"

"This year's theme is *Animal House*." She scrunched her freckled nose in disgust. "The romance and mystery writers wanted to do a Vagabond Cabaret, but the sports and humor writers turned out in record numbers to vote this year. They wanted *Animal House*, so we're stuck with a bunch of overweight smartasses and sports nuts in togas sucking up lime Jell-O shooters."

"That actually sounds like fun," Carter laughed. "It shouldn't be too hard to rig a toga out of one of the hotel bed sheets."

"Don't you mean two?"

Carter didn't follow.

"Two," Daphne clarified. "One for you and one for Khela."

"Right," he nodded, gleefully envisioning Khela tangled in a bed sheet.

"I'm going to my room to get a nap in before the ball," Daphne said, heaving her tote onto her shoulder again. "I'll see you tonight, I hope."

"Sure, me too," Carter said, waving at her.

He shouldered his way through the crowd, doing his best not to crash into chattering fans clutching signed books to their bosoms as though they were treasures handed directly from goddesses.

Khela had been situated in the middle of the center table, with five other writers on each side of her. She was the Torchbearer, so she had no books at her elbow. As befitted the queen for the day, readers purchased her books at the door and brought them to her.

She smiled and offered handshakes and hugs, but her affection for the people who'd come to see her failed to reach her eyes. The visage she presented to her fans was a mere mask of the face Carter had come to know so well over the years. She had a wider variety of smiles than any woman he'd ever known. There was the big, open smile she gave the UPS man who serviced the brownstone, and there was the lopsided, quirky smirk she reserved for the pianist living below her, who made no secret of his attraction to her.

She had a way of shaping her full lips into a plump little bow when Carter unexpectedly encountered her, and last night he'd seen what was now his favorite—the luscious, blissful smile of Khela Halliday in the throes of carnal surrender.

She greeted her readers with a beauty pageant smile that made her features appear shellacked. Her fans might not have seen the difference, but Carter knew her a little better than that. While the other authors seemed happy, and in some cases downright excited, to be signing for their fans, Khela appeared to be in agony.

His hands in his pockets, he strolled over to the signing tables. He stepped over a box of Rose Gracen's *The Rake's Redemption* and made his way down the line of authors to Khela.

She scribbled an illegible note to the fan standing before her and finished it off with an equally unreadable signature.

"Thank you so much for coming out today," she said, handing the thick hardcover back to its new owner.

"I love your books, Khela," the stout little woman said, the brown apples of her cheeks plump in a big smile. "I wrote a book myself. I let some of my friends read it, and they loved it. They said it was just as good as your books."

"You should submit it to a publisher," Khela said, accepting a book from the next woman in line.

"Really?" the stout woman said, pushing her ample belly into the edge of the table. "You think it's good enough?"

"Well, I haven't read it, so—"

"I'll send it to you as soon as I get home!" the squatty woman squealed. "After you read it, you can send it to your editor. Who's your agent? You can sign me up with your agent, too!"

Khela gripped her pen so hard, her knuckles whitened. Her shoulders tightened and slowly rose, as though their intent was to swallow her neck.

Carter lightly rested his hands on her shoulders and bent to speak close to her. "Can I get you some coffee or juice or something?" he murmured near her ear.

The welcome balm of his voice instantly relaxed her, settling her shoulders back into their normal position. Without thinking, she caressed his left hand with the fingers of her right and answered, "If you could find an iced tea, I'd be really grateful."

"No problem. I'll be right back." He gave her cheek a soft stroke with one finger as he left.

The pushy woman in front of Khela stared after Carter. "Where can I get me one of him? That is one fine lookin' youngster." She pinned her dark eyes on Khela. "And girl, is he ever burnin' for you!"

The woman whose book Khela was signing leaned forward. "He looks like Ken, from *An Angel's Prayer*, doesn't he?"

"Exactly!" declared Wallis Finchley-Locke, a native of England and a past Torchbearer winner who had built a career on Georgian historicals. She wagged a long finger, heavy with diamonds, at Khela's customer. "It's been plaguing me since I first saw him at the awards ceremony last night. He's Ken, in the flesh! Talk about an answer to a prayer."

"I think he looks more like Cale Garrett from *A Warrior's Secret*," offered the tall, blue-eyed woman whose book Khela still held open before her. "He's got Cale's caring eyes."

"I wasn't lookin' at his eyes," growled the stout woman, who had yet to leave.

"Me neither," interjected a woman in Wallis's line.

"Mmm, what it must be like to live your life, Khela," Wallis sighed. "A thriving career and a handsome man to cater to your needs. You're living the life we all write about."

Khela cringed, clamping her jaw with such violence that she heard a sharp crack near its hinge.

"Do you think he's as good in bed as Ken and Cale?" the tall woman asked the stout one as the two moved along.

"I suppose we'll find out in her next book," laughed the stout woman.

The two women passed Carter on their way out as he was returning with a tall sweating glass covered with plastic wrap. They parted, allowing him to move between them. Still moving forward, they looked back, their blue and brown eyes scanning Carter from head to toe.

Oblivious to his latest admirers, he returned to Khela.

"As I said," Wallis practically purred as Carter set Khela's tea before her. "You live the life we write about."

"No more than you do," Khela managed through the stiff smile she offered her next fan.

"Stunningly handsome men don't deliver cold beverages to me," Wallis said.

As her final, over-enunciated word fell from her lips, a cute young man with bright eyes and dimples slipped through two fans and set a tall iced tea in front of her.

The strait-laced, buttoned-down Brit's jaw fell as the young man and another waiter, moving in opposite directions, placed glasses of iced tea adorned with lemon circles and mint before each of the authors.

"I thought you all might be a little thirsty," Carter told Wallis. Leaving her speechless, he turned to Khela. "If you need anything else, just give a yell."

"Where did you find that one, Khela?" Wallis asked once Carter was out of earshot. "Studs R Us?"

"Just about," she mumbled under her breath. She glanced over her shoulder, tracking Carter's movement to the wall of windows. A trio of unpubs gravitated toward him, orbiting his heavenly body like moons.

The slender, long-haired blonde in a form-fitting wrap dress under-combed her hair with her fingers and tilted her head, to better display her décolletage. A blonde with an edgy, asymmetrical bob kept flipping her hair and stroking her throat as she guffawed at whatever was being said by her companions. The zaftig brunette, perched on four-inch ostrich Ferragamos, couldn't keep her hands off Carter. She straightened his already neat collar, plucked at his belt and even grabbed him by his chin to turn his face toward hers.

At which point Khela realized that, until the brunette literally stole his attention, Carter's eyes had been fixed on her.

———————

A gang of overzealous readers spoiled Khela's hopes for a quick getaway. They surrounded her the moment she stepped into the hotel corridor, peppering her with questions about her characters and storylines and stinging her with complaints about the same.

A persistent few thrust spiral-bound copies of their own self-published books at her, begging her to read their work or forward it to her publisher. Still others waved business cards and brochures in her face, hoping that she could donate time, books or money to their book clubs, schools or churches. January Rose, Wallis Finchley-Locke and Carmen Almeida were similarly engulfed by fans, but Khela was the only author who seemed to be withering under the attention.

One of the few men in Khela's crowd pushed an eight by ten-inch black-and-white head shot on her, backing her against the wall. "I've seen your book covers, baby," he started, a perfect smile gleaming within his flawless mocha complexion. "You need to drop the zeros and get with a real hero."

"I don't hire cover mod—" Khela began before a pair of skinny twins with matching whip-thin twisties pushed him aside.

"We're your—" started one twin, "biggest fans," finished the other.

"We write cybertechno—" said the first one.

"—paranormal romance—" continued the second.

"—under the name Echo Dawn," they giggled simultaneously. "We drove for an hour—"

"Two hours!" bellowed the first twin.

"—to come ask you if you would read our book—" said number two.

"And give us a blurb so we can sell it to a big publishing house!" they said together.

"M-My schedule is full for the next few months, so I-I—" Khela stammered before a woman carrying a stack of Watchtower Magazines pushed her way forward. *God, help me*, she pleaded, squinting her eyes shut in silent prayer.

"Forgive me for interrupting, kitten, but we've got to get going." Carter's arm fastened around her shoulders, drawing her into the safety of his embrace. "I'm sorry to spoil the party, folks, but Ms. Halliday has a very full schedule today. Please excuse her."

And with that, Carter practically lifted her off her feet, steered her through the crowd, and guided her to the bay of elevators. He took her convention tote bag from her, slinging it over his shoulder. Unwilling to give up so easily, some of Khela's fans, led by the twins, followed them.

Quick on the draw, Carter swiped his cardkey through the power box activating the VIP elevator. The doors opened, and he drew Khela inside the mirrored box. He pushed the button accessing the suites on the restricted floors, and the doors closed just as the grasping twins lunged forward.

Shaking, Khela and her reflection began to pace the tiny space. "H-HoHos," she mumbled. "I need some HoHos. Or Doritos. Cool ranch. No, nacho cheese.

When I was a kid in St. Louis, they used to make these really hot barbeque potato chips. Old Vienna, or Old Susannah or something. I—"

"—have a death wish, clearly." Carter stopped her frenetic movement by cupping her face. "Why are you so rattled? This isn't the first time you've had to deal with aggressive fans."

"It's not them." Her voice broke, and she looked up at the floor indicator to avoid meeting Carter's eyes.

"You were the most popular author at the signing," he told her.

"January Rose was the most popular," Khela corrected.

"Well, maybe her line was longer than yours, but you had a wider variety of fans. There were men in your line."

"Gay men." She reached for his shoulder and reclaimed her bag. "Gay men love my books."

"Is that bad?"

"It's good. It's called crossover appeal."

"You won an award, your keynote address brought down the house, hundreds of readers and writers lined up to have you sign their books this afternoon, and you've got crossover appeal."

The elevator came to a stop, the doors whispered apart, and Carter held out his arm to usher Khela forward. As she passed him, he added, "I don't understand why you're so upset."

"You don't have to understand," she muttered, shoving her cardkey into the power pad mounted on one of the penthouse's heavy double doors. When the security light flashed green, she pushed the doors open and walked through them, allowing them to swing back in Carter's face.

"I'd like to," he insisted. "This is the closest I've ever been to the life of a celebrity, and—"

"I'm no celebrity." She dropped her tote bag on the cocktail table on her way to the bar. "My *books* are well known. Not me."

"You wrote them," Carter persisted, watching her slam a crystal tumbler on the lacquered bar. "You can't separate yourself from them."

Breathing hard, she grabbed a bottle from under the bar and uncapped it. She sloshed a dram of pale liquid into the tumbler, plunked the bottle on the bar, and raised the tumbler. She tossed back her beverage in one gulp. Carter doubted that it had a chance to warm in her stomach before she hunched over, clutching at her throat and gut.

"Water!" she coughed, the cords in her neck protruding. "*Help!*"

Carter slowly strolled over to her and picked up the bottle. "Wow," he said, reading the label. "Knappogue Castle Irish Whiskey. Nothing but the best for the VIPs, huh?" He raised his voice to better hear himself over Khela's strangled coughing and the sound of her fist pounding the bar. He poured himself a swallow and sipped it.

"This is really good, Khela. Crisp, clean . . . slightly sweet, actually. It has a really smooth finish, unlike the peat-aged Irish whiskeys."

"Water," she hissed. "Please . . ."

Carter rounded the bar and took a bottle of Waiwera Infinity water from the minifridge. He'd barely removed the cap when Khela grabbed it from him and began chugging it. "Overpriced New Zealand water is more agreeable to you than overpriced Irish whiskey, I see."

Her esophagus no longer on fire, Khela took several deep breaths and several more sips of water. "That's the problem," she shouted at him.

"Not if you cut the whiskey with a little water," he suggested with a little laugh.

"You think this is funny? Gimme a pen and I'll really crack you up by gouging out one of my eyes. I'm not talking about the damn drinks, anyway! I can't separate myself from my work anymore, and I don't believe in my work!"

He crossed his arms over his chest. "So the logical conclusion would be that you don't believe in yourself."

She slammed her palms flat on the bar. "Don't you dare try to use logic on me, Carter Radcliffe! Logic has nothing to do with how I feel!"

He snickered. "That doesn't surprise me."

Khela left the bar and headed for the Chippendale desk in the office section of the suite, kicking off her dressy jute slide sandals as she went. She untucked her white linen blouse and unfastened the top button of her tobacco-washed silk pants before sitting down and opening her laptop. She held her head in her hands until her desktop appeared.

"What are you doing?" Carter asked from a safe distance.

"Writing a letter to my editor."

"Shouldn't you be getting ready for dinner and the ball?"

"I'm not going to dinner, and I'm especially not going to that dopey ball." She opened a blank document and began typing.

"Your letter is so important that you have to miss out on the social event of the weekend?"

"I think announcing my retirement is much more important than a bunch of middle-aged headcases running around in bed sheets."

"You make it sound like a clan ral—hey!" He went to stand behind her, to read over her shoulder. "You're retiring? Seriously?"

"I wanted to announce it at the luncheon, but I couldn't." Her fingers whizzed over the keyboard, committing to paper all the things she wished she'd said in her keynote address.

"Wait a minute here, just hold on," Carter said. "I don't understand this at all. Those people down there respect you. I met a few of them in the hotel restaurant this morning when I got back from my run."

Her fingers paused over the keyboard. "Is that where you were when I woke up?"

Her tender inquiry drew him closer.

"I agreed to spend this weekend with you, and I'm a man of my word. Besides, I wouldn't have missed your keynote address for anything."

She propped her elbows on the desk and buried her face in her hands. "I'm sorry, Carter. I'm letting this weekend get the better of me."

"I'm sure it happens to the best of them." He scrubbed a hand over her head as though she were his little brother. "The irony is that you *are* the best of them."

"Carter?"

His grin faded once he spotted the tears sparkling on her lower lashes. "Jeez, Khela, what is it?" He kneeled next to her chair, spinning it so that she faced him.

"Everyone down there, especially Daphne, would hate me if I'd given the keynote I'd originally planned." Her tears spilled over her lower lids, dotting her blouse with dark spots.

Ordinarily, a woman's tears had the power to send Carter scurrying for cover. Khela's had the opposite effect. They kept him rooted to the spot and determined to erase their cause. "You weren't going to tell everyone that romance sucks, were you?" he joked.

She chuckled in spite of her misery. "Sort of. For me, it does."

The quiet, delicate tears that heightened the rich chocolate of her eyes were the preamble to a flood that turned her into a weeping, drooling mess in Carter's arms. He stroked her hair and her back, soothing her with gentle words that made her feel doubly guilty about having been so cross with him the night before.

When she calmed enough to speak, she did so, her mouth moving against the side of his neck. "I started writing romance because I lucked into it. As I was hammering out that first book, I fell in love with it. It became something I really believed in. I don't anymore."

"You're not just talking about the Disney-distilled Brothers Grimm type stuff, are you?"

She pulled away a bit, but remained in his embrace. "I'm talking about the 'stuff,' as you call it, that my Grandma Belle and Grandpa Neal had. They weren't really my grandparents, but they adopted me when I was six. They were together for fifty-two years. They were the happiest couple I've ever seen, and it was genuine. It was everything. They understood each other. They knew each other. They had a trust and a love that I've never been able to find for myself." She laughed sadly, then revealed the deepest, most painful secret in her heart. "I make it up. I write books that let me dream about what I want because I'm scared I'll never find it in real life."

Khela assumed that her melancholy was contagious as she and Carter sat in a pensive yet comfortable silence in the limousine taking them back to Khela's brownstone. In no mood for further festivities, she had decided to go home, a decision fully supported by Carter, who had called the car for them.

The view of downtown Boston through the dark tinted windows seemed far more interesting to Carter than more conversation, and Khela respected his silence by keeping her own. His new quiet filled the luxurious cabin, making it seem even larger. He stared out as if watching the inventory of his own secret heart tumbling down the sidewalk.

When they arrived at the brownstone, Khela spent a moment in the car with Carter while the driver unloaded her bags.

"The driver will take you home," she said. "Thank you, for . . . helping me out this weekend. I owe you one."

He finally looked at her. "What you owe me is a real date."

She blinked, undecided as to which surprised her more—his calm, blunt delivery or the fact that he wanted to see her again at all. She hid her discomfiture behind lukewarm indignation. "First of all, when I said I owed you one, I meant a favor, not a future."

"Spoken like a true sourpuss." Carter slid across the seat and exited the limo. He offered his hand and waited for her to take it.

She crossed her legs and arms and stubbornly waited for him to drop the chivalrous act. Carter grinned at the impatient tap of her right foot in her fancy sandal, but then his heart surged when her hand slipped into his and she allowed him to help her onto the sidewalk. He held onto her hand and drew her close. "I had fun, Khela, and I think you did, too, at least with me. I want to do this again, only for real."

"I'm a sourpuss, remember?"

"I shouldn't have said that." He dropped his eyes and his voice, forcing Khela to move in closer to hear him. "I actually found you rather sweet."

Khela suddenly felt feverish. "I was hoping you wouldn't mention that. Ever."

"Okay, I won't mention it anymore. When can we do it again?"

She looked at her feet to hide a smile.

"C'mon, Khela," he cajoled. "What d'ya say? Let me take you out. Think of it as a favor to me. We could grab some dinner right now. We've got the car for the rest of the evening."

She had a dozen good reasons to not accept his offer. Trouble was, the number one reason was that she really wanted to accept it. That fact alone convinced her that she would be better off saying goodbye to him right there on the sidewalk.

"I'm flattered, Carter, I really am, but . . ." She swallowed, but the tiny lump in her throat only wedged itself more firmly. "I'm not interested in a relationship."

"Not interested or scared?"

"It doesn't matter, does it?" She pulled her hand from his and put some space between them. "The bottom line is that I can't go out with you again."

He shoved his hands in his pockets and rocked on his heels. Khela waited for him to respond—to argue or plead, insult or tease.

The noises of a busy Boston summer evening filled the empty silence between them as Khela tipped and thanked the driver, politely refusing his offer to carry her bags up to her apartment.

"Thank you for everything," she told Carter before grabbing her bags and lugging them up the steep stone stairs to the front door. She turned back before closing the door behind her. Carter still stood at the wide open limo door, seeing her into the building.

Only a fool would turn down a man like him, Khela thought, her heart as heavy as her footsteps as she bypassed the stairs to take the elevator. *Then again, that's me. Your typical romantic fool . . .*

———✦———

"Where am I taking you, Mr. . . . ?"

The driver waited for Carter to respond, which took awhile, since he was surfing the Internet on his cell phone. "Radcliffe," Carter finally said.

"Where do you live, Mr. Radcliffe?" the driver said pleasantly.

"Uh, across the street," he said tersely. "But I think I need to make a stop first."

"Yes, sir. Where to, sir?"

Carter Googled Khela Halliday, then selected the site most likely to give him the information he wanted.

"I really need to get this boat moving, Mr. Radcliffe," the driver said. "There's a meter maid incoming at a pretty good clip."

"Sorry," Carter said absently. "Just drive."

"Not a problem, sir."

Carter scanned the information he'd selected, then logged off and slipped his phone back into his pocket. The driver smoothly pulled the car into traffic, and Carter turned around in his seat to look back at the brownstone. High above Commonwealth Avenue, Khela was probably climbing into her loft and unpacking. Having spent time with her, Carter now realized that her top-story condo was no more than a luxury prison, and that she would never let down her hair and give a prince a fair chance.

I write books that let me dream about what I want . . .

Khela's confession moved through his head and settled deep in his chest. If her books held the key to unlocking her heart, then there was only one thing for Carter to do.

"I'd like to go to Waterstone's," he called to the driver. "It's a bookstore in Harvard Square."

CHAPTER 5

"You are the most base of thieves, one who schemes to steal that which is freely given you—my heart."
—*from* The Pirate's Princess *by Khela Halliday*

"You didn't."

"Yes, I did."

"Khela . . . you couldn't have."

"I couldn't stop myself."

"It's not right."

"I was asked to make a cake, so I made a cake. There was no guideline as to what it could or couldn't be made of."

"This isn't going to do much to contradict the general perception that you're a little bit weird."

"Are you going to bid on my cake or not?"

"I don't have much choice, do I? I'd hate for anyone else to cut into that thing and find out what you did."

Khela studied her cake with an unbiased eye as she and Daphne strolled side by side along the length of the display table. It was just as pretty as the others, though not as artistic as architect Jonathan Brady's, which was a double-fudge masterpiece sculpted and frosted to look like Trinity Church. Nor was it as ornamental as fashion designer Katrinka Klinche's chiffon-pink dome encased in a shell of spun-sugar threads sprinkled with genuine fourteen-karat gold flakes.

Khela considered her cake far more interesting than cartoonist Ray Crowley's effort, a 28-inch pyramid constructed of Twinkies cemented together with melted Hershey's Kisses and mini marshmallows.

The two-layer cake Khela donated looked like a typical, grocery-store bakery offering: smooth white frosting, puffy shell borders, red roses clustered on top.

It didn't matter which cake looked and tasted better or fetched the highest bidder. Boston "celebrities" had been asked to create them for an auction to benefit the Greater Roxbury Literacy Fund.

Katrinka Klinche had been asked to create a "fashion forward confection." Jonathan Brady had honored the Fund's request to "build an edible example of form and function."

The Literacy Fund was one of Khela's favorite charitable organizations, but having been asked to bake a cake "faithful to the spirit of true love and romance," she had done almost the exact opposite.

At least that had been her intent.

Daphne nudged Khela's elbow. "Looks like your abomination has drummed up some interest."

Khela looked over her shoulder. Through the crowd she saw two men examining the description placard set before her cake. They were both tall and broad-shouldered, and they seemed to know each other. The shorter of the two, an African-American man with nut brown skin, a shaved head and big diamond studs in his ears, stood out in a cream-colored suit with a cranberry square in his upper breast pocket. His taller friend passed a hand through his short, dark blond hair as he leaned over Khela's cake. He grasped a shiny black paddle in one hand, the gold number 88 glinting from it. Wearing a smart white shirt, jeans and a snappy black blazer, he looked more relaxed than his companion. He was dressed with casual perfection for the event, and he blended with the chic artists and wealthy Literacy Fund benefactors milling about the Stahp/Geaux Gallery of Modern Art, which was hosting the auction. When he turned in her direction, Khela's jaw dropped and her face snapped forward.

"What's he doing here?" she hissed at Daphne.

"Sniffing at your cake, looks like." Daphne grinned around the slim polka-dotted straw sticking out of her blue margarita.

"How'd he know about this event?" Khela set down her cranberry, apple and honey "mocktail" on the nearest object, the flattened, feather-covered top of a giant yellow head made of plaster.

"It was in the *Herald-Star*, the *Globe*, the *Metro*—" Daphne started.

"But why is he *here*?" Khela ducked behind Daphne when Carter and his friend seemed to glance her way. She fluffed Daphne's voluminous red mane, hoping it would act as an invisibility cloak.

"Either he really likes cake or because *you're* here. Duh." Daphne finished her drink, set the empty glass next to Khela's, and stepped to the side to expose Khela. "He knows you're here. Quit acting like a child and let's go say hi. I haven't seen him in ages, and I need my fix."

"You go. I'll wait here."

"What is with you?" Daphne stamped her foot. "There are too many hot, available, employed Beantown bachelors here tonight."

She grabbed Khela's upper arm and turned her toward a giant sheet of glass two inches thick hanging from the ceiling. A wide stripe of black acrylic paint divided the panel into equal halves. Titled *Parallel Perspectives*, the art piece made an impromptu mirror for the two women to inspect their reflections.

"We look amazing, if I do say so myself, and I'm not going to waste this Zac Posen on you."

With a twirl of her flirty cocktail dress, Daphne left Khela alone with her reflection. Khela watched her friend's disappearance in the glass. Male and female heads alike turned to track the diminutive redhead. Daphne cut a striking figure with her flaming hair and the Kelly green baby doll dress that complemented her fair complexion. Givenchy heels undercut the sweetness of the dress, leaving no doubt that Daphne was a kitten on the prowl.

─── ∾∾∾ ───

Alone in the crowded room, Khela studied her reflection, deeming it more panther than kitten. She had chosen one of her little black dresses, a fitted, brushed cotton jersey soft as cashmere. It was sleeveless with a high collar and armholes cut deeply, fully exposing her shoulders and shoulder blades. The dress was a fine advertisement for her boxing coach's push-up regimen.

The skirt hugged her hips, the hem resting just under her knees. Two notch pleats in the back allowed for walking ease and continued the line of Khela's seamed stockings. Her upswept hair was casual but chic, and with the modest champagne diamond studs in her earlobes, her whole look was sultry sophistication. The finishing touch wasn't the light application of nude lip gloss and smoky eye paint, but the black, four-inch Roger Vivier heels on her feet.

Fine, double straps circled her ankles to fasten with delicate, diamond-studded buckles. A satin rose, too big to go unnoticed yet too small to be considered ostentatious, decorated the narrow vamp. From head to toe, Khela was classy and provocative in equal measure.

Yet she would have given anything to be back at home in her office, slogging around the house in jeans and a T-shirt, lost in the pages of her current writing project. Her feet wandered along with her mind as she moved through the gallery, scarcely noticing the wacky, whimsical and ridiculous works for which the Stahp/Geaux Gallery was renowned.

She would never have done what Carmen had done at the awards dinner—discuss her storylines with others. Other than her editor, her books had only one reader before publication, Daphne, and even after ten years, it was still hard to turn a manuscript over to the best friend who was her best editor and harshest critic.

Daphne's first serious crush was on William Strunk Jr., the Cornell professor behind the classic grammar guidebook *The Elements of Style*, and she had spent a week in mourning when an illustrated version came out in 2005.

"What's next?" she'd ranted. "Dr. Seuss illustrating the Bible?"

Daphne's eagle eye for typos, grammatical mistakes and incongruities was the secret behind Khela's reputation for highly polished manuscripts.

The story occupying Khela's mind now was a brand new 'what if?' Most of her books began with a 'what if?' Her current project had its genesis in a fight she witnessed while walking home from the Boston Public Library a few weeks ago.

A wiry man and a squat woman stood on Boylston Street. The man bent over her, angrily jabbing his finger at her as he spoke words that Khela couldn't hear. It was raining, cars packed the street, their drivers honking as if that would decongest traffic, pedestrians moved in steady currents along the slick sidewalks, and no one seemed to notice the man and the woman.

Khela wouldn't have noticed them, either, if she hadn't been trying to wrestle open her stubborn umbrella. Once she saw them, she couldn't look away. She had scoured them with her eyes, noting every detail.

The greasy dirt ground into the knees of the man's jeans. The torn pocket on the woman's poncho, which looked as if it had last been cleaned when the poncho was first fashionable. The way the hard raindrops matted the man's thin dark hair to his skull, and how the woman's dark hair, heavy with rain, hung lifelessly from her bowed head. The way the man used his sleeve to wipe spittle from his mouth, and how the woman hunkered away from him, her shoulders hiked up to her ears. Khela especially noted the way water flew from the ends of the woman's hair after the man slapped her hard across the face, sending her head rocking violently to one side.

Khela had used her cellphone to summon the police, who'd been nearby, fortunately. As the man was led off in handcuffs, still cursing, Khela watched the woman. Her assailant was long gone by the time a female police officer touched the woman's chin, raising her face. And then it happened. Khela's 'what if?'

What if she'd hit that son-of-a-bitch back? she had thought.

All the rest of the way home, Khela kept having to stop to scrawl notes on the tiny pad of paper she kept handy for just such occasions, no easy task with her heavy book satchel and umbrella in her arms. She had the bones of a story by the time she'd arrived home. She was soaked through to her underwear, but didn't bother to change until she had the first rough draft of an outline. The best stories were always the ones that wouldn't let Khela go, and this was one of them.

Working on the story had been so fulfilling that she'd hardly thought of Carter in the weeks since they'd last seen each other. Hardly meaning only once . . . or twice . . . a day.

She had declined Daphne's repeated requests to visit following the convention, because she knew that Daphne would lure Carter to her apartment. Her new book was the perfect thing to keep her isolated—from Daphne, Carter and everyone else.

———◦◦◦———

Khela paused in front of a seven-foot sculpture of an old-time baseball player. The placard in front of the work read that it was Red Sox legend Ted Williams in his classic batting stance. The piece was made of Big League Chew bubble gum, personally chewed by the artist, an ardent Sox fan. Khela circled to the rear of the grayish-pink creation. To onlookers, she might have been studying the work from its other side. Khela was actually scanning the crowd for the man she desperately tried not to think about.

He stood at one of the chest-high, white melamine tables near the bar. While his friend drank one of the garish, glow-in-the-dark martinis specially concocted for the auction, Carter had his hand loosely curled around the neck of a Sam Adams. He and his friend had been at the table for all of three seconds before they were joined by an older woman in a long black dress that fit her as closely as her own skin.

The woman's frosted blonde hair was styled in what Daphne called the Cougar Do—the sporty but sophisticated flip that certain plastic surgery patients get because it showcases their rejuvenated, mask-like faces while hiding nip-and-tuck scars.

Khela was trying to shake off the first pricks of jealousy when a grinning man seemed to materialize right out of Ted Williams's back pocket.

"Boo," he greeted pleasantly.

"Blecch," Khela grunted at the truly terrifying sight of her ex-husband, Jay Frederickson.

Jay straightened his purple silk tie, and the chunky gold rings on three of his fingers glinted in the track lighting. "It's so good to see you too, Khela," he said, his voice syrupy. "Don't worry. I'm not here for anything from you. I was in the mood for a new piece, so uh, I thought I'd come by. Do a little shopping."

She tugged the program that he'd curled into a loose tube from his hand. Three of the Literacy Fund organizers' publicity mug shots were circled in blue ink: Constance Nearing-Cook, the widow of one of Boston's most successful and respected attorneys; Jamie Shouten, an heiress whose family fortune had been made in Boston shipping; and Esmé Wilhoite, the Latina divorcée famous for walking off with half of her banking magnate husband's half-billion dollar fortune upon their divorce.

"Shopping?" she snorted. "Looks more like you're hunting."

He raised his half-tone Gucci sunglasses, resting them on his head. "Are you jealous?" he whispered, girlishly batting his long, thick eyelashes.

"Please," she retorted. "Come on, let me introduce you to those chippies." She took his purple silk cuff between her thumb and forefinger and dragged him forward. "The sooner you marry some rich sucker, the sooner you'll stop sucking alimony out of me."

"Hey, beautiful, where's the fire?" snickered the man Khela almost trampled in her haste to get rid of her ex-husband.

"Holy—!" Khela gasped. She looked from the stranger to her ex and shuddered. They could have been twins, right down to the cut of their suits, their Gucci half-tones and their preference for silky, disco-shiny shirts.

"I said," Jay's doppelganger licked his lips, "where's the fire, baby?"

"Excuse me," Jay grinned, pulling his cuff from Khela's weak grasp. "I see someone I'd like to know." With that, Jay made his way straight to Constance.

"Miss Halliday," the stranger greeted, taking her hand and bringing it to his lips. "What a pleasant surprise to run into you here tonight."

"I'll bet," Khela mumbled skeptically. She wriggled her hand free and absently wiped the stranger's kiss on the back of her skirt.

"I tend to be more of a homebody, but when I was invited to attend this event, I knew I had to come out and support the efforts of this group," he went on smoothly.

"Wonderful." Khela tried to move past him, but he stepped in her path.

"I'm Sheldon Perry." He extended a hand. "It's truly my honor to meet you, Miss Halliday."

Khela gave his hand a curt shake, pinching her lips to suppress a grimace at the sight of the clear polish glossing his fingernails. Everything about him—his peanut-shaped head, yellow-brown complexion, glib manner of speech, tailored sharkskin suit and yellow silk shirt—reminded her so much of Jay that she wanted to slap him on principle.

"You know, you have really beautiful eyes, Khela," Sheldon grinned, revealing capped teeth the size of piano keys. "I know where the fire is now. In your gorgeous eyes."

"Thank you," Khela said, not meaning it one bit. "Now if you'll excuse me, I have to find my friend."

"I could be your friend," he oozed, pitching his voice low into the Barry White range. "Who knows? In time, friendship could lead to more."

Real or imagined, Khela tasted vomit at the back of her throat. "I'm not looking for more right now. I won't be looking for it later, either." *Especially not with the likes of you.*

He threw his head back and laughed. "I love a woman with spirit. A challenge!"

I think I'm gonna be sick, Khela thought.

His laughter abruptly stopped. Staring her in the eyes, he said, "So where're we going for dinner?"

"There's a buffet next to that blue display," Khela told him, referring to the series of blue light bulbs mounted on a wall-sized board on the other side of the gallery.

"I thought you might like to take me someplace a little nicer." He stepped close enough for her to count the hairs rimming his nostrils. "Someplace more intimate."

"I haven't asked you out," Khela pointed out.

"It's the twenty-first century, baby," he grinned. "I don't mind when a woman takes charge and tells me where and when we're going." He ran his tongue over his lips again.

"Ew," Khela grimaced. "I won't be taking you to dinner, Mr. Perry."

"Sheldon," he cooed, audaciously stroking her upper arms. "You got something better planned? Excellent! I'm free, baby."

"I doubt that," she muttered under her breath, shrugging free of his loose grip.

Other women might have considered Sheldon Perry attractive, well-spoken and charming, but Khela was all too familiar with his type to stumble into his sticky web of flattery and confidence. The suit he wore was probably his nicest, an Armani or Calvin Klein he'd purchased secondhand online, at a consignment shop or borrowed permanently from a friend. He likely scoured the newspapers and local magazines looking for events such as the Literacy Fund auction, events where he was sure to encounter wealthy women lonely or stupid enough to fall for the reptilian charm wrapped in his discount designer duds.

Khela knew Sheldon Perry even though she'd only just met him.

She'd been married to a man just like him.

"What do you do for a living?" she asked him, narrowing her eyes in suspicion.

He shifted his gaze from her eyes to a point between them. "I'm a broker with Manulife Financial."

Khela remembered his hands on her upper arms. His nails were tidily manicured and polished, but his palms were calloused. His hands had the look of someone who pushed a desk but the feel of someone who pushed a shovel.

She studied him closer. "You look familiar. Have you ever been to Buscador de Oro Island?"

"That sounds so familiar," he said, his brow knitted in thought. "Is that one of the Bahaman islands? There's so many of them I haven't been to, that—"

"It's off the coast of Spain," Khela said.

He loudly snapped his fingers. "That's right! It's one of the uh . . . um . . . it's on the tip of my tongue. I've been to Spain several times, and—"

"It's one of the Canary Islands," she prompted.

"Oh, Buscador de Oro, yes," he said, nodding. "I thought you said something else. I spent a few days in Buscador de Oro last summer myself, visiting one of my clients. You probably saw me on the beach."

"Of course," Khela snapped.

"Work keeps me busy, Khela," he said with a regretful shake of his head. "Managing multimillion-dollar portfolios isn't as easy as it may seem. I have to be available to my clients at a moment's notice. A Porsche I ordered recently is still waiting for me at my dealership because I haven't had time to pick it up."

The conversation was turning into a different kind of game for Khela than it was for Sheldon as she asked her next question.

"Where did you go to school?"

"I'm a Northwestern man," he boasted. "I got accepted to Harvard and Yale, but I wanted to remain close to my family."

She propped her hands on her hips. "You must have enjoyed going to school in Ohio."

"Yeah, it was fun." His eyes strayed to his watch, a Rolex, before bouncing back to Khela. "Uh, since my Porsche is still at the dealership, let's say you and I get out of here in your ride?" He leaned in close. "Or did the Fund organizers send a limo for you?"

Khela spotted Jay. He'd moved on from Constance and was chatting up Esmé Wilhoite with the gregarious animation of a used car salesman. Esmé had to be at least fifteen years older than Jay, but she was striking with her black eyes, smooth olive skin and short black bob. Khela shuddered. Esmé was a dead ringer for Jay's mother, who'd taught her son everything he knew about marrying for money.

Khela returned her attention to Sheldon. His forehead wrinkled in concentration, his glittering brown eyes raked over the crowd as though he were casing the joint. He glanced from the people assembled in the gallery to his program, matching faces and biographies, studying the booklet as though it were an LSAT prep book.

"See anything interesting?" Khela startled him into crunching the program in his fist.

"Just what's right in front of me," he responded smoothly. "Now how about us going for a little ride?"

Khela backed away from him, plainly stating, "I've already been taken for a ride by a man like you. See ya."

—⚭—

Khela circled around Ted Williams to find Daphne, who was working her way toward Khela through the crowd.

Jay slipped away from Esmé to intercept Khela. "You should be at home working."

"My work no longer concerns you," she snapped. "Everything I've written since our divorce is off limits to you."

"Yes, well every time you have a new book out, sales of the old ones increase. I've grown rather fond of cashing royalty checks."

Khela gritted her teeth so hard the hinge of her jaw ached. In order to dissolve her marriage to Jay as expeditiously as possible, Khela had agreed to his demand for half the earnings on the books she'd written in the course of their marriage, claiming that his "support, expertise and dedication" had been integral to her success. The judge ignored the fact that Khela's first bestseller had been written and published long before she and Jay married. In some ways, Khela's first book was her least favorite because its success had drawn Jay into her life.

After four years of marriage, she'd gotten to know him well enough to know why he was baiting her into a fight. "The investment didn't yield any dividends, did it?" Khela asked lightly.

"Investment? I don't follow."

"The ten minutes you spent trying to get Esmé to adopt you, marry you or let you impregnate her."

"Why do you always think the worst of me, Khela?"

"Because that's all you ever gave her, J-Fred," Daphne interjected, coming up behind him. "The auction's starting, Khela."

"Always good to see you, too, Daphne," Jay snidely retorted. "So when's your book coming out? Oh, yeah. You don't have a contract yet."

"The key word is 'yet,' " Khela said, hooking her arm through Daphne's. They sauntered to the auctioneer's white stylized podium, leaving Jay to resume his prowling.

"He's like an opportunistic infection," Daphne said. "He shows up wherever you are and tries to glom onto some other unsuspecting woman."

"They're out in force tonight." Khela discreetly pointed to Sheldon. "He's a prospector, too," she said, using their private code word for male gold diggers.

Daphne shrugged. "That suit is awful. The shoes, too."

"He's a rookie," Khela scoffed.

"How'd you get him?"

"Right from the get, with Buscador de Oro."

Daphne laughed lightly. "Good ol' gold digger island. Where did you put it this time?"

"The Canary Islands. It all went downhill from there. It was too easy to trip him up in his own lies."

Khela abruptly halted when she spotted Carter and his well-dressed friend, the cougar in tow, taking positions near the front.

"Look at her," Khela grumbled. "She's four hundred years old. She probably went to kindergarten with Adam and Eve."

"Shh." Daphne took a firmer grip on her shiny black paddle. "The auctioneer's a cutie, isn't he? He was in town a few months ago, calling the Children's Home Society auction we went to."

Khela was far more interested in Carter, and she bobbed and weaved to keep an eye on him through the sea of bidders. Carter faced forward despite the cougar's attempts to steal his attention from the auctioneer reading the description of the first cake.

The woman ran her hand through her hair and, holding her cocktail near her face, she leaned close to Carter and whispered in his ear. She laughed at whatever she said, touching her throat, while Carter took a subtle step closer to his friend, who appeared amused at the attention the older woman paid Carter.

He hates her, Khela thought, delighted.

The cougar deflated Khela's happy feeling by placing her hand on Carter's shoulder. It lingered there, possessive and knuckly, and Khela had to seriously fight her first instinct, which was to barge through the crowd and snatch out the cougar's whiskers.

"Are you okay?" Daphne asked, peering closely at Khela. "You look like you're turning rabid or something."

"Look at her!" Khela whispered fiercely. "She's all over him!"

Daphne clucked her tongue. "For God's sake, Khela, they're just standing there. Why are you so concern . . ." Her words faded.

Khela could almost see understanding washing over Daphne's face.

"Did you have sex with him at the convention?" Daphne asked.

Their nearest neighbors looked at them with interest. Once they'd turned back to the auctioneer, Khela drew Daphne in close. "No. Not really. Well . . . sort of."

Daphne's eyes became perfect circles. "That's why you're avoiding him! Dammit, Khela, why didn't you tell me? I can't believe you kept that secret for almost two months. I can't believe I didn't figure it out sooner." She lowered her voice to a conspiratorial purr. "How was it?"

"We didn't . . ." Khela rubbed her forehead in exasperation. "We just messed around a little."

"How little?" Daphne's eyes sparkled.

"Enough for me to know that it's better for me to stay away from him."

"That good, huh?" Daphne smiled.

Khela's eyes drifted shut, and for the ten-millionth time, she called up the memory of her intimate encounter with Carter. It should have weakened or dimmed from overuse, but it was almost as vivid as the moment she'd lived it. Her breath caught in her chest, she felt heat rise in her cheeks, and the warmth of yearning flooded her chest.

"Wow," Daphne muttered. "I've never seen you like this."

"Like what?"

"You're really into him."

"He's cute," Khela responded, forcing ambivalence into her voice.

"He's more than cute," Daphne said. "I want to lick him every time I see him."

"Yeah, he's nice, too." A slight smile came to Khela's face as she watched Carter peel the cougar's paw from his shoulder. "And he's funny. When we were in our suite, we got into a little bit of an argument. I said I was sorry for yelling at him, and he goes, 'I'm sorry I'm so handsome.' It was so adorable."

Daphne didn't laugh.

"I guess you had to be there," Khela said.

"You're falling for him."

"No, I'm not." The response was automatic. And not necessarily the truth.

———◦◦◦———

"Carter Radcliffe is definitely two-week worthy," Daphne grinned. "You should go for it."

Khela harrumphed. "One weekend was enough to get me in over my head. I don't even want to think about what would come of two—" She clutched Daphne's arm. "My cake is up! Get ready to bid."

Unlike some of his tongue-tangling American counterparts, Welsh-born auction caller Llewellyn Davies had a polished, cosmopolitan manner, which added to the sophistication of the event. Reading from a white index card drawn from an inner breast pocket of his tux, he said, "Next we have, uh, a cake titled simply, 'Cake.' Created by hot-air balloon operator Khela Halliday." All but Khela laughed, Daphne the loudest and longest. "Ms. Halliday has prepared a double-layer, round cake with white frosting and red flowers. She hasn't submitted an ingredient list, so you'll have to win this lovely confection to discover what exotic flavor waits beneath its fluffy white frosting."

"Exotic ain't the half of it," Daphne mumbled, earning a little shove from Khela.

Llewellyn had done his homework, calling specific patrons by name and using easy humor to goad them into higher bids. The higher the bids rose, the lower Khela's spirits sank. She tasted bits of her own heart when the bids climbed to fourteen hundred dollars.

"Fourteen, fourteen, will I see fifteen for this masterpiece of simplicity from author Khela Halliday?" Llewellyn asked, his merry blue eyes hunting for black bidding placards.

"Fifteen," drawled a familiar voice from the front row.

"No, he didn't!" Khela nearly cried.

"Yes, he did," Daphne grinned.

"Two thousand!" Khela called out in a high voice, shoving Daphne's paddle hand into the air.

"We have a decisive two thousand dollars from the pretty lass in green," Llewellyn said.

"He thinks I'm *purty*," Daphne squealed, a blush rising to swallow her freckles.

"Twenty-one," came the deep voice with the Southern drawl that made Khela's heart pound a little harder.

"You can't let him outbid you, Daphne," Khela said. "Raise him another hundred."

"This isn't poker," Daphne said, before waving her paddle and offering twenty-two hundred.

"Twenty-five hundred." Carter's precise pronunciation silenced the hum of low chatter in the gallery.

"I can't go higher than that," Daphne whispered.

"I told you I'd pay for it." *In more ways than one, it seems,* Khela added to herself, knowing that the winning bidder wouldn't exactly be getting a traditional cake. "Please, we can't let him buy that thing."

"You should have made a cake out of *cake*," Daphne admonished. "Three thousand!" she called just before Llewellyn would have banged the gavel on Carter's twenty-five hundred.

Llewellyn playfully growled. "The beauty in green is engaged in a spirited duel with the persistent gentlemen cowboy. I like a lady with spunk. Do I hear thirty-one hundred, anyone?"

"Thirty-five," Carter exhaled loudly, as though bored with the game.

"He can't afford that!" Khela whimpered. "That's probably a month's salary for him. We can't let him spend it on that cake!"

"Four thousand!" Daphne said with a saucy toss of her mane for Llewellyn's benefit.

Khela blanched at the way Llewellyn's gaze zeroed in on Daphne with laser precision. He smiled at her, flashing deep dimples.

"Four thousand five," Carter returned.

"Do I hear forty-six hundred?" Llewellyn seemed to ask Daphne alone. "Or shall I sell at forty-five hundred and get on with the business of having a drink with the lovely lady in green?"

"Five thousand!" Carter hollered.

"Sold!" Daphne called.

"Daphne!" Khela's cry was drowned by the sharp crack of a gavel finalizing the sale and the ensuing laughter of the crowd. She looked on in horror as Llewellyn leaned forward and shook Carter's hand, and Daphne fairly skipped to the podium.

"Traitor," Khela called after her.

Carter, on tiptoe, turned to scan the audience, which began to disperse with Llewellyn and Daphne drifting side by side toward the bar. Carter's narrowed eyes fell on Khela, and she ducked. With the grace of a bow-legged goose, she scrambled to the nearest hiding place, a work five feet long, six feet high, one foot thick and suspended from the ceiling with thin cables. The side facing Khela appeared to be painted gold, with a fuzzy texture.

A waiter garbed entirely in black glided by with sparkling flutes of blush champagne balanced on a black tray. Khela grabbed a glass, and was bringing it to her lips when Carter rounded the hanging art piece.

"I hope it's chocolate," he said with an unreadable smile, his voice startling her.

Khela whirled on him. "You shouldn't have bought my cake!"

"I didn't."

The grin that accompanied his response should have started Khela's alarm bells ringing.

"I bought what comes with the cake," he said.

"I don't follow." She licked the rim of her glass before she sipped from it, a trick Daphne had taught her to keep from stamping the glass with her lipstick.

Carter watched the unintentionally provocative gesture with interest.

"What comes with it?" Khela asked dryly. "Ice cream?" She snickered as she sipped her champagne.

"You."

The perfectly chilled Bollinger Grand Année Rosé left Khela in a spray of surprised indignation that dampened Carter's shirt front and dripped onto her bodice.

"For five thousand dollars, I bought that cake along with the pleasure of having the cook serve me the first slice." Carter pulled a program from his pocket and unfolded it to show her the detail she'd clearly overlooked.

Khela snatched the program and brought it to her face to peruse the lines she had failed to notice. She slowly raised her face to find him offering a smile and a neatly folded handkerchief. "You bought me," she gasped.

"For cheap," he murmured devilishly.

CHAPTER 6

"Yours was the kiss by which I've measured all others!"
—*from* Tender Memories *by Khela Halliday*

"That was a good one." Carter began mopping up Khela's bosom.

"I can do that." She reached for the square of white cotton. Her fingertips brushed his, and in that instant, a discordant chime from the artwork beside them stole their attention.

"What the hell is this?" Carter muttered, squinting at it.

Inspecting the work more carefully, Khela saw that it wasn't merely a large, blank canvas with a metallic sheen mounted in a black case. Thousands of tiny bells produced the hairy gold texture, and it was the bells that had responded when Khela touched Carter.

"Seems like you can call any ol' thing art these days." Carter moved closer to Khela. He dabbed at her collarbone, lifting the glistening beads of champagne. "Good thing you had your dress Scotchguarded."

"Yeah, good thing," Khela sighed.

He was too close, his touch too sure. He'd cut his hair since she'd last seen him; the whiskey blond scruff was much closer to his head. His topaz eyes were just as impish and intense, the fire in them playful and only slightly dangerous. The shape of his mouth still eluded Khela's powers of description and, looking at it, she enjoyed phantom memories of the delights it had once given her.

She lifted her chin a bit, bringing her mouth that much closer to his as he touched his handkerchief to her left shoulder, near her neck. His nostrils flared slightly as he drew a deep breath, and then said the very thing Khela was thinking about him. "You smell so good."

The bells aligned with Khela's upper right arm and shoulder leaped to rigid attention, reacting as though they too felt the power of his compliment. Their microscopic clappers strained toward Khela, producing a high-pitched, tinny buzz.

"What are you wearing?" Carter asked her.

"Old Spice."

"Me, too," Carter smiled. "Looks like we've got more in common than a fondness for cake."

"My junior year trigonometry teacher used to bathe in Old Spice," Khela said. "We could smell him coming three floors away." Carter's scent was woodsy and clean, with a hint of citrusy spice. It was masculine without being overpowering. Khela filled her lungs with it. "You're not wearing Old Spice."

"Neither are you," he responded. "So what is it?"

"Khela No. 1."

He stepped closer to her, his hands still low on his hips. A large patch of bells even with their torsos sprang to tinkling life.

"Is that anything like Chanel No. 5?"

"It's my scent," Khela said. "There's a boutique that'll custom design a fragrance for you. It's their Le Parfum Sur Mesure. It took about six months to create my fragrance. They won't ever sell the recipe to anyone else."

Khela's heart rate surged painfully when Carter bowed his head and stuck his nose in the space just behind her earlobe. He took a deep, quiet sniff of her, slightly moaning as he drew back.

The motion and music of the tiny bells followed his movements, reaching a crescendo when he nearly touched Khela.

"Can you detect the rose?" she asked, a shiver in her voice.

He answered in the positive with a deep "Umm" before leaning in once more.

Khela unconsciously held her breath and the bells jingled to life again in a pattern roughly matching their silhouettes.

"There's vanilla, too," he said. "And . . ." His breath caressed her neck as he breathed her in. "Sandalwood?"

"Very good," she sighed.

The bells nearest Khela's chest quivered so rapidly, their clappers seemed to ring in one single long note.

"Do they do scents for men?" Carter asked, taking a half step back.

Khela swallowed hard, at first unsure of what he'd said. Too conscious of the pressure suddenly mounting deep within her, she cleared her throat once more and asked him to repeat himself.

"Does this store create scents for men?"

"I imagine so. Yes." Khela touched the heel of her hand to her forehead, the bells playing a faint accompaniment to the elegant movement of her arm. "It's getting a little warm in here."

"Is it in Boston?" He returned his soiled handkerchief to its home.

"No, uh, Paris," Khela said. "On the Champs-Elysees."

"You went all the way to Paris just to cook up some perfume? It must have cost a fortune."

"Some people spend too much money on perfume, others spend too much on *cake*," she remarked, her voice cooling along with the activity of the bells as she cupped her right elbow in her left hand.

"Hey, my money's going to a good cause," Carter said. "The cake is just a bonus. So how often do you zip off to ol' Paree?"

Khela's bells lost a bit of life. "I've only been once, and I went there for work, to research a book."

"The guy I brought with me, Detrick Francis, he flies to Europe frequently for business." Without touching its surface, Carter slowly waved his hand across a section of the artwork. The bells released their notes as their movement followed that of Carter's hand. It was not unlike that of grass shaped by a gentle breeze. "Custom cologne is right up his alley."

"What does he do?" Khela asked.

"He's in real estate. What was your book about?" he asked, still watching the magical waving of the bells. "A

French pirate who marries the disgraced daughter of a wealthy plantation owner in order to hide from a rival bent on killing him?"

Khela forced her face and body language to reveal none of the exhilaration she felt at Carter's excellent summary of one of her books.

"Actually, it's about one of the *femmes tondues*, a woman accused of being a 'horizontal collaborator' during the Nazi occupation of France in World War II," Khela said with a touch of defiance. "She traded her body for food, and ended up with a baby sired by the enemy. At war's end, she and many women like her were punished by having their heads shaven publicly, and then, often with their babies in their arms, they were paraded through town so everyone could participate in their humiliation."

"What about the men?"

"They were the ones who did the shaving."

"No, I mean the male collaborators. What happened to them?"

Khela blinked. "Some were executed, some were beaten."

"None of them got sheared?"

"I've found no record of that in the course of my research."

"Seems like they would've wanted to execute the women, too."

" '*C'est par le ventre des femmes que la nation prospère, les femmes doivent être pures et préserver leur corps des étrangers afin d'éviter la détérioration de la nation,*'" Khela said. "It means—"

" 'It is in the belly of women that the nation prospers, women must be pure and preserve their bodies of foreigners to avoid the deterioration of the nation,' " Carter translated. "I guess it was better to humiliate them for not keeping themselves pure but keep them alive to make more French people just the same."

This time, Khela's shock and delight registered in the form of a big smile.

"What?" Carter shrugged. The tips of his ears turned pink. "I took French in school. Some of it stuck."

"It's just that . . . you surprise me," she said.

Khela stared at the last quarter inch of champagne in her glass, but she looked up when the bells signaled Carter's movement toward her. "Surprise you how?"

His scent again invaded her senses when she inhaled before speaking. "Did you read it?"

His gaze traveled slowly over her hair before moving to her face. "Read what?"

"*The Pirate's Princess.*"

Another casual shrug. "I had some time in the weeks you've been avoiding me."

"I haven't been—"

"Then you must be cheating on me."

"What?" The bells accentuated Khela's outcry.

"This has been the longest you've ever gone without calling me for a repair, so either everything is running smooth as chicken spit in unit A, or you got yourself a new Mr. Fix-It."

"You're deflecting," Khela said. "You don't want to admit that you read one of my books."

Carter wrinkled his nose as he scratched it. The tips of his ears practically glowed, even though he crossed his arms over his chest and took a more imposing stance. "So what if I did?"

"Did you like it?"

"It held my attention."

More than appreciating his forced indifference, Khela liked the fact that his ears looked as though they were on fire. "What was your favorite part?"

Carter exhaled, blowing his cheeks out, and fixed his eyes on the exposed pipes in the ceiling. "I don't know, let me think." He took his chin between his thumb and forefinger, drawing Khela's attention again to his mouth. "There were lots of good parts. I mean, you're a very good writer."

"I guess I surprise you, too."

"Oh, yes, ma'am," Carter agreed. "That you do."

"Did you like the scene in the captain's quarters aboard the pirate ship?"

Carter visibly swallowed, his Adam's apple slowly rising before settling into its normal position. The bells nearest him seemed to be laughing at him. "Which, uh," he coughed a little, "which scene was that?"

Khela's bells began to buzz when she leaned in closer toward Carter to say, in a lowered voice, "It's the scene when the pirate figures out that his marriage of convenience and his bride actually mean far more to him than he'd been willing to admit. When he realizes that he wants his bride more than any other woman he's ever met. And he has to satisfy that hunger or go mad."

"That was a good scene," Carter said, studying her lips. "Wasn't my favorite part, though."

"Oh?" Khela said, cocking an eyebrow and tilting her head slightly. She moved to brush a tendril of hair off her face just as Carter reached forward to do the same. Their hands met, and the artwork next to them seemed to shudder, the bells level with their point of contact leaping forward with such force their clappers stood out straight like tiny little tongues, their connection to the board the only thing keeping them moored in place. The bells in the vicinity of the area where Carter's hand covered Khela's started a quivery reaction that stirred every bell all the way out to the borders of the box.

Taking a firmer grip on Khela's hand, Carter pulled her farther away from the piece.

A short, bald man in an iridescent turquoise suit hastened toward them. "It's perfectly safe; nothing to worry about," he said. "It's just my Hot Box."

"I'm sorry?" Carter said.

"The bells are attached to a very sensitive panel that reacts to electrothermal emissions," the man said. "It literally responds to your body heat. This is the most activity my work has ever generated." A proud grin bloomed beneath his hooked nose. "Apparently, you two make beautiful music together."

The loose knot of Khela's and Carter's hands tightened. They looked sideways at each other and saw that they both were wearing the same sappy smile. They jerked their hands apart and struggled to find a response to the man's innocent but dead-on observation.

"I'll bet you've been waiting all day to say that," Khela scoffed as Carter drawled, "Man, you call that music? Sounds like a batch of alley cats bein' deep-fried."

"I should find Daphne before she flies off to Wales with the auctioneer," Khela said quickly.

"Yeah, I better find my wingman, too," Carter said, backing away. "I, uh, should probably go and settle the bill for my cake."

"Sure," Khela said, moving away. "Bye."

Carter and Khela went their separate ways, the distance between them increasing. No longer powered by Carter's and Khela's body heat, the bells ceased their otherworldly movement and faded into cold silence.

※

Carter and Detrick eased their way through a noisy crowd of Red Sox fans packed shoulder to shoulder in Boston Beer Works.

Nearby Fenway Park was dark on Yawkey Way while its beloved team scrapped with the Yankees in New York, but a Red Sox home run elicited cheers from the Beer Works patrons that surely carried all the way to the Bronx.

"Maybe we should have gone to Jillian's," Detrick shouted.

"We've already got a table here," Carter called back, following the pretty young waitress as she forged a path through a sea of fans in red.

She led them up a ramp to the small square tables lining the front of the restaurant. A brass railing separated the dining area from the various bars, where Sox fans sat on stools or stood, their eyes glued to the television sets mounted throughout the restaurant.

"Is this okay?" the waitress asked, placing two plastic-encased menus on a small, square table. "It's the best I could do," she said, her loud, nervous chortle sounding just like Scooby-Doo's. "Those Northeastern guys look like they want to kill me for bumping you ahead of them." She mimed an exaggerated slashing gesture across her throat. "Oh, well, anything for one of my regulars."

"I'm not a regular here," Carter told her.

"You could be," she said with a wink. "I know how to treat my regulars."

"The table is great, thanks." Carter took the chair; Detrick slid onto the leather-covered bench seat against the plate-glass window.

"Can I get you a drink to start?" the waitress asked, her big brown eyes fixed on Carter. "Name your brew. It's on me."

"I'll have a Sam Adams—whatever's on draft," Carter said.

"I'd like to take a look at the drinks menu, if—" Detrick managed to get out but the waitress was already moving away with a bubbly, "I'll get that for you right away."

Carter caught her by her apron. "My friend wants to look at the drinks menu."

The waitress noticed Detrick for the first time. Her cheeks reddened, she apologized for ignoring him, then hurried off to give him time to decide which specialty beer would best suit his palate.

"Sorry about that, Detrick," Carter said.

"You'd think I'd be used to it by now." Detrick shook his head, his shaved dome catching the bright gleam of the overhead lights. "I don't know what it is the ladies see in a 'Bama-fried cracker like you. That little minx is ready to curl up in your lap and lick cream from your chin."

Carter chuckled lightly. "Whatever it is, it don't work on all of 'em," he said, emitting a long sigh as he stared at the television set propped high in one corner.

Detrick leaned back, draping an arm over the padded back of the bench seat.

"Your honorary blackness has finally kicked in."

"What gives you that idea?"

"The writer. She's the reason you spent a fortune on that cake," Detrick snorted. "A funny-lookin' cake, at that."

"Literacy is a cause near and dear to my heart," Carter deadpanned.

"I know what you want near your heart, and it ain't literacy." Detrick scanned the custom beers on the back of the menu. "I think I'll have the Bunker Hill Bluebeery Ale."

"Didn't you have enough girlie drinks back at the auction?" Carter taunted. He opened his menu and looked over the appetizers and entrees. "If you're gonna drink beer, drink a real beer."

"Unlike yours, my palate is somewhat refined," Detrick retorted. "If I'm forced to drink beer, I don't want one that tastes like beer."

Carter chuckled. "Your palate wasn't so refined in school when we'd sneak out after lights out to choke down your Aunt Sukie's corn whiskey."

"That corn whiskey put hair on your chest, boy," Detrick said, lapsing into the Alabama accent he ordinarily took pains to hide. "Put hair on Aunt Sukie's, too, come to think of it." His gaze shifted beyond Carter's shoulder. "Your little admirer is coming back, and she's bearing gifts."

Carter glanced over his shoulder. He didn't know how Detrick had seen their waitress amidst the throng of baseball fans. But then he spotted a circular tray laden with baskets of food, a bottle of wine and two long-stemmed goblets seeming to surf the shoulders of the crowd. Then, as Detrick had, he recognized their waitress's bangled and braceleted wrists beneath the tray.

"Whew!" she exclaimed, emerging from the crowd at the bottom of the ramp. "The Sox better win tonight after all this. I hope you guys are hungry." She set the tray on the table and began serving them, placing a giant platter of nachos in front of Carter and a basket of calamari before Detrick. "The ladies are a little on the wild side tonight."

"We didn't order this," Carter told her.

"These are courtesy of those ladies right over there." The waitress pointed to one of the bars, where several women in business suits raised their glasses to Carter. He politely waved back. "And the drinks came from that lady in the leather skirt over there, under the Red Sox Parking Only sign."

Carter took a quick peek at a tall blonde in a leather miniskirt so short it looked more like an extension of her black top. She lowered her chin and kept her eyes fixed on him.

"Ooh, that one's giving you the hard look," Detrick said in a low voice. "I give it five minutes before she comes over here and starts throwing her hair and laughing at everything you say."

The waitress leaned in close to Carter, her hands on her knees. "You know what they say—the way to a man's heart is through his stomach."

"Excuse me," Detrick interrupted. "I'd like to try the wine."

The waitress seemed transfixed by Carter's face, staring at him with a dreamy smile.

"Miss?" Carter prompted.

"Hmm?" she cooed.

"Just take it back, please," Carter said quietly.

"The wine?" the waitress asked.

"The wine, the food, all of it." Carter stood, drawing his wallet from his back pocket. He lifted out two five-dollar bills and dropped them on the table. "I'm not staying."

As Carter started for the exit, the waitress shared a look of confusion with Detrick, who cast a final longing look at the wine before scooting off the bench. He dropped a bill of his own atop the two fives before hurrying after Carter.

"What gives, man?" he asked, catching up to Carter halfway to the lot where they had parked.

"I'm not hungry," Carter said.

"Since when do you pass on free food?" Detrick fairly trotted to keep up with Carter's long, fast strides. "You haven't paid for a meal in years."

Carter halted in front of another bar, this one so full its patrons had spilled out and were milling in front of the neon-illuminated front window. Every drinking and dining establishment on Brookline Street was full of Red Sox fans reveling in the hometown team's three-run lead over the Yankees.

Three women in pink and white Red Sox jerseys did a long double-take after passing Carter on the sidewalk, one of them even stumbling over her feet. His oldest and closest friend stood there staring curiously at him, but Carter had never felt more alone.

"I want more," he finally said.

"Okay, then let's go back and get more," Detrick said. "That waitress would have given you steaks and lobster on the house. She looked as though she would have cooked up a small child for you, if that was what you wanted."

"That's just it, Trick," Carter said, clenching his fists in frustration. "I don't want that. Not anymore."

"Don't want what?" Detrick said, speaking around a large group of Northeastern students that ambled between them. "I'm not following you."

Carter started walking again. "I don't want to be adored. At least not without earning it."

"What the hell does that mean?"

Carter kept silent until he could work out an explanation other than the truth: that he had just quoted a line from one of Khela's books. The line perfectly summed up the frustrations that had been niggling at him since his weekend with Khela. "Women look at me and decide who and what I am based on this," he said, jabbing a finger at his face. "I want someone who looks in here." He slapped a hand against his chest.

Detrick smiled uncomfortably. "Uh, I'm not sure what's goin' on with you, man, but I do know you need to stop watching *Oprah*."

Shoving his hands into his pockets, Carter continued to the parking lot.

"I'm sorry, Carter, I didn't mean any disrespect." Detrick hurried after him. "You gotta admit, you're behaving a little strangely tonight."

"I've just got some things on my mind, that's all," Carter responded tersely. Head down, he moved steadily forward through a rush of rowdy Sox fans going in the opposite direction. Carter's shoulder collided hard with an oncomer, spinning the solidly built man around.

"Watch it, douche bag!" the man shouted over his shoulder.

"You have a good night, too, pal," Carter called back grimly.

The man pushed up the sleeves of his red sweatshirt, revealing forearms the approximate width of a fire hydrant. "What did you say to me, hick?"

"C'mon, let it go," Detrick urged, taking Carter, who had stopped, by the arm. "You're not in college anymore. Leave the brawling to the kiddies."

Carter shrugged him off. Foot traffic around him and the man in red slowed.

"I was just being neighborly," Carter said, his calm a bit too measured.

"Watch where you're walking, hillbilly, unless you want that pretty face rearranged." The man cracked his big knuckles, displaying a chunky Boston University ring.

"Thanks for the advice, son, but don't you have some binge drinkin' and a date rape to get to tonight?"

Beer and baseball was a common recipe for brawling in Boston, a fact Carter had learned during his college days. His reflexes were much faster than those of the intoxicated collegian, so he easily ducked the fist the kid threw at his face. The kid's momentum carried him forward and he crashed into a parked car, setting off its alarm. His laughing companions scooped him up and carted him away before the car's owner arrived to deactivate the alarm.

Carter and Detrick turned into the parking lot.

"You need to work things out with that writer," Detrick said, breaking his silence as he unlocked the passenger door of his yellow Jaguar XK for Carter. "I can't go through this again. I won't."

"What the hell are you talkin' 'bout?" Carter asked.

"When you walked out on Savannah, you brawled with anybody for any reason, every chance you got." He pointed to a faint scar above and to the right of his right eyebrow. "Exhibit A. Remember this? I got it the night I had to pull you off that loudmouth in Hooters right after you saw Savannah for the last time. The only time you break out the fisticuffs is when you're pining for a woman."

"I ain't pinin' for nobody," Carter said sullenly as he climbed into the driver's seat and started the engine.

"Says you," Detrick challenged him. "I pity the fool you run into if your big cake date with her doesn't work out!"

———∞∞∞———

"What are you reading?"

Carter glanced up from the pages of his dog-eared paperback to see a man staring at him. The black eyes set deeply in his dark brown face glittered merrily, reminding Carter of a leprechaun. "Uh," Carter began, slowing his pace on the recumbent bicycle next to the inquisitive stranger's, "it's a book."

"*No!* Really?" the stranger said sarcastically, rolling his eyes. He decreased the resistance on his own bike, slowing his pace so he could talk and work out at the same time.

"A friend of mine wrote this." Carter flashed the cover. "It's just a book. And she's not really a friend; she's more of an acquaintance. Well—"

Carter's fellow bicyclist held up a hand. "No need to explain. I actually like a good romance novel myself. One of my best friends is a romance novelist. Victoria Ronaldinho?"

"Sorry," Carter said.

The man reached over and grabbed the book, taking a long look at the cover. "*A Curious Affair*," he read aloud, and then grunted his approval. "That's Khela Halliday, isn't it?"

"Yeah." Carter began his cool-down, slowing his bike from twenty miles per hour to fifteen. "You know her?"

"I've read a couple of her books," the grinning stranger said. "I loved *Satin & Secrets*, her follow-up to *Satin Whispers*. That girl has a knack for creating heroes that you just want to take home and lick from head to toe."

Carter chose not to picture that image. "Is that right?" he said. "You don't find them a little . . . unbelievable?"

"In what way?"

"Well, take *Satin & Secrets*, for example. Do you really think a man would just drop everything—his job, his friends, even his dog—to pack up and go chasing halfway around the world to find a woman who might not even love him?"

"If he knows what's good for him, he'd better," the stranger said bluntly. "I lived in the United Kingdom for a few months, and my significant other was running his design house in New York City. Long-distance relationships are for the birds, not fairies! When that man showed up one day with an ultimatum, I had a real-life romance novel moment of my own."

His curiosity getting the better of him, Carter slowed his bike to eight miles an hour. "Oh yeah? What happened?"

"That man showed up and said all the right things. He said, 'Bernard, we need to close the distance between us.' That man crossed the ocean to bring me home, and we've been together ever since. There would be millions more happy women on this planet if more men read books like those." The man chuckled. "Hell, there'd be a lot more happy men, too."

Carter's fellow gym rat looked him up and down, his gaze lingering on the muscles exposed by the torn sleeves of Carter's T-shirt before moving slowly down his well-defined arms. "Unless my gaydar has short-circuited, you are one of the last men on earth I'd expect to find reading a romance novel."

Carter's feet came to a stop, but he kept them on the bike pedals as he spent a moment catching his breath. "This is homework," he panted. "I'm more of a Tom Clancy kinda guy."

"Oh, I know what kind of guy you are," the stranger said knowingly. "Whoever she is, I hope she knows that you're willing to sit up in the middle of Boston's toniest gym studying a romance novel for her."

"I'm reading a romance novel *by* her," Carter muttered.

"Son, you are as sneaky as you are handsome. You know, they say that the way to a writer's heart is through her words."

Carter dismounted and tossed a thick white sweat towel across his shoulders. He took a couple of steps toward the rows of weight machines and then turned back. "Is that really what they say?"

"If they don't, they should," the stranger chortled.

———∞∞∞———

Carter stared at his reflection in the mirrored wall, concentrating on maintaining the proper form as he pulled the cables that hoisted the weights that would work the perfectly carved caps of his deltoids and lats. If he noticed the Lycra-wrapped gym bunnies in full makeup drifting slowly past him, he gave no indication of it.

In groups of twos and threes, they paused at the huge piece of equipment he worked at. A tall, busty blonde stood close to the mirror, making a production of rolling up the cuffs of her skin-tight exercise Capri pants. Her rear end protruded toward Carter, her invitation as blatant as that of a female baboon in heat.

Carter paid her, and the others like her, no attention.

"Need a spotter?" a perky brunette in a Patriots half-shirt asked, appearing behind Carter.

"Thanks, but I'm good," Carter told her on a sharp exhalation that helped him return the weight stack to its original position.

The brunette followed him to the next machine, one on which Carter could work his biceps and triceps. He sat on the black foam bench and leaned forward to reposition the pin in the weight stack.

"Wow," the woman said, watching Carter's movements. "You curl fifty pounds?"

"Sure looks like it," Carter said. He began his set, scowling slightly when the brunette sat behind him on the bench.

"There are better ways to work up a sweat, you know," she said close to his ear. "I'm right down the street, at the Holliston."

Carter let the weights clang back in place. The Holliston, one of downtown Boston's ritziest addresses. The woman had serious coin if she called the Holliston home. Carter picked up his sweat towel from the floor and mopped his face and the back of his neck. There was a time in the fairly recent past when he would have high-tailed it back to the Holliston faster than a chicken on fire.

But things had changed since he'd spent time with Khela at the auction last month. The pretty brunette was just the latest in a string of pretty brunettes, and blondes, and redheads, none of whom held any appeal for him. Carter mustered a polite smile of refusal.

"I appreciate the invite, but I can't," he said, directing his response over his shoulder.

"Oh, come on," the woman playfully purred, resting her chin on his shoulder and wrapping her arms around his middle. "If you show me your muscles, I'll show you mine."

Slowly standing, Carter extricated himself from the woman's grasp. "I'm sorry, ma'am," he said, calling on the power of his accent to make his refusal more palatable. "You're as pretty as a summer sky, but I'm afraid I can't go anywhere with you today."

She perched prettily on the weight bench. "What about tomorrow?"

Shaking his head, Carter grabbed his towel and his paperback and headed for the locker room.

"Howdy, cowboy!" called a slender girl who looked no older than eighteen. "Where've you been keeping yourself?"

In the span of time it took the young lady to disengage herself from the headphones connected to the CD player built into her elliptical trainer, Carter tried to peck her name from his brain. By the time she'd stopped the machine and hopped into his path, he was at least certain that her name ended in 'ie'."

"Hey, Carter!" she greeted shrilly, tugging at his sweat-dampened T-shirt. "I was hoping to run into you."

Clinging to his arm, she leaned close to him and spoke directly into his ear. "I've been coming here every day for the past three weeks, hoping to catch you here. I can't stop thinking about our night on your roof."

She took his hand and squeezed his fingers until his knuckles cracked. "You made me see stars with that telescope of yours." She grazed his groin with her knee, causing him to jump.

"Hey, now, uh . . . you," he stammered, "let's try to control ourselves here."

"I'm free tonight—if you want to stargaze some more."

Carter's blood chilled a degree or two. There were details, other than her name, he hadn't remembered about this woman. Had her smile always been so wide, so hungry and so full of teeth? Had the shine in her eyes always been this bright and feral?

Everything about her seemed exaggerated and unpleasant. He didn't even like her smell, and there was nothing wrong with her floral scent other than it lacked the spice and individuality of Khela's.

Carter shook his head slightly, more aware than ever of how flat and unappealing every woman looked to him now. "I've got plans tonight, honey," Carter said, inching away from the overeager woman. "Sorry."

"Another time, then?" she asked hopefully, backing toward her vacated machine.

Before turning the corner leading to the locker room, Carter looked back and saw the toothy woman turning her high-wattage grin on fresh prey. He was tall and stacked with muscle. She thrust out her chest and touched the man's shoulders and arms.

For a second, Carter thought the twinge of emotion he felt in his gut was jealousy. But then he quickly realized that he was completely wrong, and that the truth was more troubling. He wasn't jealous. He was interchangeable. The women in the gym treated him the way most women did, as though he were a piece of meat of no use other than satisfying their most indelicate appetites.

A pretty Asian exiting the women's locker room almost bumped into Carter, and the appraising look she gave him as he apologized made him open his sweat towel and drape it self-consciously over his chest as he ducked out of sight into the men's locker room.

CHAPTER 7

"Her gaze copied their bodies, fusing with his to lock them in that place in the heart and head where love, lust, passion and romance intersect."
— from Sybarite Seeks Same *by Khela Halliday*

Khela used the back of her wrist to swipe sweat from her forehead. After leaning her mop against the wall, she emptied the bucket of dingy water into the Toto toilet, which she'd already scrubbed until it sparkled, and inhaled deeply. Murphy's Oil Soap was one of her favorite scents, and it was perfect for Carter's visit.

Along with her cake, he'd purchased an evening with her, presumably to share her creation. Although she'd begrudged being bought through Carter's five thousand-dollar donation to the Literacy Fund, her efforts to make the night perfect surprised her.

"Not perfect," she corrected, giving the almond-colored marble counter one last polish with a cleaning cloth. "Just good enough."

This isn't a date any more than the convention weekend was a date, she told herself. She crossed the room to get to the shower stall, where she started a powerful stream of hot water. *I'm gonna shower, I'm gonna dress and then I'm gonna slap some cake on a plate and call it a night.*

She stripped off her clothes and stepped into the shower. "May as well use the good stuff," Khela said indifferently, reaching past the everyday deodorant soap to grab her eponymous body gel. She smoothed it over her legs and, noting their less-than-silky texture, she decided to use a depilatory cream rather than a razor. "Save me the trouble of shaving for awhile," she reasoned.

Khela found perfectly innocuous reasons to take tweezers to her eyebrows, tidying their graceful arches, and to paint her finger- and toenails, a task she completed solely for herself, and not because Carter might come into contact with her hands or see her feet in the course of the evening.

By the time she had chosen a cotton halter dress with a floral print, selected for comfort, not because of how it prettily displayed her back and arms, she had managed to convince herself that the evening with Carter was a business meeting like any other.

Any other that would take place within twenty yards of her bedroom.

She gave her head a hard shake, clearing it of dangerous thoughts linking Carter with her bedroom. A quick glance at the big analog clock in the kitchen prompted her to give the dining area a quick once-over. Carter had never been late for any of his maintenance appointments; she doubted he'd show up tardy for a real date.

She slapped her forehead. "It's not a date," she said adamantly. "It's just another business arrangement."

Khela tended to this business arrangement with the same care she would have shown any other. Every detail was as perfect as she could make it—bone-white china, crystal glassware and silver cutlery sparkled on the dining room table, the cake was in her warming oven along with a shallow pan of water to keep it from drying out. An Israeli muscato chilled in the refrigerator, and India.arie's rich, evocative voice complemented the orange glow of the sunset tinting Khela's tall, wide windows.

At seven on the mark, the doorbell rang. An unpleasant jolt of anxiety shot through her, forcing her to take deep breaths as she slowly made her way to the door. *It's just Carter*, she told herself as she turned locks and unlatched the security chain. *He's been here a dozen times.* She worked her face into a wide, nervous smile and swung open the door. *This is no big deal. It's just—*

"Carter," she sighed at the sight of him filling the doorway. "Hi."

He was just Carter, but Carter elevated in the weeks since she'd last seen him.

He wore jeans, leather uppers and a blue-striped button-down. His right hand rested in one pocket, the left gripped his clean-shaven jaw. He was the very picture of casual indifference from the nose down, but his eyes told a very different story.

Unblinking, they raked over Khela, making her wish for the barest of moments that she'd done something more with her hair other than pull it into a ponytail.

His greeting surprised her. "You look stunning," he said.

It was a simple statement of fact that temporarily robbed Khela of her ability to speak. "Thank you," she responded, once she regained control of her tongue. "Come in." She stepped aside to allow him to enter.

"The cake is in the kitchen," she said. "Go ahead and seat yourself and I'll—"

"Lookin' to get rid of me quick, huh," he said over his shoulder as she followed behind him.

"No, it's just that I made the cake a few hours ago, and I'm worried about the quality of the product you're getting." She hurried ahead of him and turned into the kitchen.

"Need a hand?" He paused in the archway between the kitchen and the dining room area. "I've got two good ones, and they ain't busy at the moment."

"Please, just have a seat." Khela shoved her hands into black oven mitts. "I can handle this."

The instant Carter stepped away, Khela collapsed against the stainless-steel door of her refrigerator. She suddenly felt as though she'd had the oven on all day. Rushing to the kitchen window, she shoved it open and let the breeze cool her flushed face and soothe her nerves.

"I can't handle this," she whispered anxiously.

He had been to her place dozens of times to flirt with Daphne and handle some dubious repair. This time shouldn't be any different, even if he had dropped heavy coin for the honor of spending time with her.

And that's the difference, Khela silently admitted. *The only thing broken around here tonight is me, and he's here because he* wants *to be.* After another moment of quiet contemplation, Khela was forced to admit a deeper truth. *And I'm glad.*

With truth came a sense of ease that allowed her to focus her thoughts and get on with the evening. She carefully centered the cake on a black platter and set a silver cutter alongside it. Everything else she needed was already on the table—or sitting at the head of it.

Khela exited the kitchen carrying the cake before her. She made it all the way to the table and placed the platter in front of Carter before her palms began to sweat.

"Aren't you joining me?" he asked, catching her wrist.

She expected the question, seeing as how there was only one table setting. Gently pulling her wrist from his grasp, she answered him. "This is your party. You paid for this cake, and I'm supposed to serve it to you. There's nothing in the rules that says I have to join you."

Carter held her gaze a little too long, certainly long enough for Khela to see the flash of disappointment in them. He issued a short, decisive sigh, and said, "Fair enough. Rules are rules. So is this a chocolate cake?" Leaning forward, he studied it a bit closer. "It looks kinda strange."

"It's not chocolate," Khela said uncomfortably, picking up the cutter.

"Is it vanilla?" Carter sat up straight as she bent over the table to cut the cake, inhaling the vanilla nuances of her perfume.

"Nope."

"Lemon?" he asked hopefully.

Khela made two cuts and lifted out a solid wedge of her cake. "Beef." She eased it onto Carter's plate.

He seemed to shudder, and Khela pinched back an impish smile.

"You made a beef cake?" he deadpanned.

Khela stood up straight, her right fist propped on her hip, the cutter protruding from her clenched hand. "The irony of you buying this cake is just too indescribably delicious."

"Why is that?" His jaw tightened. "Because you think of me as beefcake?"

"No, I figured this cake would go to some stranger, not someone I know."

"Oh," he grunted, a faint blush rising in his cheeks. "Sorry." He looked down at the pleasantly steaming cake on his plate and took a deep whiff of it. "Is this meatloaf?"

Khela toyed with the cutter, her eyes lowered. "It was supposed to be a joke. It's a double-layer meatloaf made with lean ground chuck, pork sausage, green peppers, onions and mushrooms. The frosting is mashed potatoes. The roses are made of ribbons of red bell pepper, and I cut the leaves from green peppers."

Carter stared at his cake, his brow slightly furrowed.

Khela shifted from foot to foot, yet again regretting her decision to make light of her auction contribution. "I thought it would be funny," she explained, twirling the cutter just to give her hands something to do. "The Literacy Fund sent me that invitation right after the writer's convention, and I just wasn't in the mood to promote romance. It was just bad timing, and I wasn't thinking about how the person who got the cake would feel about it. Now that I think about it, I'm glad that you bought it, because if someone else had I'd be even more embarrassed than I am now. So—"

Carter stopped her river of words by touching her hand. "It's perfect."

"It's a joke," she smiled wanly.

"It's a good one." He smoothly took the cutter from her and laid it on the table. Then he wrapped her hand in his.

"So you get it?"

"Coming from you, yes," he chuckled. "A romance novelist who donates a comfort food cake. It's brilliant."

"Uh . . . yeah," Khela hesitantly agreed. "Um . . . what's so brilliant about it?"

"Who but a romance writer could so vividly illustrate that the way to a man's heart is through his stomach?"

"I didn't . . . That wasn't . . ." Khela struggled to confess that his deduction had never factored into her decision to make a meatloaf instead of a traditional cake. The fact that he'd provided a decent, heartwarming excuse for her cake sent a flood of affection through her. Acting on it before common sense stopped her, she leaned forward to brush his lips with a kiss.

But before she could make contact, Carter turned his head and leaned away from her. "What are you doing?"

Scorching heat raced into Khela's face as she hastened away from him. "I was going to kiss you, to thank you, for . . . oh, my God, I'm so embarrassed."

"Don't be," he said. "It's okay. It's just that I came here for cake, not . . . sugar."

"Right." Khela swallowed hard, her cheeks still burning as she took a seat adjacent to him. "There's, uh, gravy in the little boat there, and I've chilled a bottle of wine. Please, start before it gets cold."

Carter focused on his meal to keep his mind off the kiss that almost was. It had taken every bit of willpower he possessed to refuse her kiss. But one thing he'd learned from her books was that a kiss was easy, and almost meaningless. Carter wanted more and he determined to hold out for it, just like Khela's fictional heroes. In every one of her books, whether the hero was a myopic string-bean or a Tarzan-styled alpha male, the hero settled for nothing less than his ladylove's whole heart.

"This really smells delicious," he said, using his fork to cut a hearty bite.

Khela held her breath as he chewed, then swallowed. "Well?"

"Tastes better than what my mama used to make," he said through another hearty bite. "It reminds me of the meatloaf she used to make on Saturday nights, only better."

The compliment eased Khela's mortification at having been rebuked and gave her a more pleasant reason to blush. "This is my Grandma Belle's recipe. She was born and raised in Mississippi."

Carter used his fork to emphasize his next point. "I knew you had a bit of the South in you. Not too many Yankees know about Chilton peaches, and every now and again I hear a trace of the Delta in your dialect."

Resting her elbow on the table, Khela propped her fist under her chin. "What brought you all the way from Alabama to Massachusetts?"

"School." He stopped eating long enough to touch a napkin to his mouth. "Could you pass the gravy, please?" Khela did so, delighted by his enjoyment of her cooking. Carter cut himself a second slice of the meatloaf cake, and drizzled gravy over it. He moaned after his first bite. "Lord, woman," he mumbled through a mouthful of meat and mashed potatoes. "You cook as good as you look."

"Thanks," Khela said. "What school did you go to up here?"

"Dearborn Academy," he managed, chomping on a bell pepper rose.

Khela's eyebrows shot up. "Wow. I spoke at Dearborn once, on writing. I've never seen so many Hummers, BMWs, Mercedes and Jaguars in a student parking lot."

"It was the same way—minus the Hummers—fourteen years ago when I graduated," he responded. "With honors, I should add."

"Your parents sent you up here?"

Carter leaned back and unfastened the snap of his jeans to give his full stomach room for one more slice of meatloaf. "Naw, I was recruited. My friend Detrick and I, we both got the call to come up and play football our junior year. In exchange for our speed, size and superior athletic talent, we got a full ride."

"And a diploma that would get you into any college you wanted."

His mouth too full to speak, Carter nodded until he swallowed. "Yeah, Detrick ended up at Columbia. He majored in business and finance. He's in real estate. Does all right for himself. He splits his time between Alabama and New England. He was in town last month working on a property deal for a strip mall in Woburn."

"So you decided to drag him along to watch you spend an insane amount of money on my cake."

"A 'funny-looking' cake, according to him."

"What college did you go to?"

"Boston University. Go Terriers."

"Hmm."

Carter gave his mouth a final swipe with the cloth napkin before neatly placing it beside his plate. "What's that mean?"

"There's a lot about you that I didn't know."

"Didn't know or didn't expect?"

Khela thought a moment. "Both, I guess."

"A college boy can't be a handyman, is that it?"

"No, a Dearborn boy can't be a handyman," Khela clarified. "Obviously, there's much more to you than I realized."

"You've been a writer too long, Khela." Carter took a long sip of wine before explaining further. "You don't see folks as folks any more. You see them as characters."

Khela sat back in her chair, her jaw falling. "How . . . ?"

Carter guiltily picked up his plate and cutlery. He couldn't come out and admit that in reading her work he'd recognized tenants in the brownstone, and even her friend Daphne, in the pages of her books. He fled into the kitchen, Khela hot on his heels.

"You can't make an accusation like that and just run away without explaining it," she said, taking Carter's plate from him and setting it in the sink.

"I just think that all writers probably borrow in part or whole from real life when they're creating their characters," Carter allowed, leaning against the Le Cornu stove. "Seems like a bit of truth would only enrich the fiction."

"It does," Khela agreed.

Carter crossed his arms over his chest and, staring at his feet, asked the one question that he most wanted answered. "What would you do to me to turn me into one of your heroes?"

Without hesitation, Khela met his gaze straight on and said, "I'd make you black."

———————— ∽∾ ————————

Carter watched as Khela retrieved a black lacquered platter from the refrigerator and set it on the prep island. He moved closer to investigate the colorful tidbits comprising her dessert course.

"Cake for dinner, now sushi for dessert?" he asked.

"In keeping with the theme, I thought I'd make a main course dessert." Khela pointed to each item as she described it. "The sticky rice in the California maki is actually a mini cupcake topped with shredded coconut. The seaweed wrapper is a Fruit Roll-Up. The carrot, cucumber and avocado are actually cut from jellied fruit slices, and the crabmeat is vanilla taffy with a bit of food coloring. The nigiri is a hillock of candied coconut with a Swedish fish on top. The seaweed strip around it is more Fruit Roll-Up."

"I gotta give you credit for inventiveness," Carter said. "May I?" he asked, reaching for the platter.

"Please."

Khela groaned as he popped a fat slice of candy California roll into his mouth. "I don't know where you plan to put that," she chuckled. "You look like you're going to pop."

"There's always room for sushi," he said, his cheek bulging.

"There's always room for Jell-O," she corrected.

"That, too," Carter agreed. "So, um, why would I have to be black to be your hero?"

"The book I'm working on now is an African-American romance." Khela picked up a piece of coconut nigiri. "My hero is black. If I use a real person to flesh him out, that man has to be black. Other than that, you have most of the qualities I'd like my hero to have."

"Oh, yeah? Such as?"

"Well, you're reliable. You're straightforward. And honest." Seeing Carter's self-satisfied expression, she added, "And you're really not all that good-looking."

Carter's head jerked up. "What's wrong with my face?"

"Your eyes. I think one is a little tiny bit higher than the other."

"Anything else?"

"Your hair is too short. It emphasizes the roundness of the top of your head."

"It'll grow out. Problem solved. What else?"

Khela rolled her eyes. "There is nothing else. I just made up that stuff about your eyes and your hair. You're stunning, Carter. Quit fishing for insults."

"So I'm hero material after all?"

"No. You're very handsome and you know it. My hero is very handsome and doesn't know it. That makes a big difference."

"I see." Carter said pensively. "You're sayin' that I've got an Adonis complex."

"I didn't say that at all," Khela retorted, nibbling the end of her nigiri.

"But you think I'm hung up on my looks."

"I didn't say that, either."

"Then what *are* you saying?" He closed the distance between them to meet her eye to eye and toe to toe.

"I'm saying that I would like to experience the kind of love I write about," she said plainly. "I don't think I could have that with you."

"Why not?" he asked softly, searching her eyes.

Because your looks and my money are a bad combination perched on her tongue, but she turned it into, "We don't complement each other."

"Because you look at me and see some dumb Mr. Fix-It, and you're the sophisticated novelist?" He took a step back, and Khela's feet moved her in his direction.

"I never said that," she insisted. "I never even thought about it like that! Is this the reason you bought my cake? So you could come here and ambush me in my own house?"

"This is *my* house," he countered. "I'm the one who takes care of it, and—"

"Why are you yelling at me?"

"You wrote me off after the convention because you've become a victim of your own competence!"

"I have not!" she fired back. "*What?*"

"You said you want the kind of love you write about," he began. "So you think you should be with a sheik who captured you for his harem and forsakes his four hundred other wives for you? Or that you're the emotional and physical salvation of some sea captain whose dark personal secrets have condemned him to a life of solitude at sea?"

Scowling, Khela marched back out to the dining area and grabbed the bottle of wine and Carter's empty glass.

"You ignorance is showing," she muttered as she poured wine into the glass. "Those aren't even plots to any of my books."

"The plots don't matter!" Carter exclaimed, joining her at the tableside. "The boy gets the girl in every one of those books. It's the details that make the difference between them. You've managed to capitalize on the simple formula of boy-meets-girl and eventually lives happily ever after. You take yourself too seriously."

Khela slammed down the wine glass, splashing wine onto the dark, polished surface of the dining table. "Do you take your tinkering seriously? Don't insult what I do. It might not save lives, but it can definitely make life easier to bear. Reading is one of the oldest, most personal forms of entertainment and leisure, and—"

"Romance novels are just soft porn for women," Carter stated flatly.

"—romance is the ultimate escape," Khela continued as if he hadn't interrupted. "Men are perfectly happy with sex. Women want romance."

"And sex," Carter put in.

"And tenderness."

"And sex."

"They want honesty and bare emotion!"

"And . . . sex?"

"Serious romance authors are some of the smartest people you'll ever meet. We do more than entertain. We do our best to bring our stories to life by loaning our own very real experiences to our fictional characters! Do you know how much research goes into a romance novel, especially a historical romance? We take our readers directly to times and places they would never otherwise experience." Khela stopped, but only to breathe, fueling her next volley. "January Rose writes romantic ethnic westerns that blur the line between commercial and literary fiction. Her books are sharp and brilliant in detail. She's Harper Lee, Louis L'Amour and Nora Roberts in a single African-American skin."

"Who's Nora Roberts?"

Rolling her eyes, Khela went on. "If I set a book in ancient Rome, you'll come away knowing how the Romans dressed, ate, fought, worked, played and—"

"Had sex."

"You would smell the dust kicked up by a centurion in the midst of battle, and you'd taste the wine and honey on the pouty lips of an emperor's handmaiden."

"So you distill important lessons in Western civilization through cheap paperbacks," Carter reasoned.

"Why do you have such contempt for me?"

"Why are you so scared of me?"

Khela scoffed. "Scared doesn't mean what you seem to think it means. Annoyed would be a more apt description of how you make me feel."

"How do I annoy you?"

She stared at him for a moment, torn between the truth and a diversion. The truth burst from her. "You make me feel things that I know I can't follow up on," she blurted. "You give me an itch that I just can't scratch."

"I don't think itch means what you seem to think it means," Carter said, choosing his words deliberately. "Lust would be a more apt description of what I make you feel."

Grunting in frustration, Khela balled up her fist and punched Carter in the stomach. It was like striking the side of a cliff, and she hugged her aching hand to her chest.

"Love and lust combined is what makes women hungry for sex," she said, allowing Carter to take her hand. "You men are too stupid to realize that, and women are tired of explaining it to you over and over. The best thing any man could do for the woman in his life is to read a romance novel with an open mind and pen and paper in hand to take notes."

Carter gently massaged her aching knuckles. "Are you willing to at least consider the possibility that in your books, you've created the kinds of men who intrigue you personally?"

Dropping her eyes to their clasped hands, she murmured, "If I fall in love with my hero, then so will my readers."

"With your books, you're God. You build a man from scratch, making him exactly what you want him to be. You can't do that in real life, so no man will ever be as good as the studs in your books. You need a man who'll show you that the real thing is better than the sterile neatness of what you put in your fiction."

"Are you talking about sex scenes?"

"I most definitely am," he responded defiantly. "Sex is raw and slippery and sticky and—"

"Not in my books."

"Then you ain't doin' it right."

"Have you ever read any of my books?" she demanded. He offered a sheepish smile.

"Then shut up," she snapped, snatching her hand back. "You don't know what my men are like, and you don't have the first clue as to the kind of man I need!"

"What you like and what you need are right here, honey." Carter pressed her hand to his chest and took her about the waist, pulling her against him. She stiffened and would have protested had Carter not sealed her complaint with a kiss. Her lips parted against his, to welcome rather than disagree with him. Her arms went around his neck, her fingers into his hair. He backed her onto the table, shoving up her skirt to give her legs the freedom to wrap about his hips.

Khela, sighing against the explorations of his mouth, let her head fall back to give him easier access to the sensitive terrain of her neck. His shirt bunched in her hands, Carter allowed her to draw the obtrusive knot of heat between his legs into the soft cradle between her own. The tips of her breasts rose to meet the pads of his thumbs through the thin fabric of her dress. With each movement of her skirt, her custom scent and the one organic to her rose to infuse his lungs. Every part of her fit his hands perfectly, fit his mouth exactly.

Instantly addicted to his kisses, Khela broke free of them only to gasp for air and, if need be, to beg him for still more.

Carter read her mind, mumbling between kisses to her earlobes. "What now, sweetheart?" he drawled, his voice low and as seductive as his kisses. "You gonna run from me again?"

"No," she exhaled, cupping his backside and giving it a good squeeze.

"Tell me what you want."

Everything! was the answer that clanged in her head, but what she said was, "Two weeks."

Carter raised his head from her bosom. "Come again?"

She grinned, a little, at his choice of words. "I want two weeks."

His eyes searched hers, gauging whether she was joking. "You want to spend two weeks with me?"

"Yes. That's all it usually takes."

"For what?"

For your true color to appear, and it'll probably be green, she thought. "Two weeks," she repeated. "Take it or leave it."

He spent another long moment holding her flesh in his hands and studying her troubled gaze. "Starting when?" he finally asked, his hand inching toward the hot juncture of her thighs.

Khela moaned, the sound both throaty and silky, as his fingers found their moist mark. "Starting there . . ." she gasped, her legs falling wide.

CHAPTER 8

"It was love at first write."
—*from* Teacher's Pet *by Khela Halliday*

"I'm black, you know."

Khela laughed so hard she would have fallen off Carter if he hadn't tightened his grip on her waist. He flexed his abdominal muscles as he shifted a bit on the bed, his new position wedging him deeper. Khela's thighs and belly quivered in response to yet another wave of pleasure cresting within her. Carter helped her reach its zenith by palming the weight of her breasts, kneading them and pinching their hard buds at exactly the right moment to force Khela to lock around him, wringing still more from him.

Their first coupling had occurred volcanically atop the dining table. Frenzied with hunger, they hadn't bothered to fully undress, satisfied with mere shifts in panties, the unzipping of jeans. Their initial appetites appeased, they took their time the second time, with Carter fully savoring every inch of Khela as he peeled her dress and panties from her body. The third time, in Khela's sizeable whirlpool bath, became a silly interlude that began with wine and leftover candy sushi and ended with Carter demonstrating all he could accomplish in the three minutes he could hold his breath underwater.

This, the fourth time, was simply showing off.

"Funny," Khela gasped, covering him with her body to await the return of a normal heartbeat, "you don't look black."

"I got my honorary blackness in high school." Carter lightly stroked her back with the pads of his fingertips, raising goosebumps along their path. "Detrick gave it to me."

"Well, that was awfully generous of him," Khela laughed. "Was it a birthday present? Christmas?"

"Nah, nothin' like that," Carter exhaled, Khela sinking and rising along with his torso. "Detrick and I came from the same place, which was no place compared to our classmates. We were two 'Bama country boys among Boston Brahmin babies and the imported sons of foreign oil magnates."

"Did you come from the same school in Alabama?"

"Nah. I went to Speake High. Detrick's outta Hubbard."

"Would you two have been friends if you'd stayed in school down South?"

Carter shook his head, but then realized she couldn't see him, not with her ear pressed to his heartbeat. "Probably not. Detrick is the best thing I got outta my two years at Dearborn. We hated each other when we first met, though."

"Why?"

"I thought he was a cocky sumbitch who cared more about his personal stats than he did about the team."

"Was that all?"

"What else would there be?"

"He's black."

Carter rolled onto his side and faced Khela. "You think I have a problem with black people?"

She grinned. "Not at the moment."

"I'm serious, Khela. Do you think I would've disliked Detrick because he was black?"

She sat up, as did he. "No, I . . ." She rubbed her temple with two fingers. "I don't think you're a racist, but you were young then, and from the South, so—"

"I must've been a bass-ackwards, prejudiced cracker," he finished for her.

"Don't put words in my mouth. I've never thought that about you. You said that you hated Detrick when you first met him, so I just jumped to—"

"The wrong conclusion."

"I'm sorry. It wasn't fair. People make assumptions about me all the time, and I hate it. I shouldn't have done that to you. Tell me how you and Detrick became friends. Go on with your story."

Khela rearranged the pillows at her headboard and guided Carter to rest against them. With the top sheet covering her torso, she sat facing him. "What position did Detrick play on the Dearborn football team?"

"Left out, for the most part," Carter chuckled. "That was the problem. He was the best receiver on the team, but the coaches only played him if we were down. There were a lot of good players on the team whose parents were boosters. The coaches were more inclined to play fellas whose mommies and daddies paid for team buses, uniforms and vacations."

"Vacations? Are you kidding?"

"Nope. One of the boosters sent us to Sanibel Island for spring break our junior year. They thought it would help the team bond."

"Did it?"

"Nope. The rich kids hung with the rich kids, the climbers hung with the climbers and tried to hang with the rich kids, and Detrick and I sort of kept to ourselves—until the brawl."

"That sounds interesting."

"Quincy Latin was our biggest rival, and their football and baseball teams were in Daytona the same week we were," Carter said. "Get a bunch of drunk, over-privileged, under-aged jocks from rival schools together, and you got yourself a recipe for hell."

"Was there a girl involved?"

She had guessed right, surprising Carter. "How'd you know?"

"There's always a girl involved."

"Detrick was talking to some local girl, a little green-eyed blonde who worked in the surf shop on the beach. A couple of the Quincy guys didn't like it, so . . ."

"Who threw the first punch?"

"Quincy. I jumped in when four of them went after Detrick."

"You were the only one who came to his defense?"

Carter nodded.

"And you didn't even like him?"

"It wasn't a matter of like or dislike. He was my team-mate and he was outnumbered. It wasn't fair."

"Who won the fight?"

"Quincy tore us up. That's how I ended up with this lovely detour in the middle of my nose." He tapped the barely noticeable bump on his nose. "There were six of them and only two of us."

Khela put her hand over his, giving it a squeeze. "Your nose was broken?"

"Got one of my teeth knocked out, too," he said. He curled his lip and tapped one of his upper canine teeth. "This is an implant."

"I hope you gave the other guy as good as you got."

He chuckled. "I never would have pegged you for the bloodthirsty type. But yeah, I got some good ones in. So did Detrick."

"Was he hurt badly?"

"Detrick can take a punch better than any man I've ever known," Carter said. "They couldn't hurt him. Not on the outside, anyway. It's what they said that got to him. He'd been called names like that before, but not by prep school kids who were supposed to be educated."

"Ignorance is everywhere," Khela sighed. "You know that."

"Detrick and I have been friends ever since," Carter smiled. "We became blood brothers the hard way."

"Being blood brothers doesn't make you black."

"It was a gift," Carter insisted. "Those Quincy frauds thought they'd dish out seconds the next night. Detrick and I were ready for them. You ain't gonna whup two

155

'Bama country boys twice in a row. Me and Detrick and two rolls of quarters did the trick."

"You threw quarters at them?"

Carter gave her the sort of grin one would bestow upon a charming idiot. "We put the quarters in our fists. Instant hammer hand. We didn't have any more trouble from Quincy."

"Did any of your other teammates help you guys out?"

Carter shook his head. "They weren't going to risk their pretty faces for Detrick. Or me, for that matter. I wasn't the only guy on the team who thought Detrick needed to come down a peg or two. See, Detrick was the best guy on the team and he knew it. Called himself Detrick 'The Trick' Francis. He was fast, he had power and he had an ego bigger than the Patriots' defensive line. He wasn't as bad after the Florida trip, though."

"You still haven't explained how you came to be black," Khela reminded him.

"Right. It was after our first game, senior year. We played Quincy Latin—"

Khela whistled through her teeth. "I'll bet that was some match up."

"It was. We beat them, 56-10. Detrick rushed for three touchdowns. He met some girls after the game, and they invited him to a party in Jamaica Plain. He invited me along to be his wingman. When a Snoop Dogg song came on and I started dancing, Detrick said I fought, played ball and danced like a brother. He poured a beer over my head and said it was my baptism into official blackness. We've been best friends, brothers, ever since."

After a long moment of silence, Khela looked at him and said, "That's the goofiest thing I've ever heard."

Carter laughed and pulled her into his embrace. "I'm black and I'm proud, and right now, I'm the luckiest man in the world."

"Why's that?" Khela murmured against the warmth of his chest.

"Because I've got you in my arms," he said. "I feel like I've waited a lifetime for this."

Khela lightly took his chin and turned his face toward hers. "That's very sweet."

"I'll bet you had all the boys chasin' after you in high school."

She barked a laugh of astonishment. "I was the invisible girl in high school. I was good in math and science, I was the editor for the school literary magazine and I didn't have any friends. I hit the geek trifecta by the time I was a sophomore. I used to spend my summers reading and the school year writing weird short stories when I was supposed to be taking notes in class."

"So you've always been a writer?"

She nodded. "I was a little bit of a handful when I first went to live with Grandma Belle and Grandpa Neal."

"You spent a few years in the child welfare system before you were adopted, right?" Carter stroked her arm. "You don't have to answer that if you don't want to. It's none of—"

"It's okay," she said, clasping his hand. "I never talk about it. That was my problem when I was really little. I couldn't articulate how I was feeling, so I acted out. I'd fight anybody, break things, cry, yell at everyone, and then not speak for days. I was a little mess when I got adopted. One day, after I'd torn my pretty pink room to shreds—again—Grandma Belle gave me a blank notebook and a box of crayons. She told me to draw pictures of what I was feeling the next time I wanted to have a fit. It helped. I eventually started putting my thoughts and feelings into words. I started writing stories, and I've been writing ever since."

"What became of your parents?"

She looked him in the eye and said, "My mother died of an overdose and my father is incarcerated. They were both out of my life by the time I was two." Khela didn't blink, determined not to miss any part of his reaction.

"What did he do?" Carter asked softly.

"He was involved in an armed robbery where the victim was killed. He didn't pull the trigger, but he was there, so he was charged with first-degree murder."

"How long did he get?"

Khela swallowed hard. "Life."

"You got a rough draw. You should be proud of how you far you've come."

"I'm just another black girl with a drug-addict mother and a daddy in jail," Khela said bleakly. "I could win a Nobel Prize and I'd still be the daughter of a druggie and a jailbird."

"What did your Grandma Belle and your Grandpa Neal do for a living?" Carter asked.

"Grandma Belle was a nurse and Grandpa Neal was the custodian at the high school my father attended, until they retired. They went to the same church as my father's parents," Khela said. "Grandpa Neal had always liked my father. My father was in detention a lot, and he very often had to help Grandpa Neal with some of the school maintenance. When my mother died and my father was sent up, none of my real grandparents or aunts or uncles wanted me. I guess they thought I'd turn out like my parents. When Belle and Neal found out that no one else wanted me, they went out and found me. And the rest . . . is my history."

"Sounds to me like you had amazing parents," Carter said. "You got the short straw at the start, but you finished up very well. Belle and Neal get the credit for that, not the pair who made you."

"I know." Her lower lip quivered, but she kept her tears at bay. "I was so lucky."

Carter lay a warm, heavy hand on her thigh and asked, "Do you ever see your daddy?"

Khela squirmed a little, but Carter's comforting hand settled her. "From what I've been told, he left while my mother was still pregnant with me. He never wanted me, and he never wanted to see me when Grandma Belle and Grandpa Neal would take me to the prison in Jefferson City. I refused to go anymore when I was ten. I went on my own when I was twenty-two, right before my second book was released. I'd done an interview with a women's magazine, and when the reporter asked me about my parents, I told her that they were both dead. I felt so guilty. Grandma Belle and Grandpa Neal had passed, so I wasn't lying entirely, but I knew the reporter wasn't asking about them."

"It was nobody's business but yours," Carter said.

"It was unfinished business. That's why I went to see him. It was so hard," she admitted, her voice breaking. "He knew who I was immediately. His first words to me were, 'You look just like your mama.' "

"Your mother must have been very beautiful," Carter remarked tenderly.

"I don't know if she was or not," Khela said. "I don't remember anything about her."

"What else happened with your daddy?"

She gave him a forlorn shrug. "Nothing. He asked me if I came there because I needed money, and I said no. I told him that I just wanted to see him. He said, 'You seen me. Now what?' There were so many things I wanted to ask him, so many things I wanted to know. He was all I had left, and after meeting him, I realized I had nothing. I immersed myself in my writing. I'm never lonely when I'm working on a book."

"You got something now, baby," Carter assured her. "You got Daphne, you got me and you got thousands of readers who look forward to reading your books."

When she continued to stare at him, her dark eyes glistening with unshed tears, Carter gently stroked the back of her hand and asked, "What's on your mind?"

"You really are the most beautiful man I've ever seen. Inside and out."

In a move both quick and inelegant, Carter rolled her onto her back, pressing his weight upon her as he parted her legs with his knee. He pressed hard kisses to her neck and clenched his fists in her hair. His abdominal muscles bunched as he positioned himself for their union, and still he avoided eye contact with her. Her trust in him meant so much that he felt he couldn't look at or speak to her without shedding his own tears. In a language they both understood, one without words, without inhibition and without hesitation, Carter thanked her for her trust, and Khela thanked him for his acceptance.

"I didn't think you would do it," Daphne said, smiling appreciatively. "I'm glad you did, because God knows you needed it, but I didn't think you would actually do it."

Khela rested her forearms on the table, splaying her fingers toward Daphne. "Look," she said defensively, loud enough to capture the attention of the young couple nursing macchiatos at the neighboring table, "it happened before I realized it was going to happen. I like him, okay?"

"Okay," Daphne grinned.

"He's very sweet," Khela continued, still sounding defensive.

Daphne hung one elbow over the back of her chair. "Oh, really?" she leered.

"I don't mean sweet that way." Khela blushed, her complexion darkening to match her berry-colored tank top. "Well, he is sweet that way, too. He must have eaten a lot of pineapple or something, because—"

"Details," Daphne said, holding up a hand. "Too many details."

"I thought you liked the details," Khela said, taking a sip of her iced mocha coffee.

"Not this time. You and Carter are my friends. I don't need to know the intricacies. Progress reports will do just fine."

"Progress reports?"

"Just keep me posted on how things develop." Daphne chuckled lightly. "Let me know when to pick out a maid-of-honor gown."

"Never," Khela said. "I'm giving him two weeks. We'll have some laughs, some moans and sighs, and then part as friends. You know how it works."

Daphne's smile vanished and her eyebrows drew a bit closer together.

"What?" Khela asked nervously. "You don't approve? It was your idea."

"I know." Daphne uttered a sharp sigh. "And I was wrong."

"This should be good." Khela loosely crossed her arms on the tabletop and waited for Daphne to explain.

"I've seen the two of you together, and it's worth more than two weeks," Daphne said in a rush. "Yeah, I'm the big fat flirt who teases him and toys with him, but Khela, you're the one he looks for. When he sees you, his whole face changes, his whole body changes. Remember the time I got him to come to your place by stopping up your toilet with Q-tips and cotton balls?"

"How could I forget? Carter had to unstop the clog from the outlet pipe in the basement. No one in the building could use any of their toilets until he turned the main water valve back on."

"I knew what I was doing because my dad is a plumber," Daphne said. "With a snake, that clog would have taken no more than ten minutes to break up. Carter spent half the day on it so he could spend the time with you, and you kept yourself hidden in your loft the whole time."

"That's asinine," Khela said. "If he wanted to spend time with me, there are better ways to go about it than playing in the toilet."

"Are there?" Daphne asked skeptically. "You close yourself off so much, Khela."

Khela started to protest, but Daphne spoke over her. "No, you do. You've always had one foot in the real world and the other in the worlds you create. You live in a great apartment in a great city filled with fascinating people, yet you haven't done any entertaining since your divorce. Sometimes I think you prefer your fictional characters to real people."

"Fictional characters don't sit in Starbucks pointing out my social deficiencies. So yes, from time to time, I do prefer the people I create to my real friends."

"I'm not trying to insult you, Khela."

"This is you not trying? You're very good at it just the same."

"Stop trying to pick a fight with me. I'm going to say what I have to say."

Khela gnawed her lower lip, dreading what Daphne would tell her.

"He's in—"

"Love with me?" Khela squeaked. "No, he's not. He's in it for the same reason I am—to have a little frisky fun."

"I was going to say that he's infatuated with you," Daphne said. "I think two weeks is more than enough time for him to fall in love with you. If you'll let him."

"I'm not the boss of him, Daphne. I can't control his feelings."

"But you can control how much of yourself you give to him. You know how it works, Khela, better than most people. I'm just asking you to be careful. I don't want to see you hurt again."

"You just said that Carter's the one who might fall in love, not me."

Daphne gave Khela a somber smile. "Honey," she said slowly, softly, "you're already in love with him."

Khela opened her mouth, sucking in a big breath of air to power her denial. But the words wouldn't come. She sat there, mouth open, ignoring every version of "No, I'm not" running through her head.

"Yes, you are," Daphne said simply. "You gave it away during your keynote address at the luncheon. When he came into the room, you came to life. Everything about you seemed lighter and brighter. That doesn't happen when you look at a man if you don't love him."

Khela stared out at the pedestrians and cars moving past the coffee shop. All different shapes, sizes and colors, the twin rivers of machinery and humanity moved in opposite directions in a silent dance with a very unique rhythm.

Khela studied the moving panorama, picking faces to zoom in on. A dark-haired man in a business suit, a blond man in a track suit, a bearded man in a UPS uniform, a redheaded man carrying a backpack, a bald man swinging a briefcase . . . they each caught Khela's eye, but in the flat, disinterested way fish in an aquarium might catch her eye. They moved in her line of vision, but their appearance meant nothing to her.

It was so different with Carter. He entered a room and his presence seemed to charge the air. Every part of her would come to life in a way that made her realize how truly numb to the rest of the world she had become. None of the passing faces compared with Carter's, and not just because he was freakishly handsome. No other man's eyes sparkled as Carter's did; she knew no other man who had his unhurried yet powerful walk. And no other man's voice, when shaped into its native Southern drawl, could curl her toes just by uttering her name.

Khela propped her elbows on the table and clapped her hands to her face. "Oh, God," she whimpered. "I think I do. I think I really, really do."

Daphne patted her forearm. "What's the problem? This is a good thing!"

Khela's hands fell heavily to the tabletop. "There's nothing good about being in love with Carter Radcliffe!" she said, her voice breaking as tears trickled over her lower eyelids. "I'm not good at love."

"How do you know?" Daphne laughed, handing her a few coarse brown paper napkins. "You've never been in love, not really. Until you find it, you don't know what real love is. Most people settle for thinking they're in love, or hoping they're in love. Then they go and get married, and they're all surprised when it falls apart."

"Exactly how much thought have you given this?"

"Lots." Daphne dropped her eyes. "Lots and lots," she said somberly.

"Is there something going on with the auctioneer that you'd like to talk about?"

"No." Daphne stirred her lukewarm coffee. "Yes." She sat up straighter, leaning closer to Khela. "He wants me to go back to the United Kingdom with him."

Khela's eyes widened in alarm. "For a visit?"

"Forever." Daphne gazed absently at the world outside Starbucks, twirling the end of a lock of her fiery hair around her fingertip. "He's asked me to marry him. It's sudden, but we know it's right for us."

The iced lemon pound cake Khela had scarfed down earlier suddenly felt like lead in her stomach. Her skin felt cold and hot at the same time as she asked the first question that popped into her head. "You're leaving me?"

"Why am I not surprised that you would somehow turn the most amazing, surprising, wonderful thing to happen to me into something about you?"

Stung, Khela's stomach clenched around the leaden cake. "What?"

"For as long as I've known you, you've turned everything about me into something about you."

Khela sat back in her chair, distancing herself a bit from the ice in Daphne's stare. "I don't know what's brought this on, but—"

"The romance conference in Chicago, for starters," Daphne interrupted. "I wanted you to go there and be my moral support, not outshine me."

"That's not what—"

"I know you didn't mean for it to happen, but it did." Daphne's nostrils quivered, a tell-tale sign that tears would soon follow. "Ever since then, you've been the one with all the fame and fans and—"

"You've been harboring this jealousy for ten years?" Khela cried, her apprehension growing.

"Men!" Daphne continued, a touch of hurt in her anger. "As soon as guys find out you're a romance novelist, all they care about is getting me to introduce them to you. Llewellyn is the only man I've ever dated who never asks me about my 'writer friend Khela.' He thinks I'm funny and beautiful and talented—"

"I've told everyone who would listen that it was luck and timing, not talent, that got me my first contract. I know how gifted you are, Daphne. You're a crackerjack editor and an even better writer. Your background in comparative literature gives your writing an intellectual edge that mine won't ever have."

Still staring out the window, Daphne finally let her sobs burst free. Khela could hardly understand her as she sputtered, "Talent doesn't always translate into success, does it? Lew thinks I'm beautiful and smart and fun, but I don't bring anything more than window dressing to the table. I edit books for a living. I put the polish on diamonds that belong to other people. I get a decent paycheck for it, but I don't get any credit." Daphne used the cuff of her sleeve to wipe her nose. "Lew's one of the most respected antiquarians in Britain, did you know that?"

"No, I didn't." Khela took Daphne's hand and held it tight. "You haven't told me much about him. I haven't even seen him since the cake auction. Now I know why I haven't seen much of you, either."

Daphne turned her wounded gaze on Khela. "I didn't want him to meet you. The minute he met you would be the minute I lost him."

"How can you say that?"

"Khela, you have those big, soft brown eyes that take in everything around you, yet you can't seem to see the effect you have on men when you walk into a room," Daphne wept quietly. "And you're smart. On the fly, in front of an editor from the biggest publishing house in the world, you pitched a book that you hadn't even conceived of before you sat in that chair. You turned a hobby into a successful career, and you don't just rest on your laurels. Your crazy cake raised five grand for the Literacy Fund. The donation you made to Wednesday's Child will provide scholarships to ten kids who age out of the child welfare system." Daphne gave her eyes another swipe with her sleeve. "You're smart, sophisticated and polished, and every man who meets you, wants you."

"Okay, even if that were true, which it isn't, you have to look at why they want me," Khela argued. "Exhibit A: J-Fred."

"You were young when you married him. You didn't know any better."

"You were the same age I was and you saw right through him. You warned me about him, but I didn't listen. It was those big, straight teeth that did it. You knew that he was looking for a payday." Khela paused until she could go on without shedding tears of her own. "You knew that he didn't love me."

"Same as I know that Carter's half in love with you," Daphne said softly. "Be good to him, Khela. Don't hold the offenses of other men against him."

"I'm not punishing him for what J-Fred and the other prospectors I've dated have done," Khela said. "But I won't be fooled again. I won't get burned again. I'm just not sure how to go about avoiding it."

"Don't hold him to the two weeks."

"You think I should break it off with him? Already?"

Daphne grinned sadly. "I think you should give him more than two weeks. Give him a real shot, Khela."

"Like you're giving Llewellyn a shot? Is that what this is about?"

"I'm going to marry him," Daphne said, her smile finally radiating true happiness.

Khela nearly fell off her chair. "You've known him for four weeks!"

"Four weeks and five days," Daphne calculated. "He proposed last night, and I accepted. We've decided on a Labor Day ceremony here in Massachusetts, and then I'm going to live in a manor in the English countryside. I've got a little over two months to organize a wedding and pack up my apartment."

"So you are leaving me," Khela whispered.

"And I don't feel guilty about it at all, so don't try and make me. But I don't want you to be alone. Even more than that, I don't want you to be afraid to love a really good man."

"How can you be so sure that Carter's so good for me?"

"Because I see how happy he's made you. When you talk about Carter, you look the way I feel about Llewellyn."

Khela gripped the sides of her head. "I don't get this. I just don't get it!"

"You don't have to," Daphne said softly. "From the first time we met, Lew and I felt connected, as though we'd found something we'd been longing for and missing. Since we met, we've spent almost every day together. Sometimes, he makes phone calls and works on the Internet while I sit across from him, editing my latest assignment. We're so comfortable with each other, whether we're working or playing. He took me on a buying trip to New York City, and I took him to Richmond Heights to meet my parents last weekend."

"How do your mom and dad feel about you moving so fast with this guy?"

"They respect my judgment, even if they don't agree with it," Daphne said. "I hope you will, too. I know Lew is right for me. Same as I know Carter is right for you."

❦

Calareso's was Khela's favorite neighborhood market. Her adoptive parents had lived on modest means, but they had instilled in her the adventurous palate of the serious foodie. Khela was the only kindergartner in the small suburb of Rock Hill, Missouri who took feta cheese and black olives to school for lunch and had red pepper hummus with rice and sunflower chips for an after-school snack.

Calareso's was the one store in downtown Boston that reminded her of Grandma Belle's pantry while at the same time giving her access to many of the exotic foods she'd come to enjoy in the course of her travels as an author.

The tiny store, no bigger than the average corner market, was chock full of the most delicious and unique offerings imaginable. Dried herbs, homegrown by the Calaresos themselves on their farm in Billerica, adorned the front windows. Each section of the store had its own unique aromas. Fresh herbs and cut flowers competed for prominence in the produce section while hand-packed spices from the Far East, West Africa and the Mediterranean dominated the ethnic foods aisle.

The seafood section smelled of brine and the ocean, but not of fish, despite the presence of low barrels of ice piled high with live clams, mussels and oysters. Lobsters in a glass tank seemed to sense their eventual fate, scrambling over one another, reaching for the top of the tank as though knowing escape lay there. The glass display case housed still more fruits of the sea, with sea and bay scallops stacked high next to more exotic fare, such as mako shark and mahi mahi.

Khela had once spent an hour browsing the canned meats and sauces aisle, admiring the fanciful or just plain fancy bottles and jars and other packaging, imagining how she could use them in her stories. She'd once purchased a pricey bottle of imported balsamic vinegar because the bottle came with a security band sealed with purple wax and stamped with an ornate letter "V." That stamp had inspired one of her most popular books, *The Pirate's Princess.*

Calareso's was the one place where Khela could find her favorite English condiments from Crosse & Blackwell, such as mint sauce for roasted potatoes and sweet peas, alongside her favorite American relishes and jellies from Stonewall Kitchens. Her cart already contained big jars of Stonewall's red pepper jelly and roasted garlic and onion jam.

Right next to the fresh artisan breads were tinned squab and venison, and an olive bar featuring savory morsels from as far away as Morocco and Sicily.

Though Khela had no taste for squab or venison or imported olives, she liked knowing that she could get them if she ever needed to describe the taste for one of her characters.

Their shopping cart was stacked high with a week's supply of groceries. Fresh fruits and vegetables in green plastic bags rested atop the boxed and canned goods she and Carter had chosen. They were on their way to the bakery to select a loaf or two of Tuscan bread when Khela drew up short.

"Great," she muttered. "There's only one check-out open and Mangela is manning it."

Carter glanced at the tall, thickly built cashier at register two and chuckled. "Mangela?"

"His name is Angela," Khela said, grasping Carter's upper arm as she hid behind him. "But Daphne and I started calling her Mangela because she's so masculine. He hates me. She's the only thing I hate about this store."

"Why does she—he—that person hate you?" Carter asked, trying not to stare.

"Why do snakes bite?" Khela said. "Because it's just her nature. She was fine with me until he overheard Daphne and me talking in line one day, and she asked me if I was a writer. I said yes, and he's been evil to me ever since. She read one of my books and really gave it to me one day. I came in to buy some monkey bread, and the next thing I knew, Mangela's berating me about *Teacher's Pet.*"

While listening to Khela's rant, Carter searched his memory for *Teacher's Pet*. Then it came to him. *Teacher's Pet*, Khela's fifth novel and first Cameo Sizzler, was about a grad student who carried on a secret affair with her recently divorced English professor.

The book's sex scenes were so tantalizing, Carter imagined he saw steam rising from its pages every time he opened it. It had the wit, sassiness and humor that he had discovered in Khela, but it also had love scenes that left him so tense with pent-up desire that most nights he couldn't sleep until he'd given himself some relief, usually while looking at Khela's photo on the inside back cover of the book.

"She said that it was the most far-fetched, ridiculous book he'd ever read," Khela went on. "She went through it almost page by page while she rang up my groceries, criticizing just about everything I'd written."

"You should be used to criticism," Carter said. "You've been at this a long time."

They stepped up to the glass bakery case and studied the loaves of bread, cakes, pastries and cookies prettily lined up along the five shelves.

"Mangela screamed at the top of her lungs how stupid she thought I was for giving my English professor—he was the male lead in the book—a Porsche. She said it was improbable that an English teacher would make enough money to own a Porsche. Shows what Mangela knows about the income of tenured professors."

"Why didn't you explain that in the book?"

"Because the kind of car he drove wasn't integral to the plot. It was merely used to illustrate his character. He was a 40-year-old, graying, balding, recently divorced man who went out and bought himself a gunmetal grey Porsche. What he bought was more important than describing his financing for it."

"Sounds like she's criticizing creative choices and not the actual writing," Carter said. "Just because she doesn't know any professors with Porsches, they must not exist."

Khela tossed up her hands in relief. "Exactly! I get that all the time, people questioning what I write as though I get my ideas from stone tablets handed down by God. I make stuff up—"

"Hence the word fiction."

"—based on my own experiences and the ones I steal from people around me, and the news, and television.

Almost all of my characters come from people in my life, although—"

"I recognized Daphne and the concert pianist who lives under you in two of your books," Carter interrupted again.

"—I try to disguise them so I don't get sued!" Khela went on. "You can't complain about a character's *car* when the book is about a professor's erotic encounters with a much younger graduate student. That's not a constructive critique, that's just . . . just . . . I don't know what it is!"

"Sorta seems like a personal attack to me," Carter offered easily. "Maybe she's jealous of you."

"Yeah," Khela glowered, cutting her eyes in Mangela's direction. "That ol' bald-headed thing is jealous that I was born with ovaries and a va—"

"What can I get for you today, cutie pie?" interrupted the overly cheery woman behind the bakery counter. She leaned forward, resting her ample bosom atop her crossed forearms.

With her white apron and flour dusting her nose and cheeks, Khela thought the woman looked like she had been sculpted from hefty pillows of biscuit dough.

Khela ordered one loaf of Tuscan bread, one large French baguette and two loaves of monkey bread. By eating an entire loaf of it for breakfast, Carter had demonstrated a particular fondness for the sticky ring made of cinnamon-and-butter-soaked lumps of sweet bread.

"Cutie pie," Carter mimicked with a snicker when the counterperson retreated to fill the order. "No one has called me 'cutie pie' since I was in kindergarten."

"She's a baker," Khela said. "It makes sense that she would give you a nickname with 'pie' in it."

"So I guess she might call you Sugar Buns?" Carter asked with a laugh.

"The really funny thing is her name," Khela said.

"Is it funnier than Mangela?"

Khela shushed him, afraid that he'd spoken too loudly. "Don't invoke her name. He's got a sixth sense when it comes to stuff like that."

"Well, what's the counter lady's name?"

"Honey Baker," Khela grinned.

"No way," Carter responded. "Are you kiddin' me?"

"Nope," Khela giggled. "I just love that."

"It fits, that's for sure. That's like finding a mechanic named Otto Carr."

"There's a reality show about plastic surgeons, and one of the physicians on it is named Dr. Alter," Khela said.

"That's a good one," Carter said, nodding appreciatively. "Dr. Cutter would be good, too."

Khela shook her head. "Naah, too obvious."

"How about a dentist named Dr. Payne?" Carter suggested.

"Or a policeman named Booker?"

"A shrimp boat captain named Fisher," Carter countered.

"A seamstress named Taylor."

"A scuba diver named Schwimmer."

"That's really reaching," Khela giggled.

"Okay, an actor named Hamm."

"That's really good."

Carter lowered his voice and aimed his words at Khela's left ear. "A porn star named Wood."

"A prostitute named Hooker," Khela whispered.

"We have to stop this," Carter chuckled. "I think I'm getting a little slaphappy hanging around with you."

"I need slaphappy," Khela said, gathering her waxed bags full of bread. She thanked Honey Baker and set her selections atop her other groceries. "First Daphne, now Mangela."

"Did something happen to Daphne?" Carter asked, rolling the cart toward Mangela's checkout.

Khela swallowed hard when she saw Mangela do a double take. The cashier leveled a sinister smile at Khela before handing change to her current customer.

"I'll wait for you outside," Khela said.

"No, you don't." Carter grabbed her hand tightly, preventing her escape. "I can't believe you're scared of a cashier."

"She's not an ordinary cashier!" Khela argued. "He's vicious, and she hates me! Normally, criticism rolls off my back. I don't expect everyone to love my work, but I don't expect someone to crap all over it to my face as if what I wrote was a personal affront to them. Or him. She just makes me very uncomfortable because I can't look her in the eye and tell him to go to hell."

"Yes, you can," Carter told her.

"And the very next day, I'll read about it in the Herald-Star's *Psst!* gossip column," Khela replied. "I wouldn't put it past her to call up the information line and tell Meg LaParosa what a big bitch I was to him."

"Will you please stop that he-she stuff? You're con-fusing me." Carter pushed the shopping cart to the con-veyor belt, pulling Khela along behind him. "Hey," he said, greeting the cashier, who stood with arms sullenly crossed, wearing a nametag reading HI, I'M ANGELA.

"Haven't seen you in a while, scribbler," Angela said, ignoring Carter's greeting. "Been hiding out in your fancy apartment writing more of your silly little tales?"

Carter was prepared to defend Khela, but he was dis-armed by the sound of Angela's voice. It reminded him of Lou Rawls with laryngitis. He slowed in the process of loading the groceries onto the conveyor belt to study Angela a bit closer.

Her flawless chocolate complexion was her best fea-ture. Her hair was shorn close to the scalp, giving her head a mere shadow of dark coloration. Even though it was June, she wore a natty pink ascot that complemented the mint green of her Calareso's smock. Carter wondered, but really didn't want to know, what the accessory might be concealing.

Angela palmed a honeydew melon with ease, and the sheer size of her hands and broad span of her fingers sur-prised Carter. After punching the melon's price code into the register, she dropped Khela's carefully chosen fruit into a brown paper bag standing open at her side.

"Could you be a little more careful there?" Carter asked.

Khela flinched, fully expecting Angela to retrieve the melon and break it over Carter's head.

Angela's brown eyes, wide, deep-set and lashless beneath her sloping forehead and prominent brow ridge, seemed to flash with anger.

"Sure thing, boss," she finally said.

She next rang up Khela's Tuscan bread, making a point of stabbing it with her thumb as she placed it with exaggerated gentleness into the bag with the melon.

"I don't know what your problem is, but I'm about ready to call your manager over here and tell him about a little lady with a very big attitude problem."

"Aren't you the big hero come to the rescue," Angela said, her voice softening a little. "Why haven't I seen you around here before?"

"I'm more of a Stop & Shop kinda guy," Carter said. "I can't see my way to paying five dollars for a loaf of bread."

"I hear you," Angela said. "I work here and I can't afford to shop here." She laughed, and the sound boomed throughout the front of the store. "Your little writer friend there shops here all the time. Some people sure like to be good to themselves."

"If you got it, spend it, 'cause you sure can't take it with you," Carter said.

Behind him, Khela rolled her eyes, sickened by the heavy dose of Southern charm Carter was wasting on the meanest cashier in the world.

"Miss Thing hiding in your back pocket sure has got it," Angela said, her voice low, conspiratorial. "She was in here last week buying beef tenderloin at twenty-two dollars a pound. Of course, if she was buying it for you, then I'll bet it was worth it."

"Isn't there some sort of customer-cashier confidentiality code you're supposed to adhere to?" Khela demanded, stepping out of the safety of Carter's shadow. "Who are you to judge what I buy and how much I pay for it, and why the hell do you have to talk about me while I'm standing right here?"

Angela innocently batted her eyelids. "I didn't see you there, Ms. Halliday."

"Folks in Boston have the reputation for being rude," Carter began graciously, "but you might want to rethink the way you treat Miss Halliday. One of these days, she might decide to put her writing skills to work on a letter of complaint to your manager." He set the three bags of groceries in the cart. With a wink at Angela, he said, "Just something to think about, darlin'."

Angela appeared to do exactly that—think about whether she wanted Khela to compose a letter of complaint to her manager. "That'll be one hundred and eleven dollars and sixty-two cents," Angela said politely. "Would you like that to go on your account?"

"Please," Khela said.

Angela, her broad mouth widening in a smile, swiveled a mounted keypad to face Khela, who punched in her personal account number and hit ENTER. A moment later, Angela ripped the receipt from the register and held it out to her.

"Thank you very much," Khela said pleasantly.

"Have a very wonderful day," was Angela's saccharine response before turning to her next customer.

"She wasn't that bad, once I showed her who's boss," Carter said, gathering the bags into his arms before they left the store.

Khela returned the cart to the cart lot near the entrance. "You called him a lady. That's when she stopped hassling me and started trying to charm you."

"You're sure about that?"

"Of course I am." Khela got the door by stepping in front of its electronic eye. "When you try so hard to look like a lady, and a handsome man comes along and calls you one, I imagine it goes a long way. Of course, your sweet way of threatening to get her fired probably did show her who was boss."

"You?" Carter asked.

"No," Khela chuckled. "*You.*"

"You know, if Miss Angela upsets you so much, you don't have to shop here," he suggested. "I think you like scrappin' with that gal. Everybody else tells you how much they love your books, but that one doesn't cotton to 'em."

Khela hid a guilty smile. "I appreciate her candor, to be sure. And she's interesting, too. She's a *real* character, unlike so many of the other characters I spend my time with."

CHAPTER 9

"A lover doesn't have to be your friend,
but the best lovers start out as best friends."
— from Mr. Wrong *by Khela Halliday*

Balancing three paper bags of groceries in his arms, Carter used his chin to shift the greens on the beets in the center bag to keep them from obscuring his view as he stepped off the curb and into the street. He stopped, waiting for a break in traffic. But Khela, walking beside him, was staring at her feet and continued forward. Blaring its horn, an oncoming Yellow Cab showed no sign of stopping. Dropping the bags, Carter lunged forward and yanked Khela from the path of the speeding taxi.

"Cockass!" he yelled after the taxi before turning his full attention back to a shaken Khela. "Wanna tell me what's got your eyes turned so far inward that you've forgotten how to cross a street?" Carter's heart throbbed painfully as he walked her a short way to a bench at a bus shelter.

She seemed to have trouble catching her breath, but had little to say once she had. "Someone's going to steal our groceries."

"Let 'em." Carter squatted before her. "You've been odd and moody all day. What's on your mind? Is it still Mangela?"

She shook her head, fixing her gaze on something beyond Carter's shoulder.

He cupped her face, gently urging her to look at him. She obliged, and his concern shattered her emotionless façade.

"Hey, now," he said tenderly. He used the pads of his thumb to strike away the tears seeping from her eyes. "Is it really as bad as all that?"

"It's not bad at all," she croaked. "It's good. Daphne is getting married."

Carter's face broke into a wide smile. "That's a good one," he chuckled. "You almost had me there."

"I'm not kidding," Khela wept. "She told me yesterday afternoon. She's running off with that auctioneer. She's leaving in a few weeks. They're getting married, and then he'll be taking her to the other side of the Atlantic."

"Seems kinda quick to me," Carter said.

"Duh!" Khela agreed, giving voice to her inner adolescent. "And he's a lot older than she is."

"How old is he? Fifty?"

"He's thirty-seven, but he looks fifty, doesn't he?"

"No," Carter grinned. "I was just being a smart ass."

A big navel orange rolled into the street, and Khela recognized it as hers since it had a hole in it about the same width as Angela's thumb. She got up and retrieved one of the bags lying on its side at the curb.

Carter collected the other two bags, shoving a cello-wrapped package of celery hearts and a box of whole-wheat spaghetti back into a bag. They continued to Khela's building in silence until they reached the front door.

"You and Daphne have been together a long time, haven't you?" Carter asked, standing aside as Khela unlocked the massive door.

"Since freshman year in college," Khela answered. "We were assigned to the same dorm room. We're total opposites, but we hit it off right away." Clutching the heavy bag of groceries to her chest, Khela used her foot to hold the door open for Carter. "Apparently, she's secretly hated me ever since."

"I doubt that." Carter walked ahead of Khela and pressed the UP button for the elevator. "You two are thicker than thieves. Daphne's crazy about you."

"You got the crazy part right," Khela scoffed, entering the elevator. "She accused me of being completely self-centered. She says that I turn everything she tells me about her life into something about me."

"Do you?" Carter used the toe of his sneaker to press the button for the top floor.

"I can't believe you think that—"

Khela's complaint was cut off when Carter set down his bags, cupped Khela's face and brought his lips to hers. Khela's bag tumbled out of her arms, once again spilling its contents. Her arms went around Carter's neck, his hands went to her waist, and Khela found herself pressed against the back of the car.

Carter's hands moved over her backside on their way to her thighs, where he clutched her, to help her boost herself onto the brass rail along the back of the elevator.

Carter's lips sought her throat, then traveled farther south, to the opening of her crisp white sleeveless shirt. "We can't do this here," she breathed hard in his ear. "Someone will walk in on us."

Smiling, Carter shot out a hand and activated the emergency stop button. The elevator whined to a halt, bouncing slightly as it hung by its unseen cables. Carter returned to Khela and began unfastening the prim white buttons on her shirt.

"The day you moved in, I fantasized about what I could do to you in this brass box," he told her.

"Sex in an elevator is such a cliché," Khela moaned as his tongue dipped into her ear.

"You call it a cliché, I call it a dream come true," Carter murmured. "Every time I ride this elevator, I think about what it would be like to take you for a ride in it."

His confession gave Khela an extra thrill, but she masked her enjoyment by smiling at the roof as Carter exposed the white lace cups of her bra. She surrendered to him, her body and mind devoted to the pleasures he offered so generously.

This was the third of the fourteen days she'd given him, and Khela found herself hoping that day four would never come, only because it meant they would be one day closer to parting ways. In satisfying one of his fantasies, Carter brought to life one of Khela's, which was to experience the kind of spontaneous couplings she wrote about. Carter was gentle, unhurried and completely devoted to satisfying her. His touch sure and knowing, he exhausted her with his loving.

"It's like something from one of my books," she sighed, fastening the buttons of her shirt as he embraced her from behind. "Real men never give women the kind of attention you just gave me."

"Is that so?" Carter asked innocently. "Are you speaking for all women, or just your own experience?"

"I'm speaking for myself and all of the women who write telling me that their husbands and lovers don't listen." Khela zipped up her khaki shorts and then shoved her foot into the Keds sneaker that had flown off in the middle of their romp. "In my books, when my heroine tells the hero what she wants, he does it. He doesn't make faces or act stupid, and he's certainly not selfish." She pressed her body to Carter's, hooking her arms under his to hug him. "You could give lessons in how to make a woman feel like the only woman in the world."

"The only woman in the world for *me*," Carter quickly clarified.

Khela slowly drew away from him, unsure whether she should be confused or surprised. "That's . . . uh . . . th-that's just about the nicest thing any man has ever said to me," she remarked with a soft laugh. "It actually sounds like a line from one of my books."

Carter bent down and once again picked up the groceries. "We'd better get these dairy products up to your fridge," he said in a rush. "Can't have your fancy mozzarella going bad before you get a chance to eat it."

"You're gonna love that fancy mozzarella once I put fresh basil, sliced Roma tomatoes and white balsamic vinegar over it."

Carter deactivated the emergency stop, declaring, "I would never pay twelve dollars a pound for a little knot of cheese."

"Say that with a straight face after you taste it," Khela challenged him as the elevator lurched into motion, jostling her into Carter. "There's only about four ounces there. Just enough to taste."

"That's one of the things I love about you," he said. "You introduce me to the finer things in life."

Khela righted herself, her smile fading as she turned to face the elevator doors. Carter continued talking, but his last words, *The finer things in life*, echoed between her ears, deafening her to whatever he was saying.

———❧———

"Are you going to get that?" Carter asked over the tenth ring of the phone sitting on the ornate cherry wood table near the dining room table.

"No." Khela stubbornly turned away from the phone. "It's just Daphne again."

Carter, rattling the silver bag of Scrabble tiles, shook his head. "You should talk to her. She obviously wants to talk to you. And she'll be gone before you know it. Labor Day isn't that far off."

Khela watched him set five new tiles on his rack. She had been delighted when he'd agreed to play her favorite board game, and he kept her on her toes with the words he spelled. FOLKS had left him five tiles short, but he closed the points between his score and Khela's to sixty-five.

Ordinarily, Khela had a cutthroat, take-no-prisoners approach to Scrabble. If she won by two hundred or more points, so be it. But her heart wasn't in the game, not with Daphne calling every few minutes.

"Khela," Carter said, a plaintive note in his voice.

She scowled at her tiles, trying to ignore the incessant ringing of the phone.

"She obviously knows you're here. The only way you're going to get her to stop calling is to talk to her."

"What am I supposed to say?" Khela asked petulantly. She jostled the wooden table when she slapped down six tiles, one covering a red triple word square, to spell JINGLY while turning Carter's FOLKS into FOLKSY.

Carter calculated Khela's score, which put her up another ninety-three points. "In all the years you've lived here, I've never known you and Daphne to have a fight."

The phone stopped ringing, and Khela stared at it as if it had betrayed her somehow. "She pitched the biggest jealousy fit in Starbucks. It was sickening."

Carter started to speak, but Khela talked over him. "Do you know how many times I offered to give her manuscripts to my editors?"

"Three?" Carter randomly suggested.

"Try three dozen, but she always refused!" Khela gave the three Is in her tray a disgusted sneer. "She wants to get published on her own, with no help from anybody. Even if I gave her a leg up by getting her work in front of an editor, it won't get published unless it's good. I don't know why she won't let me give her a shortcut."

"Some folks like doing things all on their own," Carter said. "Considering all the strangers who ask you to forward their work to your publisher, you should be glad that Daphne doesn't want to hitch a ride on your coattails."

"Daphne is ten times a better writer than I am, a hundred times! She's a good storyteller *and* a good writer. Do you know how rare that is?"

"Aren't they the same thing?"

Khela fussily pinched her lips together and glared at him. "Of course not. Almost anyone can open their mouths and tell a story that holds your attention. Very few people can sit at a keyboard and create stories that do with words what Monet did with paint."

"Or what Mozart did with music."

Clearly appreciating his understanding, Khela relaxed, the tension leaving her face. "Exactly."

"The best writers tell beautiful stories beautifully," Carter said.

"Who's your favorite author?" she asked him, the new topic mollifying her unhappiness over her fight with Daphne.

"You are."

She rolled her eyes. "Okay, who else besides me?"

"I've always liked F. Scott Fitzgerald."

Khela's eyebrows rose. "Really? I would have pegged you for a Hemingway fan."

"He's too macho for me."

"You're macho," Khela giggled. "It's one of the things I like best about you."

"Don't confuse macho with manly," he advised.

"Point taken," Khela said. "It's your turn, you know."

"I know." Carter's gaze moved from his tile rack to the game board and back again. "You didn't give me much to work with in your new word, and there's not much I can do with no vowels."

Khela grabbed Carter's wrist and glanced at his watch. "Are you hungry? If we leave now, we can beat the dinner rush at Pizzeria Regina."

Carter began packing up the game. "You bought all that overpriced cheese just to let it sit in the fridge? Let's eat in tonight. I'll cook."

"Shoot, I won't turn down an offer like that," Khela grinned. "You can cook, can't you?"

"What do you think?" Carter asked suggestively.

"I think there's not a whole lot you aren't good at."

He closed the Scrabble box and took her hand, clasping it atop the box. "That's about the nicest thing you've ever said to me."

"Well . . ." Khela cast her eyes down shyly. "It's true. You surprise me with the things you know and the things you can do."

"You thought I was just another pretty face?"

Khela looked at him, unsure if she'd actually heard a note of sadness in his question. "You're more than just another pretty face. You have one of the best faces I've ever seen."

Rising from the table, Carter pulled his hand from hers. "I kinda wish you'd stop saying that."

"Saying what? Did I say something wrong?"

He took the Scrabble box and returned it to its home atop Monopoly and underneath Yahtzee on the oak bookcase spanning one wall of Khela's living room. "How do you feel about pasta for dinner?"

"I thought you said you could cook," Khela said, hoping to douse the flicker of tension that had suddenly risen between them. "Boiling pasta isn't cooking."

"You gotta cook to make a good sauce." He went to the kitchen and began opening cabinets and the refrigerator, collecting the items he would need. "Mind if I use some of the vine-ripened tomatoes?"

"Go ahead," Khela said. "Just leave me two of them."

She sat back in her comfortable wing chair, listening to Carter's movements in the kitchen. The wall dividing the kitchen from the living and dining room areas kept him out of sight, but his quiet humming and murmured words reached her ears. And touched her heart in unexpected ways. The soft Southern purr of his accent took her years back to the summer vacations she spent in Mississippi and Alabama visiting the older relatives of her adopted family.

Her Great Aunt Sugar in Tupelo had been born in Mobile, Alabama, and had moved to Mississippi after marrying Grady Robertson, a man from Jackson. While there was no mistaking the part of the country from which Sugar and Grady hailed, their dialects couldn't have sounded more different to Khela.

Grady's was clipped, while Sugar's was languid. Sugar had a touch of the Gulf in her speech, and no matter how hard Khela had tried to copy it, she couldn't make her mouth form words into such lovely sounds.

Carter originated far from the Gulf, but his accent so reminded Khela of her happy summers down South that she couldn't help thinking of sleepy June days spent at hidden ponds, fishing for crawdads at mud holes with a bit of pork fat tied to a shoelace. Listening to Carter's soft musings from the kitchen, Khela found herself day-dreaming of long, lazy rides on the tire swing hanging from Sugar's biggest oak tree—and bellyaches from eating green plums from the tree in the backyard.

Her family down South had always been exactly that—her family. She had none of their blood, but they had proven that family you choose can be more precious than family you're born to.

The man in her kitchen gave her a sense of home and family that ran deep, and Khela wanted to hold on to it, to revel in it. She wanted it to last longer than another week and a half.

She practically launched herself out of her chair and zipped into the kitchen, determined to renegotiate their two-week agreement. His greeting stopped her short.

"This stove is unbelievable," he said, turning away from his simmering pots. "One of my other tenants wanted a Le Cornu, but when she realized how much it cost, she settled for a good old-fashioned General Electric. The best will outlast the rest, that's for sure. I'll say it again, if you got it, spend it, because you can't take it with you. And judging from this stove, you definitely got it, Khela."

He set down his wooden spoon, which was dripping with pasta sauce, and crossed the kitchen to get a box of spaghetti from the center prep isle. He kissed Khela's cheek as he passed her, oblivious to the serious set of her eyes and mouth.

She crossed her arms and leaned against the wide archway. "Could you stop looking for dollar signs?"

His smile faltered. "I'm not looking for them, Khela. They're all over this place. You can't spend thousands on a fancy French stove and a Toto toilet from Japan without having people notice."

"People like who?" she asked, her voice a bit too high and strained. "Who could I possibly be trying to impress? Other than Daphne, you're the only person who's spent any real time here since I got divorced. My ex picked all these pricey appliances. *He's* the one who sat around thinking of ways to spend *my* money. I confess a fondness for one-of-a-kind perfume and certain specialty foods, but guess what? I earn my own dough and I won't apologize for how I spend it. J-Fred—"

"Who?"

"Jay Fredericks," Khela explained. "My ex-husband. Daphne calls him J-Fred because when we divorced he made sure that he took a hearty settlement with him. I got the condo and everything in it, and he got a lump sum payment and a percentage of future royalties on all the books I wrote while we were together."

"I'm sorry," Carter said, going to her.

Her dark eyes gleamed as she held his gaze. "Don't be. I'm not. I'm grateful for what I have. I just wish Grandma Belle and Grandpa Neal were here, or that Jay had been willing to have a child to spend money on instead of a toilet and a stove."

"Family means so much to you, doesn't it?" he asked, stroking her hair.

She hid her face in his shoulder until she could look at him without shedding tears. When she faced him again, she changed the subject. "How do you know how much my appliances and toilets cost?"

"I'm the one who takes care of them, remember?" Carter said, respecting her reluctance to answer his question. "I do my homework so I can learn how to repair them if something gets busted or breaks down."

His reasoning made perfect sense, but Khela remained unconvinced that Carter didn't find her income more attractive than he found the rest of her. Nonetheless, she said, "Forgive me for overreacting. I guess I'm . . ."

"A little hungry," he offered generously. "Hunger makes your mind play tricks on you."

She gave him a grateful smile. "Your sauce smells wonderful."

He wiped his hands on the blue cotton towel tucked in his waistband. "It's an old family recipe." He went to Khela and took her in a loose embrace. "It's not from my family, though. I picked it up from the owners of a little trattoria in the North End. I used to go there a few times a week for their linguine with red sauce and the chocolate-covered cannolis. When they decided to retire and close the place, they gave me their recipe for red sauce."

"They must have really liked you." Khela's gaze fixed on his lips, which were almost close enough to kiss.

"I was a good customer." Carter bowed his head a bit. "And the owners had no children. I guess they didn't want the recipe to die with their restaurant."

"So now it'll live on through your family," Khela whispered, tilting her face upward.

"Once I have one," he murmured before pressing his lips to hers in a soft, sweet kiss that sent Khela's hands to his backside.

Though no less tender, Carter's kisses intensified, pushing Khela's niggling reservations to the farthest recesses of her mind. He kissed her as though he wanted her to stay kissed long after their two weeks ended, as though each kiss would be their last and needed to surpass the one that came before it.

Carter mumbled against her lips.

"What?" she managed, breaking for air.

His lips moved to her throat. "I said, we need to talk about the two weeks."

"I agree," Khela gasped when his hands covered her breasts, his fingers working the magic that never failed to start her blood moving faster through her veins.

"It's a mistake," she said simultaneously with his, "It's not right."

They abruptly separated, shocked speechless. Before they could elaborate on their brief but meaningful exchange, the doorbell started to chime, the ringing every bit as insistent as the earlier ringing of the phone.

"Let me . . ." Khela said awkwardly, pointing with both index fingers toward her front door.

"Sure," Carter said quickly, turning and going back to the stove.

It's not right! Khela repeated in her head, her expression betraying bafflement and disbelief. *What the hell does he mean, "It's not—"*

She unlocked the two deadbolts and the knob latch and opened the door to find Daphne. From the neck down, she was the picture of a mild New England summer in a pale green sleeveless tank top and matching Laura Ashley walking shorts. But from the neck up, she looked as if winter's fiercest nor'easter had settled in her face.

Khela's eyes instantly filled in response to Daphne's obvious misery. The tear-slicked green of Daphne's gaze met the watery shine of Khela's, and without a word, they fell into each other's arms, their apologies overlapping.

The caterwaul brought Carter from the kitchen, and he stood a ways back in the foyer, waiting for the women to release each other.

"Do all your fights end like this?" Llewellyn Davies asked, stepping into view.

"Maybe," Daphne sniffled. "This is the first fight we've ever had."

Khela wiped her nose on the back of her hand. "This is the last fight we'll ever have."

"It's good to see you two getting on again," Carter said, coming forward to give Daphne a brief hug. "How are you, Daphne?"

Her narrowed eyes shifted from Carter to Khela and back to Carter. "I think I should be asking you guys that question."

"We can jibber-jabber later." Khela eyed Llewellyn over Daphne's shoulder. "Who's your friend?" she asked playfully.

If her smile was the sun, Daphne could have warmed and illuminated the earth for millennia as she took Llewellyn's hand and proudly drew him forward. "Khela Halliday, Carter Radcliffe, this is Llewellyn Davies. My fiancé."

"I've heard . . ." Khela started, shaking his hand, ". . . pretty much nothing about you."

"Yes, I imagine we have quite a lot of explaining to do," Llewellyn said, offering a self-conscious smile.

Khela boldly sized up the man who was planning to marry her best friend. Llewellyn looked much different now in jeans and a black polo shirt than he had the night of the cake auction, when he'd emceed and called the event in a natty tuxedo. Black was a good color for him because it complemented his fair hair and complexion. About Carter's height, Llewellyn was fit, as all Daphne's love interests were, but he wasn't as heavy with muscle as her men tended to be. His expressive blue eyes and accent were the features that stood out most to Khela because he had those traits in common with Carter.

"Why don't you and Mr. Davies come in and join us for dinner," Khela said, moving aside to allow Daphne and Llewellyn to enter. Carter briefly shook Llewellyn's hand before closing the front door and following everyone into the living room. "Carter's been slaving over the stove for hours, preparing some secret sauce he picked up from an old Italian couple in the North End," Khela added.

"I haven't been slaving," Carter said. "That's the beauty of the recipe. If you've got fresh tomatoes, fresh basil, garlic, salt, pepper and olive oil, you've got yourself the best red sauce on the planet."

"Or gravy," Daphne said. "That's what they call it up here in Boston."

"I thought gravy was made from the drippings of roasted meat," Llewellyn said, joining Daphne on Khela's overstuffed loveseat.

Daphne rested her hand on his thigh, and he put his arm around her shoulders. Watching them, Khela envied the natural ease of their affectionate gestures. Every time she held Carter's hand, every time she hugged or kissed him, an undercurrent of urgency powered their contact. Their physical encounters seemed too intense, and Khela reasoned that it was because they had to enjoy as much of it as possible before their two weeks expired.

That urgency added an extra thrill in the bedroom, but Khela wanted more. She wanted with Carter what Daphne and Llewellyn seemed to be sharing in her living room. She wanted that sense of safe and generous ownership, that knowledge that she had the rest of her life to enjoy touching him, and not just a few days.

She sighed heavily, drawing everyone's attention from Daphne's attempts to school Llewellyn on the various forms of "gravy" in New England.

"You okay, Khela?" Carter asked.

It's not right, she heard in her head.

She nodded, even though she felt anything but okay.

"I'll throw the pasta in the pot, and we'll get some dinner on then," Carter said with a lazy clap of his hands. "Wanna give me a hand, Lew?"

"Uh, certainly," Llewellyn said as Carter went back into the kitchen. He turned to Daphne, lowered his voice and said, "I can't understand a bloody word he says. What does he want me to do?"

"He wants you help him boil some water," Daphne said with a grin. She sent Llewellyn off with a pat on the hand and a kiss on the cheek. Khela noticed the diamond engagement ring glinting on Daphne's finger, and the second Llewellyn disappeared into the kitchen, Khela took his place on the loveseat and brought Daphne's hand to her face.

"Oh, my God," Khela said. "Did he rob Queen Elizabeth to get this rock?"

"It's pretty, isn't it?" Daphne smiled. "It's a little over one carat, and the band is platinum."

"European cut." Khela admired the way the big rock caught the pink light of the sunset from her living room windows.

"It's American, Art Deco circa 1925," Daphne rattled off knowingly.

"You sound just like the wife of a renowned antiques expert," Khela remarked.

"Well, it kind of rubs off." She turned her head, as if she could see Llewellyn through the wall. "I've gone on buying trips to Vermont and Philadelphia with him. I never really had an interest in furniture other than what was needed to fact-check some of the books I've edited. But when Llewellyn finds a piece that excites him and starts telling me what the object is made of, how it was constructed by artisans whose craft is long lost, and its provenance, it excites me, too. It's easy to fall in love with what he loves. He talks about Victorian end tables the way other men talk about beautiful women."

"I wish I had time to get to know him better," Khela said. She took Daphne's hand and held it to her heart. "I'm really happy for you. I didn't think I would be, but seeing the two of you together makes me a little less worried."

"When I'm with him, I feel as though I'm the most important woman in the world," Daphne said.

Khela's emotions built up forcefully, almost choking her. She smiled stiffly, unable to work words past the knot in her throat.

"Lew and I want you to be a part of the wedding ceremony," Daphne said.

"Tell me when and where," Khela croaked. "I'll be there."

"I'm looking forward to seeing Carter in a tux again," Daphne said.

Khela sat forward. "Carter? Why?"

"Well, you're going to bring him, aren't you?"

"It hadn't occurred to me, no. I don't even know if he'd want to go, or if he can take the time off work."

"You sound as if you don't want him to come."

"That's just it. I don't know what he wants."

"We're talking about you, not him. What do *you* want, Khela?"

Khela's gaze wandered to the windows, the floor, the direction of the kitchen and finally back to Daphne's face. She fidgeted uncomfortably, her face tightening in an effort to hold back tears.

"Oh, honey," Daphne cooed, taking Khela in her arms. "I thought everything was going so well!"

"It is," Khela wept quietly. "That's the problem. Everything has been too perfect. I don't want to think about it ending."

Daphne pulled away and stroked Khela's hair. "It doesn't have to," she chuckled. "I already told you what I think. You just have to believe it for yourself. That gravy-making man in there is crazy about you. You've got him totally domesticated. He's not going anywhere."

"Right before you got here, we decided to have a talk." Khela sighed sadly. "He said it wasn't right."

"What isn't right?"

Khela shrugged. "The two weeks. You guys got here before I could get a fuller explanation."

"Maybe Lew and I should leave so you and Carter can get to the bottom of this," Daphne offered.

"No, don't." Khela dismissed the notion with a wave of her hand. "I want to get to know your Mr. Davies a little better."

As with every mention of her fiancé's name, Daphne perked up, her whole face radiating with the inner light of her adoration for him. "You'll really like him, Khela. He's an expert on Georgian and Victorian furnishings."

"That'll come in handy for your historical romances." Khela stood and straightened her white twill miniskirt.

Daphne laughed. "Yes, I'll have the most authentic rooms in stories about Georgian-era sea captains and thirty-year-old Victorian virgins."

"I hate it when you downplay your writing skills," Khela said, leading the way to the dining room. She opened the pine hutch and handed four white porcelain plates to Daphne. "Your stories are—"

"I know, I know," Daphne said, taking the plates and arranging them on the long pine table, two on each of the longer sides. "I 'take great care in establishing my settings,' and I 'have an unerring grasp of the societal mores' of my time periods, and of course, I 'have a sure and clever touch with witty dialogue.' "

"Daphne," Khela said, clutching four settings of silverware.

"You know, I should have those lines from my various rejections printed onto T-shirts. I'd make a fortune, I bet."

"I was going to say that your stories are too unique, which is probably why they haven't been contracted. You write literary fiction for a commercial market."

"So I'm not published because no one wants my work," Daphne said bleakly. "Great."

"You're not published because you haven't found the right editor on the right day at the right house," Khela explained. "Of course, you have to send your work out if you want to get published."

Daphne accepted two knives, two forks and two table spoons, which she then laid beside the two plates on her side of the table. "I send my work out," she said breezily. "Sometimes."

"Each no is one step closer to a yes," Khela sang with a grin.

"You've been saying that for the past ten years."

"Ever since we first heard that line at the romance conference in Chicago. It's true, too."

"Not for you. Your first step was a yes. You don't know what it's like to get rejected over and over again, Khela," Daphne said. "You hit it out of the park with your first book. It's hard to take advice from you."

"Do you know what a publisher told Stephen King about *Carrie*?"

"No, but I have a feeling you're going to tell me," Daphne said.

" 'We are not interested in science fiction which deals with negative utopias. They do not sell.' Millions of books sold, two movies and one sequel later, and I'll bet that publisher wishes he could hop into his Wayback machine and unwrite that rejection."

Daphne moved aside a bit, allowing Khela to set crystal wine goblets on the table. "I'm going to miss your pep talks," she said softly.

"You'll still get them. Only they'll come by phone and e-mail."

"It won't be the same." Daphne strolled a few feet to the windows. Cupping her elbows in her hands, she stared down at the traffic flowing along Commonwealth

Avenue. "I'm going to miss all this. It never occurred to me that I'd ever leave New England, never mind go all the way to Old England."

"I thought you were going to Wales," Khela said, hiding her grin as she lit four votive candles snug in crystal holders on the table.

"You know what I mean," Daphne said. "I always figured that I'd become a real author if I lived in Boston. So many great writers called this little state home and found inspiration here."

"Yeah," Khela said. "Ben Affleck and Matt Damon did pretty well for themselves with *Good Will Hunting*."

"I meant people like Louisa May Alcott," Daphne said.

"And Denis Leary," Khela said.

"Ralph Waldo Emerson," Daphne said.

"Dr. Seuss," Khela offered.

Daphne faced Khela, her arms crossed over her chest. "Erle Stanley Gardner."

"Lesley Stahl."

"She's a journalist, not an author," Daphne scoffed. "Now you're reaching. Nathaniel Hawthorne."

"We hate him," they deadpanned together, and then collapsed into laughter.

"Great writers call the world home," Khela said, joining Daphne at the windows. "Connecticut tries to steal Mark Twain, but he belongs to Hannibal, Missouri. You can write in Wales, but you can always call Boston home." Khela locked her arms around Daphne and planted a noisy kiss on her cheek. "You'll always have a home here. I'm not going anywhere."

"Not even if Carter wants to move back to 'Bama?"

"Especially if Carter wants to move back to Alabama."

CHAPTER 10

"All the best things about you can't be seen with the eyes."
— *from* You're The One For Me *by Khela Halliday*

Dinner was exactly what it should have been, a gathering of good friends and new friends. Showing that his appreciation for food was just as keen as that he possessed for furniture, Llewellyn praised Carter's sauce, comparing it favorably to one he had enjoyed in a small town in Caprese during a summer abroad spent as an apprentice for an Italian antiques trader.

"You do a lot of globetrotting in your line of work," Carter observed as he refilled his and Llewellyn's wine goblets with a palate-pleasing merlot he'd unearthed in the back of Khela's pantry.

"In recent years, yes," Llewellyn said. "Travel is a perk for a bloke who spent the first twenty years of his life in the midlands of England."

"How did you get into antique dealing?" Khela asked.

"Purely by accident," Llewellyn said. "I was reared by my maternal grandmother. She died the year I started university, and she left me a house full of furnishings, paintings and heirlooms that had been in our family since Richard III offered his kingdom for a horse. I kept her diaries—" Khela and Daphne shared an approving glance. "—all of her most treasured heirlooms, and in accordance with her will, I had certain items—a dresser, a vanity table and a bed—appraised for auction. My grandmother was not penny rich but she had quite a lot of good sense. Authorizing the sale of specific pieces of furniture assured that I would have the resources to support myself until I finished school. As difficult as it was to part with her things, I became enamored with the research and expertise involved in antiques. It's rather like being a detective, really, learning the origin of a piece and how it came to be where you find it. It's quite thrilling to discover something long thought missing or crafted by a little-known master artisan. While I was in school I took an apprenticeship with a renowned antiquarian and learned the trade from him while I completed my business degree. I started my own business five years ago, and it's been thriving since."

"So you kind of just stumbled into your dream job?" Khela said.

"The best surprises are the unexpected ones," Llewellyn said, taking Daphne's hand and kissing the back of it. "You never know when something or someone will come into your life, changing it for the better."

Carter raised his wine glass and made a toast. "Here's to surprises."

Glasses kissed with delicate clinks, and Llewellyn addressed Carter. "This building has wonderful features. Daphne tells me that you're the caretaker?"

"Well, this brownstone is one of the buildings I take care of," Carter said. "I've also got a townhouse across the street."

"I'm familiar with Baltimore's rowhouses and New York City's brownstones, but Boston seems to have no distinction between brownstone, townhouse and rowhouse," Llewellyn said.

"Essentially, almost all of the residences you'll find along this section of Comm Ave are townhouses," Carter explained. "A townhouse can be attached or detached and, although it might not exactly resemble its surrounding houses, it'll be scaled about the same height. A rowhouse is a string of adjoining townhouses. A brownstone is a townhouse or a rowhouse with a façade in brown sandstone, or pudding stone, which is unique to Boston."

"So townhouse is an overall term," Llewellyn summarized, "with rowhouse being a subset of that, and brownstone a further subset of both."

"You got it, Lew," Carter said with wink.

"It's like frogs and toads," Khela said. "A toad is a frog, but a frog isn't a toad."

"Or rectangles and squares," Daphne added. "A square is a rectangle, but a rectangle isn't a square."

"Bloody hell, I think we need more wine!" Llewellyn declared to the approval of his dinner companions.

"I got a special adoration for this brownstone," Carter said as Llewellyn refilled everyone's wine goblet. "It's got a lot of character. I fell in love with it the first time I walked through the front doors."

"I can see why," Llewellyn said. "Is the mahogany paneling in the foyer original to the structure?"

"Sure is," Carter replied. "The copper ribbons on the dormer windows are original, too."

With that, the two men spent the rest of the meal discussing the unique details of the brownstone the way other men might discuss their favorite sports teams.

"They play well together," Daphne said, following Khela into the kitchen to make coffee.

"Llewellyn is a good example for Carter," Khela said, retrieving a small brick of coffee from her freezer. "If he wanted to, Carter could turn his love for this building into a business of his own the way Llewellyn did with antiques. Every brownstone on this street could use someone with his expertise at restoration and repairs."

"Maybe he's happy just being a super," Daphne considered.

"Carter's not 'just' anything. He's so smart and personable, and he's so good with people." Khela pulled a pair of scissors from her utility drawer and snipped open the coffee, which expanded with a fragrant puff once the vacuum seal was broken. "I'm accused of hiding from life by sitting up in my loft writing books, but Carter's doing the same thing by spending his days keeping up this building."

"He's doing what he loves," Daphne said. "Same as you."

"I guess," Khela said dubiously. "It's just seems weird that a Boston University graduate would want to polish banisters all day."

"At least he looks good doing it," Daphne chuckled.

"Amen to that," Khela laughed.

"Ladies," Llewellyn said, entering the kitchen with Carter. "I apologize for abandoning you to ready dessert on your own. Mr. Radcliffe and I are at your service."

"Would you take the cheesecake from the fridge, Carter?" Khela asked.

Without answering, he did so, keeping his silence even as he set the cake in front of her on the counter.

"That's actually a cheesecake, right?" Daphne asked. "It's not a tuna casserole or a cleverly disguised shepherd's pie?"

"It's classic New York cheesecake," Khela said, smiling. "Carter can vouch for it. He was with me when I bought it." She glanced at Carter, who stood slightly apart from the others, leaning against a counter, staring at nothing in particular. "Carter?" Khela prompted.

He responded with a noncommittal grunt of acknowledgement.

"Okay . . ." Khela sighed under her breath, at the moment unwilling to investigate Carter's sudden detachment.

After coffee, cheesecake and pleasant goodnights, lovey-dovey Daphne and Llewellyn went on their way, leaving Carter and Khela alone with unasked questions looming unspoken between them.

"Your sauce really was amazing," Khela said as she began clearing the table.

"Lew asked for the recipe." Carter started collecting wine glasses from the cocktail table in the living room.

"At least I think he did. I could hardly understand a word that boy said."

"He said the same thing about you, yet the two of you got on famously," Khela chuckled.

"Well, when two fellas find themselves in the same boat, they row together."

Khela, the empty bread basket and butter dish balanced in one hand, stopped midway to the kitchen. "What does that mean? 'The same boat?' "

"Lew probably spent the day listening to Daphne rant about you same as I spent the day listening to you go on about Daphne."

Khela's jaw stiffened. "I'm sorry I spoiled your day."

Carter rolled his eyes toward the vaulted ceiling and scrubbed his fingers through his hair. "Did I say that my day was spoiled? Don't start hearing things I didn't say."

"I heard you loud and clear earlier," Khela said archly, continuing into the kitchen.

Carter heard the bread basket and butter dish land upon a hard surface—either the granite countertops or the hardwood of the center prep island. Steeling himself for battle, he entered the kitchen.

Khela stood at the sink, using the sprayer to rinse out the pot Carter had used to make his sauce.

"Is there something you want to say to me?" he asked.

"Nope."

He leaned a hip against the counter farthest from Khela. "That 'nope' sure sounds like 'yep'."

She whirled around, her right elbow striking the metal water pitcher and sending it clanging to the tile floor. "Why did you say, 'It's not right?' "

"Why is what not right?"

"Us! Our two weeks!"

The following silence filled Khela with sick fear. Carter just stared at her. And then, very quietly, he said, "You called it a mistake."

Khela looked at him, chewing the inside of her lower lip until she could work out a reasonable response.

Carter slowly neared her as if afraid she might lash out with one of the heavy or pointed cooking utensils within her reach.

"Why is it not right?" Khela persisted.

"I didn't mean it in a bad way," he said.

"I didn't mean what I said in a negative way, either."

"So what did you mean?"

"You first."

Carter bought two seconds of thinking time by clearing his throat. "It's not right to assign a time limit to something that should develop naturally."

"I agree," she all but whispered. "It was a mistake for me to think that two weeks would be enough time with you."

Carter's heart soared with the purest of emotions for Khela, but the feeling took on a sour note with her next words.

"Every time I look at you, I just want to touch you, and I want you to touch me," she said. "You're so beautiful."

Deaf to the earnestness in her words, Carter heard only the meaning of them. "You want me," he said, his voice breaking as he closed the distance between them. "Is that it?"

"Yes," she sighed heavily, her heart pounding against her ribcage.

"Is that all?"

"No." She would have backed up if the stainless steel rim of the sink hadn't been blocking her.

"Well, what else is there?" He swallowed hard, his throat working visibly. His strained tone and movements began to concern her. "Is this what you want from me, Khela?" he asked, pressing her right hand to his cheek. "And this?"

She found her left hand pressed to the rock-hard bulge behind the button fly of his jeans.

"You're the writer, Khela. You don't have any words for me now?"

Her forehead wrinkled in confusion and her mouth worked to form a response, but she couldn't make herself say the three words resting on her tongue.

Still grasping her wrists, he spun her, pressing her abdomen to the edge of the sink. He slid a hand under her shirt, running it over her flat belly to raise it, exposing her. Her reflection in the wide window above the sink added to her pleasure, the sight of her breasts in Carter's hands sending an extra erotic charge through her.

The back of her skirt went up next, and her panties went down. Khela felt a slight tremble in his hands when they went to her hips to guide her against him. She widened her stance, his hot breath and fierce kisses at her ear.

She couldn't see what he was doing behind her, but she realized that he had lowered his own garments when she felt him, insistent, hard and weighty, at the back of her left thigh. With one hand at her breast and the other at her hip, he used his foot to part her legs further.

His hands and lips seemed to sizzle over her skin, readying her for his passionate invasion. Molding her breasts to the shape of his hands, he filled her.

Reaching over the sink to grab the windowsill, Khela moved against him, swallowing him to the hilt, silently begging him to send her to that place of sheer bliss that she shared only with him.

Carter stared at her reflection in the window. With her features etched in the full glory of her passion, she was simply the loveliest thing he had ever seen. He wrapped his arms around her, plastering himself to her, convulsing within her with a loud groan that made her cry out as she reached the pinnacle of her own pleasure.

Khela shivered afterward, physically spent by the power of the moment. She felt as though she'd been claimed, once and for all. There were no other men in the world, certainly no other man for her. Still slightly panting, she righted her clothing and turned to Carter, to tell him.

He was pulling up his sports briefs and jeans. His cold gaze and the hard set of his jaw silenced Khela. Without looking at her, he buttoned his fly and reached past her, to wash his hands.

Khela was suddenly self-conscious in the face of his impersonal tone.

"Did I do something wrong?" she asked.

"No, I think I did," he answered. "I'm going home."

"What?" she blurted.

"I need to go home." His eyes, suddenly somber, seemed to look at everything but Khela. "I need to sleep in my own bed tonight."

She stared at him for a long moment, confused. Obviously something had happened to bring on this sudden change in him. She racked her brain trying to determine what it could possibly be.

"Do you need any help cleaning up?" he asked, still not meeting her eyes.

"Carter," she said, her shoulders sagging. "I don't understand why you're being this way."

"What way?"

Khela's ire began to rise, hardening the edges of the concerned confusion she was feeling.

"One minute you're screwing my brains out," she said, making the intimate act they had just shared sound as ugly as possible, "and the next you act like you hate me."

"I don't hate you, Khela."

"Then what's the matter?"

"Look, I just need to go, okay?"

He started for the bedroom, and Khela followed him. "No, it's not okay. Tell me what's the matter!"

"I just need some time alone, woman, is that so hard to understand?"

In the bedroom, he gathered up the clothes he'd left at her place piece by piece over the past few days. He shoved them into a black nylon duffel bag and then went into the master bathroom to retrieve his toiletries, Khela on his heels.

"Are you coming back?" she asked, nearly frantic.

"I don't know." He brushed past her and went back into the bedroom. He tucked his toiletry kit into the duffel bag, zipped it and slung it over one shoulder.

"The least you could do is tell me why you're leaving so abruptly," Khela demanded, hurrying ahead of him to block his exit. "Don't I deserve at least that much?"

His eyes lingered on hers, and the longer he looked into them, the more his face relaxed. Her familiar Carter had returned, and Khela almost smiled at the tenderness in his expression.

"There's my darling beefcake," she lovingly teased.

His face stiffened. "I gotta go, Khela."

"Why?" she said, throwing her hands up in frustration.

"Because I'm disappointed, that's why."

Frozen in shock, Khela was still rooted to the carpet long after Carter had left without so much as a look back.

———⚬⚬⚬———

Carter walked home.

After leaving Khela, he took the stairs down to the lobby to avoid the wait for the elevator. Crossing the highly polished floor, he made a note to water the braided ficus trees flanking the heavy double doors, one of which he flung open. He took the wide, cement steps two at a time, pausing at the curb. Traffic never stopped on Commonwealth Avenue, so he waited for a lull before he trotted across the westbound side of the street, dodging the overly bright headlights of oncoming cars and buses.

The mall, the gorgeous, eight-acre park situated between the east- and westbound lanes of Commonwealth Avenue, was empty, but Carter didn't dawdle as he crossed it. Traffic was heavier in the eastbound lanes, so he walked right into it, easily navigating his way past the slow-moving cars.

He walked two houses east to a five-story limestone townhouse and went up another steep flight of cement steps. He didn't need a key to gain entry. Like every other resident, he had only to type his personal security code into the electronic keypad mounted on the mahogany door frame. Carter had considered installing a similar system in Khela's building, but her brownstone was older, and it would have taxed the electrical system and compromised the integrity of the home's design to an unacceptable degree.

The top-floor apartment of his Victorian Gothic townhouse had a bit less square footage than Khela's, but it had finer architectural details—pointed arches and bay windows—characteristic of George H. Clough, the noted architect who designed Boston's first police station. Carter used his keys to unlock the door of the rooftop unit; upon entering, his eyes landed on the one feature that had sold him on the entire building: the fireplace. The wide, deep, black marble cavity boasted a mantel made of Rosa Aurora marble, which had the unique characteristic of growing harder as it aged.

Carter took off his shoes in the foyer, leaving them and his duffel bag neatly by the door. He shuffled across the thick, dark carpeting and fell heavily onto the sofa. It was deep and wide, and he knew already that he would not be getting up anytime soon.

He smoothed his hands over the silky-soft black microfiber covering the cushions, then placed one of the throw pillows on one arm of the sofa and rested his head on it, staring at his fireplace. The back of the sofa faced a wall of tall, wide windows, through which lay all of moonlit Boston. In front of him Carter had a view of the cold hearth of a fireplace he hadn't used in months.

So many times, he had started a fire and sat staring at it, wishing with his whole heart that he had someone, a very specific someone, to share it with. He closed his eyes and replayed his most well-worn fantasy.

Khela, her hair in its usual ponytail, her feet in white anklet pom pom socks, curled up on the sofa with Carter's head in her lap. Her slim, elegant fingers stroked his hair, her touch igniting sparks hotter than the ones given off by the fire that would be burning in his fireplace. In this humble fantasy, they would have sat for hours talking, watching the flames dance to the music of the popping and crackling logs.

But Khela had gone and done him one better, allowing him more than the sweet fantasy of sharing a fire with her. She'd given him full access to her body and home, to her life, and after overhearing one comment, he'd walked out on it. And why?

In the solitude of his own home, in the quiet company of his innermost thoughts, he could freely admit why.

Because he was disappointed.

Khela was everything he'd ever wanted in a woman. She was independent, smart, knowledgeable—so knowledgeable that he often felt like a third-grader in her company. She was beautiful, loving, funny, attentive, alluring. There was nothing wrong with her.

Except for the way she made him feel. Or rather, the way he felt when he was with her.

"It's just seems weird that a Boston University graduate would want to polish banisters all day," he murmured, speaking aloud the words that had been playing on a loop in his head ever since he'd overhead Khela speaking them. He'd distilled only one meaning from them—that she believed him to be wasting his life.

His whole life he had been told how attractive he was, going back to the embarrassing *Aren't you the prettiest little boy?* from one of his grandmother's church friends, to Khela's *There's my darling beefcake.* He had heard it all from female—and occasionally male—admirers of all ages, races and descriptions.

He had never thought of himself as better looking than anyone else, but he couldn't deny the preferential treatment he had received throughout his life. Teachers had seemed kinder to him. Negotiating higher grades had always been a piece of cake for him. If not for football and baseball, he would have been obese in high school from all the free cookies, Rice Krispies treats, cake and ice cream the lunch ladies plied him with.

And girls—from his first day at kindergarten, when Elaine Sharp got into a hair-pulling match with CaraAnne Finley over who would be his Line Buddy for recess, to tonight, when Khela had called him her beef-cake—they had always been drawn to him.

He had enjoyed the attention and had endured the razzing from his male friends. In college, modeling agency scouts had tried to recruit him with the same enthusiasm as football and baseball scouts. Using his face to earn a living had appealed to him even less than using his athletic skill, so he'd stayed in school and earned his degree with the intention of doing what most people did: to get a job, get married, buy a house and fill it with as many children as he could.

That plan fell apart when he discovered that his own fiancée wanted him for the only reason so many other women had—because he looked good. His love for her had not mattered, nor had his earning potential. She just wanted a hardy sire to continue her family's line.

He needed Khela to see him differently than everyone else did, certainly more than Savannah did. And definitely as more than just someone who polishes banisters.

He'd done nothing to show her that there was more to him than home maintenance. Daphne had always been the one to call him, to stare at him under the pre-tense of making repairs. Khela had never invited him for coffee, or to lunch. His parting behavior tonight had probably done little more than reinforce what she likely believed about him. That his usefulness was limited to one thing, and that thing wasn't something upon which lasting relationships were built. It wasn't something upon which families or lifetimes were built.

He rolled off the sofa and went into his bedroom, going directly to the stack of Khela's books atop one of his oak nightstands. He'd read them in order, starting with *Satin Whispers*, her first book, and ending with *Soul Surrender*, her latest.

He'd read them all in an attempt to learn how to be the kind of man she wanted, and he now realized that he'd overlooked one important characteristic shared by all of her heroes. None of them polished banisters for a living.

He pulled his favorite, *Sybarite Seeks Same*, from the stack and flopped down on the bed. Its hero, Collin Drew, was an executive with an affinity for the finer things in life, but he had a good heart and used his wealth to support causes he believed in. That was a quality Khela had given the character which she herself practiced.

The fictional Collin Drew was someone who commanded respect not just because he was attractive, but because he was confident, accomplished, successful and generous. There were qualities behind his pretty face that made him worth the love of a good woman.

"Don't hate me because I'm beautiful," Carter whispered, chuckling sadly. "Hate me because I'm useless."

———

Daphne's apartment, a two-bedroom walkup in the neighboring town of Cambridge, looked as if a tornado had blown through it. Half-filled boxes perched on her lopsided plaid sofa and clear storage bins full of books, clothing, bed and bath linen occupied most of the hardwood floor in the living room.

Wielding a fat black Sharpie, Daphne kneeled before a 35-gallon storage bin and neatly wrote the word COATS on the top and sides.

"There aren't coats in this box," Khela said, standing over it. "It's full of blankets."

"I'm trying to thwart thieves," Daphne said, standing. "Most of this stuff is being put into storage. I'd rather have someone steal a box of blankets, thinking that they're my coats, than have my coats stolen. I've got a vintage Halston that I got for ten dollars at an estate sale last spring. I'd die if it got stolen."

"If it's that important, you should take it to Great Britain with you," Khela said, sitting on the sofa to tackle sweaters heaped on Daphne's glass coffee table.

"I'm only planning to take what I'll need after we get married," Daphne said, resting her hands on her hips, her hair swinging as she turned her head to scan the room. "The rest of my things are going into storage until Lew and I send for them or come back to ship them. I have so much left to do. I don't know how I'll get it all done in the next few weeks. I didn't realize I'd acquired so much stuff in the nine years I've lived here."

"I remember when you picked out this apartment," Khela said. "I still don't know why you didn't want to room with me when you moved here. It would have been just like in college."

"That's why," Daphne said. "Because it would have been just like in college. I wanted to stand on my own two feet. And there was no way I could cover half the rent for your condo on what Houghton Mifflin was paying me."

"I didn't want you to pay rent," Khela said, folding one of Daphne's cashmere sweaters and placing it in a storage bin lined with thin cedar panels.

"You got me the editing job at Houghton," Daphne said. "I didn't want to take anything else from you."

"*You* got that job," Khela insisted. "All I did was tell the executive editor that you had edited all of my books."

"Well, your endorsement got me in the door. I would still be writing resumes in Brentwood, Missouri, if you hadn't recommended me to Houghton Mifflin."

"So let me send one of your manuscripts to my editor at Cameo," Khela offered. "All editors care about is a story that will sell. They don't care how it got on their desks."

"But I care." Daphne, still on her knees from marking her bins, capped her pen and sat back on her heels to face Khela. "I want to make my own success as a writer. I don't want it handed to me because some editor is afraid that Khela Halliday will leave Cameo if she doesn't sign her friend Daphne Carr."

"Do editors really think that way?"

"Some do," Daphne answered. "I never did. I flew solo before I got to the point where I felt any kind of pressure to acquire manuscripts for my list for reasons other than because the story and writing were good."

"One good thing about being a self-employed, in-demand editor is that you can do your job from anywhere," Khela said with a sigh. "Even the United Kingdom."

"It's only a plane ride away," Daphne said. She moved to sit beside Khela on the taupe corduroy sofa. "You're in the UK at least once a year on book tours anyway."

"I think I'll be going more frequently now that I don't have to worry about room and board," Khela laughed.

"So you're coming around? My whirlwind romance with Lew isn't bothering you so much anymore?"

Khela slumped against the back of the sofa. "One of my books is about a woman who married a man three weeks after she met him. At least you've known Lew twice that long."

"That doesn't answer the question."

Khela thought about her answer for a long while before she said, "I want you to be happy. And loved. And very well cared for. I think Lew can give those things to you."

"I finally know what you know, Khela. I get it now."

"Well, explain it to me," Khela said, "because I have no idea what you're talking about."

"You capture the very meaning of romance in your books," Daphne started. "Your characters are so human. They have faults and flaws, they have moods and quirks. But when you match them up, the most unlikely pairs find a common denominator that enables them to overcome any obstacle. That thing is a feeling. It's love. No matter how different two people are, love can always bring them together. Your books illustrate that so beautifully. I know what that feels like now, because it's what I have with Llewellyn. I can put it in my books now, to give them the depth they didn't have before."

"You make it all sound so wonderful," Khela said wistfully.

Daphne leaned forward to fold a sweater, a furry hot pink rabbit fur. "You have the same thing with Carter, don't you?" she asked. "You guys seemed so happy when we all had dinner."

Khela left the sofa to go to Daphne's small dining table, where she began wrapping a plate in old *Herald-Star* newspapers. She had wrapped three more plates before she could answer without bursting into tears.

"Carter walked out on me that night. I'm still not sure what happened. He said he was disappointed. I don't know if he was disappointed in me, the evening, or what."

Daphne rushed to Khela's side. "You haven't talked to him in all this time? It's been almost three weeks!"

"I haven't got the nerve to call him, and he certainly hasn't called me." Khela buried her face in her hands, smudging her cheeks and forehead with the cheap newsprint ink from her fingertips. "I don't know what I did wrong. One minute he was making love to me, the next, something in his eyes died and he just took his things and left."

Daphne stroked Khela's arm. "That doesn't really sound like Carter."

Khela began pacing. "Well, he did it, and I just don't understand why!"

"Oh, honey," Daphne soothed. "You have to talk to him. That's the only way you'll find out what's going on."

"I'm not sure I want to know," Khela said sadly. "I'm scared of what he'll say. Maybe—" She stopped before she could voice the worst thought she'd had since Carter walked out.

"Maybe what?" Daphne asked gently.

"Maybe I was right all along," Khela said softly. "Maybe he was interested in me only because of what I do, not because of who I am. You know how it's been for me, Daphne. Men want me because I'm a romance novelist and they think I know all sorts of thrilling sex secrets, or because I've got a little money in the bank."

"I'm not wrong about Carter," Daphne insisted. "I was more sure of it during dinner. He really loves you."

"Then why did he leave?" Khela whispered, Daphne's image blurred by the tears welling in her eyes.

Daphne pulled Khela into her arms. "You have to talk to him, sweetie."

"No, I don't," Khela said stubbornly, using her fist to grind away her tears.

"Yes, you do," Daphne said emphatically. "I can't run off with my prince until I know that you've patched things up with yours."

"Why am I not surprised that you would somehow turn the most horrible, devastating, awful thing to happen to me into something about you?"

Khela's question had an achingly familiar ring, and it took Daphne a moment to recall when she'd heard it. Once she figured it out, she playfully pushed Khela away with an affectionate, "Bitch."

Carter ducked under his opponent's wild, round-house right cross and landed a left uppercut to the man's flabby right jowl. Grunting and growling like a wounded wildebeest, the heavy man huffed and puffed furiously, hooking his fingers into claws to lunge at Carter.

Shorter, faster and in far better shape than his opponent, Carter dodged left. The bigger man's momentum carried him into the rusty dumpster resting against the back of the nightclub, adding another big dent to its pocked side.

Standing a good fifteen feet away, Detrick gave his watch a sleepy-eyed glance.

"Carter, boy, would you hurry this up?" he urged.

Detrick's articulated words cut through the cheers of encouragement the bigger man's friends were giving him as he picked himself up off the grimy cement of the alley behind the Purple Shamrock in Faneuil Hall.

"I can't take you anyplace," Detrick sighed, flicking a speck of dirt off the sleeve of his white summer suit. "Especially after you break up with a woman."

The big man lumbered to his feet, a fresh rip in the knee of his blue jeans. He had landed one good blow, his first, which Carter had invited him to throw when they had retreated into the alley to settle their differences over who had been next in line for service at the bar.

That first blow was the only one Carter had allowed his opponent to land. It had connected sharply with his right cheekbone, leaving a deep gash that would likely require the attention of a plastic surgeon. For now, the bright, hot pain flaring from his cheekbone was a refreshing change from the sharp agony of three weeks without Khela.

Carter poured all of his toxic emotions into his battle with the big collegian—his distrust of Khela's motives in granting him two weeks of intimacy, his emptiness without her, his disappointment with her failure to call him since he had walked out on her and his own stubbornness in refusing to contact her.

Carter's tanned biceps flexed against the cuffs of his short-sleeved Polo. He bounced a bit on the balls of his feet, his fists clenched, waiting for the big man's attack. When it came, Carter met him with a left jab that landed squarely on its mark.

Like an overripe tomato, the big man's nose exploded. Droplets of spittle and blood spattered Carter and the man's friends. The friends laughed good-naturedly as they paid off the wagers they'd made on the fight. They collected their friend and hauled him back into the nightclub.

"That was disgusting," Detrick said. He started to offer his handkerchief to Carter to dab up the blood on his knuckles, but he reconsidered and tucked it back into his pocket. "When you get home tonight, you'd better call that woman."

"It'll be too late to call when I get home," Carter said, knuckling away a trickle of blood on his cheek.

"Not if we go home right now." Detrick then started for Congress Street, where he had been lucky enough to park his Jag at a meter.

Swaggering with pride, Carter fell into step alongside Detrick. "That fella had to be two-fifty easy," he laughed. "That'll teach him to tangle with a 'Bama boy."

"You're giving 'Bama boys a bad name, pal," Detrick said derisively. "We need to get your face cleaned up before you get an infection."

"Nah, I'm fine," Carter insisted. He spat on the sidewalk, and had no discernible reaction when he saw that the spit was laced with blood. "Let's go to the Squire."

"I am not driving all the way out to Revere," Detrick said. "If I want to watch a naked lady dance, all I need to do is go back into the Purple Shamrock and invite home that lovely waitress I was talking up before you decided to come out here and play Rock 'Em Sock 'Em Robots."

"Then let's go to Chinatown," Carter suggested. "We can get some dumplings and split a scorpion bowl."

Detrick stopped beneath the orange-gold glow of a streetlight. "One, you have already had more than enough to drink. And two, the only reason you want to go someplace new is to fight someone new. And if we go to Chinatown, chances are pretty good you're gonna get your ass handed to you. Some Asian man is gonna run across the air and Matrix you in the head, or he's gonna come out of the kitchen with a Ginsu knife and cut you into six pieces before you know what happened."

Detrick took two more steps, then turned back.

"And you're crazy if you think I'm going to collect your bloody body parts and put them in my Jag. You're lucky I'm taking you home with Big Boy's blood all over you."

"C'mon, Detrick," Carter pleaded. "It's early."

Detrick started walking again.

"Lightweight!" Carter called after him.

Slowly, deliberately, Detrick turned and walked back to Carter, and fired the weapon he'd been holding back.

"I'm going home now, and if you're smart, you'll let me take you home, too," Detrick said with practiced calm. "I'm not going to another club or bar with you tonight, or any other night, as long as you're hellbent on fighting the world because you're too afraid or too stupid to fight for the woman you love."

"You don't know what you're talking about," Carter spat at Detrick's back when he again started for his car. Detrick kept walking, and Carter trotted to catch up to him. "You think I love Khela Halliday?"

"I know you love Khela Halliday," Detrick said.

"What makes you so sure?"

"You didn't step out with a regular-sized cat tonight," Detrick explained. "You provoked a brawl with King Kong. If that ain't love, I don't know what is."

"I didn't pick that fight," Carter said.

"No, but you didn't try to avoid it, either. If you need to let off some emotional steam, go to Sam's Club and get yourself a *real* punching bag. I haven't seen you scrap like that since we were in Florida for spring break."

"Yeah, and I remember you gettin' down and dirty back then to show those Quincy frauds which way was up," Carter said.

"We were seventeen," Detrick said, exasperated. "I've matured in the past fifteen years. I'd rather walk away from a fight than get some lummox's blood on my suit."

"I was just lettin' off some steam, Trick," Carter said, managing to sound a little contrite.

"There's better ways of doing that. Like picking up the phone and calling the person you really want to spend all that emotion on."

"You're right," Carter agreed, a bit defiant at Detrick's reference to Khela. "The next time some young bulldog wants to step outside with me, I'll just be mature and keep my dukes to myself."

Narrowing his eyes, Detrick peered suspiciously at Carter. "Good," he said warily. "It's about time you started acting your age, although I have a feeling that the operative word here is *acting*."

CHAPTER 11

"Forgiveness is the only antidote for disappointment."
—from Every Tomorrow *by Khela Halliday*

"I'm really not in the mood for this." Khela made no move to exit Daphne's VW bug. "I have a deadline. I should be at home working on my manuscript."

"Your book isn't due until November," Daphne said, engaging the emergency brake of the lime-green five-speed. "One night out isn't going to kill you. You need a distraction."

"Not from work," Khela said. She stared at the stately brick Colonial Daphne had driven them to in Lexington.

"I'm not trying to distract you from work," Daphne said.

"I don't need a distraction from Carter, either. I haven't thought about him in . . . a while now." *As long as five minutes can be counted as a while.*

"Look," Daphne said, opening Khela's door and tugging her out by her arm. "This is the last time I'm going to see most of the women in my writing critique group. I could use a party, and I know you could, too. Can you just push Carter out of your mind for an hour or two and have a good time? Can you just try, for me?"

"Well, fine, if you're gonna put it like that," Khela said.

She closed the car door and, heavily dragging her feet, she followed Daphne to the front door. Daphne rang the doorbell. Ten seconds later, she was greeted with an ear-splitting scream from an earthy Italian woman whose wild mane of long, wavy hair was the brunette version of Daphne's.

"Hey, babe!" she said, smiling wide and sloshing an aromatic pink concoction from a pink plastic cup as she hugged Daphne. "How's my little affianced friend?"

"I'm good, Sofia," Daphne said, kissing each of her cheeks. "How are things out here in the 'burbs?"

"It's only nine o'clock and this whole town is dead," Sofia answered disdainfully, ushering Daphne and Khela inside. "It's too dark and quiet out here. I miss the lights and the noise of the North End. I even miss that old bum who used to pee under my stoop every day." She tilted her head and looked upward. "Actually, I don't miss the bum too much. But I do miss being able to just hop the T and meet you for lunch at Gagliardi's. Ohmigod, I haven't had good chicken parm since Eugenio moved us out here."

Khela closely listened to Sofia's thick and unmistakable Tewksbury dialect. Her vowels were heavily exaggerated, the consonants almost nonexistent. Where Khela's Midwestern tongue would have clearly stated, "chicken parm since Eugenio moved us out here," the same words fell from Sofia's tongue as, "chicken pahm sints 'genio movt tuss ow hyah."

Finally recognizing Khela, Sofia screamed again. "You brought her!" she cried, shoving past Daphne to gather Khela into her arms.

Crushed against Sofia's hefty bosom, Khela couldn't breathe. Sofia drew back and took her by the shoulders. She looked her up and down, then hugged her again, forcing a loud groan from Khela.

"Ladies!" Sofia squawked, leading Khela and Daphne through the foyer and living room, which shocked Khela with its hot pink, white and zebra fur design palette. "Daphne brought her! We've got a real author in residence tonight!"

Help! Khela mouthed over her shoulder, her eyes pleading with Daphne for rescue.

———⁓⁓⁓———

Khela had been to numerous parties with Daphne: Longaberger baskets, Pampered Chef, Yankee Candle. Khela drew the line at Tupperware, being perfectly happy with the disposable storage ware she bought at Calareso's, but she'd spent nearly an entire royalty check at a Tastefully Simple party.

Any gathering that involved sampling delicious breads, chips, dips, soups and entrees that could be made in minutes with ingredients stocked in the average kitchen was just the party for Khela. Tastefully Simple's Bountiful Beer bread was a staple in her kitchen, and the ten seconds she spent mixing it up made her feel as though she was actually cooking.

No ordinary food, cookware or basket party for Daphne's last hurrah with her critique group. Sofia had gone the extra mile and organized something different—an Aphrodite's Feather party.

The other partygoers, at least twenty of them, had been settled in Sofia's animal-print themed sitting room long enough to have consumed a pitcher or two of apple, mango and watermelon martinis. Khela faintly heard the blender whirring in the kitchen, convincing her that the gregarious and hospitable Sofia was determined to work her way through every fruit in the horn of plenty before the night was over.

"Eugenio's manning the bar tonight," Sofia said, flicking a hand adorned with rhinestone-studded fake fingernails toward the kitchen. "He gets his Super Bowl party in February and I get my B.O.B. party tonight."

"Who's Bob?" Khela wondered aloud.

"Battery-operated boyfriend!" Sofia's guests raucously chorused.

Khela would have fled if Daphne hadn't grabbed the white Peter Pan collar of her smart little black dress.

"Don't leave," Daphne said in voice so low only Khela heard her. "You'll hurt Sofia's feelings."

"Ladies," Sofia began, her glossy red lips in a smile so big it distorted her words even further, "we have a special surprise guest here tonight." She breathed hard, and seemed on the verge of hyperventilating. "I want you all to give a warm welcome to Miss Khela Halliday!"

Sofia screamed her name as though she were introducing the halftime act at Gillette Stadium.

Khela's name, echoed by Sofia's guests, traveled through the hot-pink room. The women, all aspiring romance novelists, were more than familiar with Khela's books, and her presence had quite an effect on them. They set down their drinks and gave Khela a hearty round of applause.

"I loved your last book!" said a woman with a platinum-blonde bob.

"*Sybarite Seeks Same* is my favorite romance of all time," said a younger woman wearing overall shorts and green Doc Marten boots.

"Thank you," Khela said graciously, eager for them to move on to another topic.

"Why don't you two take a seat over there," Sofia suggested, directing Khela and Daphne to an unoccupied loveseat covered in faux leopard fur.

While they picked their way past women on the sectional sofa snaking along two walls and the ones sitting on cheetah-print beanbags on the tiger-striped area rug, Sofia introduced the party consultant.

"Ladies, this is Friend Oceanwater, and she will be conducting tonight's party," Sofia announced.

Khela bit the inside of her lip and kept her face forward, certain that she would bust out laughing if she looked at Daphne.

Friend was a short, somewhat barrel-shaped woman in a skin-tight black tank top and a muddy brown dirndl skirt. At first glance, Khela thought that Friend was crazy to be wearing matching tights in June. But peering closer, she realized that Friend wasn't wearing tights at all, that in all likelihood, Friend hadn't shaved her legs since . . . ever.

"I think she's part Wookie," Daphne whispered.

Khela thought she might pop a kidney from the effort it took not to laugh.

"Hello, everyone," Friend said, clasping her hands as she took Sofia's place beside a long table covered by a black satin cloth. "I'm so, so glad the Goddess has allowed us to come together this way tonight." She closed her eyes and aimed her nose at the blindingly white ceiling, breathing sharply through her nose. "Praise be to the Goddess."

"Is this voodoo?" a heavy-set, older, African-American woman in gold-rimmed glasses asked loudly. "I didn't come here for no voodoo."

"It's all right, Mrs. Willmore," Sofia soothed. "Friend is a Wiccan."

"A what?" Mrs. Willmore demanded.

"She's a witch," volunteered the woman in the green Doc Martens.

Mrs. Willmore set her martini glass on a low table sculpted to look like the disembodied foot of an elephant. "I'm gettin' up on outta here. I'll see you at work on Monday, Sofia. Thank you so much for the hooch, but I don't truck with no witches."

"May the Goddess bless and be with you as you travel through the dark heart of night," Friend said, her benevolent smile unchanging as she bid her unique farewell to Mrs. Willmore.

"You can take your God-S," Mrs. Willmore responded, pronouncing the word the way Friend had, "and get on somewhere."

"Wiccans aren't witches," Khela said. "They're more like . . . herbalists."

"Is that right?" Mrs. Willmore asked, stopping in her tracks.

"Sure," Sofia said, nodding at Mrs. Willmore and the other women, who took the hint and seconded Khela's assessment.

"Don't leave, Edith," urged an older redhead, who appeared to be Mrs. Willmore's geriatric Daphne. "You'll miss out on the free samples."

Mrs. Willmore's eyes seemed to glint behind her glasses. "Free samples? You didn't say anything about free samples at the salon this afternoon, Sofia. I guess I could hang around a little longer, find out what all this feather stuff is all about."

"Great, great," Friend said, her Laura Ingalls braids swinging as she slightly swayed from side to side as if listening to music that only she could hear. "Now that we're all at ease, I'd like to help each of you get in touch with your inner goddess."

With the skill and panache of a master magician, Friend snatched the satin cloth from the table.

Mrs. Willmore screamed.

Her redheaded friend sprayed a mouthful of cranberry martini across the room.

The woman in the Docs laughed so hard, she rolled off her beanbag.

Khela and Daphne leaned forward, to get a better look at the items displayed on the table as Friend, an earth-child Vanna White, used her right arm to introduce an eye-popping array of B.O.B.s.

There were colorful bottles, tubes and jars of various substances, but it was the B.O.B.s that captivated, frightened or amused the ladies.

Friend picked up a stack of purplish-pink catalogs and began handing them out. "Aphrodite's Feather is dedicated to pleasure," she recited in her airy sing-song. "Pleasure is good. Pleasure is necessary. Pleasure is meant to be shared. Sometimes there's no one to share it with, and Aphrodite's Feather offers a complete line of high-quality, affordable personal solo fulfillment items."

"Solo fulfillment," Khela said. "I like the sound of that."

"I'd like to start by introducing you to a few of our Partner Pleasures," Friend said. She selected a thick, bright red tube that looked and moved like a glob of jelly. "This is one of the party favors you'll all be taking home tonight, and—"

"Favors!" Sofia shrieked. "I forgot to hand out the favors." She scurried from the room, and a few seconds later scurried back with a black shoebox. She handed out mechanical pencils, which at first glance looked like ordinary office pencils.

But then Khela looked at the eraser. The little rubber item topping the end of the pencil was a green glow-in-the-dark phallus.

"Maybe I should hand these out at my next book signing," Khela murmured to Daphne.

"I dare you," Daphne giggled.

"Use the pencils to fill out your order forms," Sofia told them. "And remember, I get twenty-five Aphrodite dollars for every hundred dollars of merchandise you guys buy, so buy lots!"

"What's that jelly thing for?" Mrs. Willmore asked Friend, who casually played with the peculiar red tube.

"This is a gift for the man whom you bless with favors from the goddess within," Friend smiled.

"What the hell is she talking about?" Mrs. Willmore asked. "All I want to know is what that blood clot she's playing with is for."

"When you're sharing oral pleasures with your partner, sometimes your jaw grows tired," Friend explained further. "This unit, the Trouser Wowser, is filled with a biodegradable gel that holds temperatures for up to forty-five minutes. If your partner likes it cold, you can put it in the refrigerator for ten minutes. Don't freeze it, because it could rupture."

Friend paused her spiel to give Daphne the chance to stop giggling.

"Or, you can microwave it for forty-seconds. But no more than that," Friend warned, wagging a prim finger. "You don't want to burn your mister's mister."

Friend passed the gel tube around, allowing the ladies to get a feel for it. Literally.

Mrs. Willmore wrinkled her nose. "I hope this thing hasn't been used," she muttered.

Khela politely declined the chance to fondle the Trouser Wowser. Daphne took it, and after juggling it, playing catch with it, stretching it, sniffing it, and seeing if it would bounce, she rubbed it on Khela's bare knee.

"Great," Khela hissed. "Now I have to take a bath in hydrogen peroxide when I get home."

"Can we skip all the For His Pleasure stuff?" requested the short-haired woman in the green Docs. "I have a her at home, not a him."

"Yeah, let's get to the good stuff," Mrs. Willmore agreed. "I wanna see something with an engine."

The other ladies laughed and clapped, but they quieted when Friend picked up a black box the size of a flute case.

"Now we're talkin'," Mrs. Willmore said, nudging her redheaded friend with her elbow.

"This is one of our most popular items," Friend began as she removed the lid from the long box.

All the women, even Khela, leaned forward to better see what Friend would show them.

They all sat back, somewhat disappointed, when she displayed a long ostrich plume that had been dyed lilac.

"This is the Tickler," Friend said. "And it's unisex." She paused for laughter that never came.

"We're all romance writers here," Sofia whispered loudly. "It'll take more than a feather to stoke our imaginations, hon."

"You'd be surprised at how the simplest tools can provide the biggest thrills," Friend said.

"Cleopatra knew that," Khela said.

"Pardon?" Friend replied.

"Cleopatra is credited for being among the earliest women known to own a B.O.B., only she did it literally, with a calabash filled with buzzing bees," Khela explained.

"Bees or a feather," another woman remarked, "I don't know which is worse."

"The toy is only as good as the person wielding it," Friend said, waving the feather as she might a magic wand. "Could I have a volunteer?"

The women froze, afraid that the slightest twitch of muscle or wink of eye would draw Friend's attention.

"I'll do it!" came a male voice from the kitchen.

Eugenio, sweat glossing his bald head, bounded into the sitting room.

"Ugh. Honestly, Eugenio," Sofia complained. "Didn't I ask you to man the blender?"

"Please, Eugenio, sit," Friend said, offering the black folding chair she had sat in during Sofia's introductions.

Eugenio, smiling snarkily, happily sat. He revealed his anticipation for whatever was to come by rubbing his knuckles along the black nylon of his track pants. He gleefully tapped his toes, his white athletic shoes noiseless against the white carpet.

Friend took the feather and guided it to hover over Eugenio's bare forearm. "Imagine lying in bed on a hot summer night with the man who brings out the goddess in you," she crooned in her dreamy, high-pitched voice. "He looks at you, and he sees the goddess of his dreams."

"If she says godd-ESS one more time, I'm going to up-CHUCK," Khela whispered to Daphne.

"You take Aphrodite's Feather," Friend continued, "and you invite the warrior inside your man to come out and play." She stroked the feather lightly along Eugenio's forearm.

He giggled like a kindergartner, pulling his arm back and scratching the place the feather had touched.

"Oh, are you allergic to feathers?" Friend asked.

"No, it just tickles, that's all," Eugenio said.

" 'Genio!" Sofia cried, aghast. "God, you're so annoying!"

"I think I'd like to buy one of those feathers," Khela said offhandedly.

Everyone, even Eugenio, looked at her.

"I don't know, I think it's broken," Eugenio said. "A feather doesn't really cut it, at least not for me."

"The toy is only as good as the person wielding it," Khela interjected. Liking the sound of the phrase purloined from Friend, she asked for a closer look at the feather. Friend handed it to her.

"How would you use Aphrodite's Feather?" Friend asked her.

Everyone watched Khela run the vane, the soft, flat, web-like part of the feather, along her palm. Holding it by its stem, she pulled it through the circle formed by her thumb and forefinger.

Instantly, she pictured Carter as he'd been the last morning they had awakened together. The night had been mild, and they'd slept with the windows open. Carter, his long, lean body at complete rest atop her tangled bed sheets, looked like one of Rodin's greatest works made real.

Khela clutched Aphrodite's Feather between her fingers, and slowly brought it to Carter's chest. In sleep, his hand batted at it, likely annoyed by its slight tickle. Khela, smiling now, brought the feather lower. With its tip, she traced the dark-gold trail of hair arrowing toward Carter's thighs. He absently rolled perfectly flat on his back, subconsciously craving more attention as evidenced by the response of flesh yet to be touched.

Khela lay the feather gently on him, allowing the downy softness of the vane to settle upon him before she drew the feather along his full length. His body began seeking her even before he completely awakened, and Khela helped him out by placing herself upon him.

"Gimme that feather!" Sofia said, snatching it from Khela, thus pulling her out of her reverie. She hadn't realized that she had shared her imagined scenario until she saw the faces of her audience. Mrs. Willmore's color was high, but not as flushed as that of her redheaded friend, whose cheeks blazed.

Friend had finally stopped her odd swaying, and Eugenio sat rapt and slack-jawed in his chair.

"C'mere, 'Genio," Sofia demanded, grabbing his collar as she passed his chair. Eugenio stumbled over his own feet as he tried to keep up with his wife. "We're going to try out this feather, babe!"

Daphne looked at Khela, who blushed fiercely.

"You'd better make up with Carter," she advised. "Quick."

~~~

"Are you sure you want to do this?"

Khela licked her lips. She could still taste the fruity martini she had consumed at Sofia's, but she couldn't tell if it had been apple, mango, watermelon or raspberry. Her taste buds were dead. Every part of her had felt dead ever since she had shared her feather fantasy.

Idling in front of Carter's building, Daphne waited for Khela's answer.

Startling Daphne with her agility and speed, Khela hopped out of the car, her black handbag dangling from her shoulder. "I want to do this, and I want to do it now, while I have the guts," she said, leaning into the window. "I'll see you when I see you."

"I'm going to wait until he buzzes you in," Daphne said.

"Great, hon," Khela said, mimicking Sofia. Her high-heeled black Mary Janes tapping out her progress, she climbed the steps leading to the walkway to Carter's townhouse.

Once she found Carter's name on the resident directory, she pressed the buzzer corresponding to his apartment for a good minute.

"He's probably not home!" Daphne called, leaning across the seats to shout through the passenger window when Khela got no response.

"It's Saturday night," Khela hollered back. "He better be home. If he's out with another woman, I swear, I'll—"

"You'll what?" Carter demanded angrily, throwing wide the front door. Khela jumped back, releasing the buzzer.

"See you later," Daphne shouted. "And good luck."

Khela watched Daphne pull slowly into traffic before turning back to Carter, who stood with his arms crossed over his chest. "I'd like to talk to you," she said with a calm she didn't feel as she stared at him. The sight of him restored all feeling to her, and her heart throbbed painfully as she waited for him to say something.

"Come on up," he finally said, dropping his arms and offering his hand.

～⁓～

"What are you doing here?" Carter asked, breaking the awkward silence they had suffered during the elevator ride to his apartment.

Khela, her heart hammering against her chest, tried to calm it with deep breaths as she moved through the foyer and into his living room. His wasn't the apartment of the typical building superintendent, unless that super happened to be related to Warren Buffett. The carpet beneath her feet was so thick Khela almost felt as though she were walking on a mattress.

Carter's furnishings were tasteful, simple and comfortable-looking. The extra-long sofa, which faced a gloriously large fireplace, complemented the width of the big bay windows, which offered a look at the Prudential Center. Carter fit his environment perfectly, dressed in a white button-down with the sleeves rolled up to his elbows, khaki trousers and white socks.

Strolling past Carter, Khela went to the fireplace. She caressed the glassy smoothness of the marble mantel. Her brain flashed her an image of a snow-covered Boston day spent sharing the warmth and crackle of a fire with Carter.

She shook her head, ridding herself of the image as she continued her self-guided tour of the place. She went into the dining room with its dark pine table, chairs, hutch and buffet. She passed the bathroom without entering it, but noted its location, and she entered his office. Through the opposite door she spied the foot of a high, wide bed, but the office held her interest.

It was so unlike hers.

Khela's bedroom and office had blended into the same space, the loft area high above the rest of her living quarters. The place where she worked and the place where she slept were inextricably linked, much to her detriment. When she was seriously working, she often wanted to be sleeping. When she was sleeping, she often dreamt of working.

Carter had achieved a healthier balance in keeping his workspace completely separate from his personal space.

"You're very good at compartmentalizing your life, aren't you?" she said coldly, brushing past him to get back to the living room.

"I don't appreciate your tone," he responded once he caught her near the fireplace.

She whirled on him, fire in her eyes. "I don't give a crap about what you think about my tone. I haven't seen or heard from you in weeks. You're lucky I'm speaking to you at all."

"I didn't invite you here," Carter said.

"Fine," she snapped. "Bye."

He caught her by the arm and pulled her to him as she tried to pass him. "Don't go," he whispered into her hair. "I'm glad you came over. I needed to talk to you. I just couldn't figure out how to start."

"An explanation would be a good place."

His arms went around her, and Khela detected a slight tremble in his body. Instinct trumped anger, and she held him tight.

"I'm sorry," he murmured, his lips moving at her right temple. "I'm so sorry."

"About what? Calling me a disappointment?"

"I wasn't referring to you," he said, drawing back to face her. "I'm the disappointment."

"You're not making any sense."

He cupped her face. "You said you thought it was weird that a Boston University graduate would want to polish banisters all day."

It took her a moment to place those words. After she had, she put her hands on his neck, gently choking him. "If you're going to eavesdrop, you should listen to the whole conversation, not just the part of it that gives you an excuse to walk out on me."

"I want to be the kind of man you deserve."

In her Mary Janes, Khela was tall enough to touch her forehead to his. Carter's hands moved into her hair, cupping the back of her head.

"I deserve a man who makes me feel as though I'm the only woman in the world for him," Khela whispered.

Carter tilted his head to kiss her, but she stopped him with a finger to his lips.

"And a man who'll talk to me if there's a problem, not run off and sulk like a spoiled child."

"Nothin' I can do now but say I'm sorry," he said, his hands tightening in her hair. "I'm so sorry, Khela."

"Me, too. I wish you'd heard everything I said that night."

"If it's all the same to you, I'd just as soon get on with the business of making up the days we missed out on in our two weeks," he said.

"No."

"No?" he chuckled in disbelief.

"I want more than two weeks," Khela stated.

———— ·∾∾· ————

"When you said you lived across the street, I had no idea it was in the penthouse apartment," Khela said. She accepted the glass of wine Carter had poured for her, and she took a sip of it as he joined her on the sofa.

"You didn't give me a chance to explain," Carter replied. "This isn't the super's apartment. It's the apartment for the building owner." He dropped his eyes to his own wine goblet, swirling the pinot noir.

Khela's eyes became perfect circles. "You . . . Y-You're . . . You own this townhouse?"

He nodded. "I own yours, too."

Khela's stomach flip-flopped. Her heart seemed to stop beating. She set her wine glass on a black leather coaster atop his low cocktail table before she lunged across the sofa and let him have it. "In three years, you couldn't be bothered to tell me that you were my landlord?"

Laughing, Carter caught her fists. "You make your rent checks out to CR Management," he said. "You never associated that C and R with me?"

"When we met, you didn't exactly look like the owner of a five-million-dollar Boston property."

"Thank you. I'll take that as a compliment."

"No wonder you never seemed interested in money," she said. "You're probably worth more than I am."

He shook his head vigorously. "Nope, never. You're worth a hundred of me, Khela."

"So underneath that cool and confident façade, you've got the same insecurities as everyone else," Khela said.

Groaning, Carter let his head fall back. "I totally walked right into that."

Khela took his face and returned his gaze to hers. "I adore you exactly the way you are."

"I thought you wanted me just because you thought I was hot."

He expected her to laugh, or at the very least, to make a smart-ass comment. The last thing he thought she would do was caress his cheek with her fingertips, and touch his lips in a delicate kiss.

"What do you want?" she asked.

"For now?"

"For always," Khela said.

"I want to be happy."

"What would make you happy?"

"Someone who accepts me whether or not she understands me. Someone who'll accept me for my faults and not punish me for them. And who'll make me a better man without changing who I am."

"That's odd."

"Why?" he asked against her lips.

"Because that's what I want, too."

Carter offered her a sweet smirk. "You want to be a better man?"

"I want *you* to be a better man."

CHAPTER 12

*"True love survives chaos, madness, spite and greed.
True love solves all."*
—*from* A Proper Princess *by Khela Halliday*

Carter brewed a pot of strong coffee, which gave them the fuel to talk through the night. The pale grey light of the approaching dawn tinted the heavens beyond the silhouettes of the familiar skyscrapers, where thousands of commuters would soon begin their workday.

Once their words had been exhausted, their bodies seemed to follow. Communicating only by offering his hand, Carter invited Khela to leave the fat armchair she'd been sitting in. She took his hand and allowed him to lead her into his bedroom, where he unbuttoned the back of her dress and helped her out of it. He unhooked her black bra, carefully slipped the straps from her arms, and he laid it neatly on top of her dress, which lay atop the pine Harbury accent bench at the foot of his bed.

Left in only a dainty pair of sheer black panties, Khela's skin prickled under Carter's bold scrutiny. His fingers grazed her abdomen, making her skin jump, on their way to her hips, where he hooked them into the waistband of her panties. Slowly squatting, Carter drew her delicate panties down the length of her legs. She bent and rested a hand on his shoulder to maintain her balance as she stepped out of them.

Carter neatly folded them and placed them with her bra.

Knowing that his eyes were tracking her movements, Khela went to the bed and slid beneath its lightweight duvet. The massive sleigh bed was a near-perfect square and slightly bigger than a standard king. Through heavy-lidded eyes, Khela watched Carter undress, enjoying every second of what seemed like a great unveiling.

His belt came off first, and he put it on the bench with Khela's clothing. Next, he unbuttoned his button-down, shrugging out of it with the bored ease of a man in no special hurry to climb into bed with the woman he loved and craved. His eyes on Khela, he took off his pristine white T-shirt.

She shifted her head on his pillows, giving herself the perfect view of his bare torso. Bracing one hand on the big burled pine dresser facing the foot of the bed, he bent and removed his socks, apparently in deference to one of her long-ago observations that there was nothing funnier than a man wearing only his socks.

His pants and sports briefs came off last. Khela sighed at the sight of his nude body. He appeared to have grown only more beautiful in the time they had spent apart. His long legs, shapely in the distinct way that only a man's legs can be, brought him to the bed. His strong arms, the biceps and triceps working gracefully under his tawny skin, pulled back the duvet.

Khela welcomed him into the silken warmth of his bed, a place now made most inviting by her heat and presence. Carter aligned his body with hers. She rested her head on his right bicep; he clasped her backside, plastering her hips to his. He worked one of her legs between his and embraced her, assuring that her heartbeat was as close as possible to his own.

He nuzzled her hair, breathing deeply of her, reacquainting his senses with every detail of her. His abdomen moved hard against hers, and Khela took his face in her hands.

"Are we all right?" she whispered, her dark eyes searching his lighter ones.

He nodded, afraid of what else would spill out if he dared speak.

"I missed you," she said, her voice as soft and gentle as a caress.

Carter kissed her then, his tenderness planting the seed for a belief Khela thought herself incapable of, that love—the kind she wrote about, the kind she wished for—actually existed.

Sliding slowly down her body, Carter continued to cover her with chaste kisses, occasionally darting out his tongue to taste a specific part of her, or learn its texture anew. His warm breath, firm lips, taunting teeth and talented tongue at her breasts left her gasping for more of him.

He eagerly obliged, disappearing under the duvet to dot her taut belly and lower abdomen with kisses. He positioned her fully on her back before settling between her thighs. Khela caught a glimpse of his hunched shape beneath the covers before she closed her eyes and pushed her head into the soft pillow.

Carter braced the backs of her thighs on his shoulders, and he held her hips in his hands, as though presenting the feast of her body to himself on a platter.

Khela shivered in anticipation, hungrily awaiting what would come next. Through the duvet, she clutched at Carter's head and back, her spine arching upward. Friend Oceanwater had introduced them to dozens of tools that would accomplish the simple goal of sexual release, but Khela was confident that Friend and Aphrodite's Feather had nothing that could surpass Carter's ability to please.

He parted her wet folds by stroking upward with the bridge of his nose, anointing himself with her slippery perfume. He finished the stroke with the flick of his tongue, eliciting a sharp intake of air from Khela. Carter smiled against her dampness within the tent of the duvet. Pulling her thighs as widely apart as possible, he held her to his lips and tasted her, his tongue probing, swirling, lapping and thrusting.

The duvet protected Carter's skin from Khela's fingernails, which would have dug into him from the strength with which she was clutching his head. Carter held her tightly, breathing hard and fast against her, almost as hard and fast as the movement of his tongue and jaw.

He fully exposed her, and then gently clamped his teeth on the pulsating nub no longer hiding within its hood of slick flesh. He gave it a tiny tug, flitting the tip of his tongue over it, and Khela responded with a guttural moan that echoed off the walls and high ceiling.

Her thigh muscles hardened, her back curved, and her hands clenched into tight fists, and for one short second she was utterly still. But then her hips began moving against Carter's mouth and chin, working her into the hottest, most heavenly frenzy.

He fit his tongue into her in time to feel the violent constriction of her dark tunnel. Her body undulated, and Carter wished he could see her from outside the covers. He imagined how lovely she looked in the throes of rapture, and he found himself erupting in an amateurish display reminiscent of his earliest adolescent fumbling under the covers in the quiet of night.

Explosion after explosion rocked through her until her flesh became so sensitive, she could only whimper in mindless bliss as he continued to expertly gnaw at her.

"Carter," she exhaled weakly, "please. I can't . . ."

He pushed aside the duvet. "Do you want me to stop?" he asked against the warmth of her inner thigh.

Yes, was in her mind, but her love-starved nerve endings forced out a breathy, "No." For the first time ever, Khela's eruptions stacked, building higher and higher, the sensations intensifying until she felt she would shatter. Something within her did indeed break, and to her surprise, it turned out to be the very last of her reservations about giving herself, in total body and mind, to Carter.

He sank once more into the heaven between her thighs and, as the light of the golden sunrise flooded over them, Carter took Khela to a place where her cries of pleasure sounded like the songs of angels.

———∽∾∿∽———

They finally left the bed just after noon for a picnic in Carter's living room. White carryout containers from Rami's covered the coffee table and sat on the floor around them and their plates. Carter, dressed only in grey sports briefs, scooped up the last of the baba ganoush with his finger.

"I think the carton is edible, too," Khela joked. "Go on, try it."

"Hardy har har," Carter said. Passing on tasting the box, he did turn it upside down to shake the last bits of eggplant into his mouth.

"Have you ever been to Rami's?" Khela asked him.

Having scoured his plate clean with a piece of pita, Carter moved on to the next container. "I've never had food like this before. What is it? Greek?"

Khela marveled at how good ol' Southern boy ignorance and urban sophistication resided side by side within him. "How can you have lived in Boston for so long without sampling some of its Middle Eastern cuisine?"

He shrugged. "I just like American food better, I guess."

"I've never seen you lick your plate after eating a hamburger," Khela said.

"Okay, so this is a little tiny bit better than a hamburger," he admitted. "What was in it? I can't really tell."

"Eggplant, lemon juice, cumin, olive oil, parsley, tahini—"

"Tahiti?"

"Tahi*ni*," Khela repeated more clearly. "It's a sauce made of sesame seeds."

"I bet tahini would taste good on pork rinds."

He said this with a straight face, but then he started laughing and Khela knew that he was just teasing her.

"Have you tried the penis stew?"

Carter's laughter abruptly died. "They put real penis in a stew?"

"Well, how do you make *your* penis stew?" she asked with a sardonic smile.

Carter's face wrinkled in disgust. "Man, that's nasty."

"I'm kidding. Rami's doesn't make penis stew. You'd have to go to Malaysia or China to find a restaurant that delivered penis stew. You could probably get bull, goat, deer—"

"I don't need to hear the flavors," Carter laughed.

"Try one of the spinach borekas," she offered, handing him one. "They don't taste a thing like penis."

He took her wrist and held her hand in place so he could nibble the potato and spinach-filled turnover right from her fingers. When he finished, he licked her fingertips, sucking every crumb of pastry, every tasty bead of filling, from them.

Khela purred her approval. "Would you like to try a meat kabob?"

Tugging her by her wrist, Carter pulled her into the hollow formed by his crossed legs. "I like the theme you got goin' here." Grinning suggestively, he took her hand and wrapped it around his personal meat kabob.

"Ooh," Khela murmured through prettily puckered lips. "This could feed a family of eight."

"Try nine."

"Friend Oceanwater had a table full of B.O.B.s built like this," Khela whispered against his neck. "Tell me, what power source does *this* require?"

Carter closed his eyes and expelled a low moan. "It's manual," he sighed. "Good old-fashioned elbow grease gets the job done every time." He opened his eyes. "What's a B.O.B?"

"Battery-Operated Boyfriend." Khela put a little more elbow into the movement of her hand in his lap. "I think some of the girls went home with a couple of them last night."

Carter reluctantly moved her hand aside. "Exactly what did you and Daphne do last night?"

"We went to an Aphrodite's Feather party." She slid off his lap and onto the floor, nearly sitting on a shallow box of pitas.

"What's that?"

"It's, um . . ." She tapped her chin with her index finger. "It's like a Tupperware party, only instead of storage containers and measuring cups, you get to see samples of vibrators and edible panties."

"Oh," Carter said, reaching for a pita. Then he spun around and faced Khela. "What?"

She fell over laughing, upsetting her glass of Mideastern-style lemonade. Carter quickly grabbed a pile of white napkins from the coffee table to clean up the mess. After picking up the flecks of mint and the orange blossom that had garnished and flavored the beverage, he used bottled water to dilute the remaining liquid. He dabbed at it until no traces of it remained in the carpet.

"All better?" Khela asked after he'd wadded up the soiled napkins and stuffed them into the empty baba ganoush carton.

"Thank God, I had the carpet treated with a stain guard," he said.

"It's just lemonade, not sulfuric acid," Khela commented. "Or cat pee. Or ketchup. Or grape—"

"I get it, smarty," he chuckled. "I like to keep my things nice."

"You do realize that children will destroy this place," Khela said.

"Children? What children?"

"*Your* children. When you have them."

"Oh, I won't be livin' here when we have kids. This is my big-city bachelor pad, my playboy penthouse. Our kids are gonna have a house with a big ol' yard to run 'round in."

Khela kept her eyes on her half-eaten falafel. She didn't want him to see how his use of "we" and "our" affected her.

Carter had chosen those words deliberately. "You do want to have kids some day, don't you?" he asked when she continued to avert her eyes.

"Absolutely," she said, finally meeting his gaze squarely. "I grew up with parents who chose me, so I always felt that I was the most special little girl in the world, at least to them. I want someone who belongs to me completely. I want to know what it feels like to have someone with my eyes looking back at me. Or who flashes my smile at the world. I want someone who'll love me, no matter what."

"You got that, girl." Carter stood on his knees and cupped her face. "You got that right here, and then some," he said, covering her mouth with his and easing her onto his cushy, spotless carpet.

———

Sitting in the rear of the Crispus Attucks High School auditorium with Khela's shoulder handbag on his lap, Carter squirmed uncomfortably. Every seat in the cavernous space was occupied by a student, teacher, parent or guest who wanted to listen to Khela, who had been invited to the school as part of its Weekend Mentor Lecture Series for Seniors.

Carter knew nothing about Crispus Attucks High, other than what he discovered upon their arrival—that it was a public school in the Dorchester section of Boston and two armed security guards patrolled its parking lot during weekend functions. His own alma mater, Dearborn Academy, was as different from Crispus Attucks as an ostrich from a shark.

Dearborn's 60-acre campus was nestled in the quaint bedroom community of Concord, where median housing prices were close to $900,000. The rowhouses neighboring Crispus Attucks High were vacant, condemned, or occupied as evidenced by raggedy furniture, broken toys, uncollected newspapers and garbage strewn across patchy front lawns. Underneath their ugliness, the red brick structures had so much character, so many beautiful architectural details. Riding past the houses, Carter had wished that he could adopt the buildings as one would neglected children.

He had pushed the depressed state of the neighborhood to a deeper part of his mind once Khela had taken the stage in the auditorium. Just as she had inspired the authors at the convention, she encouraged the new seniors of Crispus Attucks to put pen to paper and record their innermost thoughts, wishes, prayers and dreams. She demanded that they record their histories in stories, songs, drawings—anything. The form of the record didn't matter, only that the record was kept.

Carter didn't have enough fingers and toes to count off the number of guest speakers he'd been forced to sit through in Dearborn special assemblies—politicians, professional athletes, CEOs—there was always some parent eager to blow balloon juice about their career to a captive audience of fourteen-to-eighteen-year-olds.

Glancing at the purple print-out of the high school's lecture calendar, Carter saw that a reverend had spoken the previous Saturday and a parole officer was on deck for next week. Carter wondered if other speakers drew the same turnout as Khela.

The lecture was the only reason Khela had left his apartment after their lunch interlude to go home, shower and change before meeting Carter in front of the brownstone, where they hailed a cab that took them into Dorchester.

Students milling outside the school prior to the lecture had given him long looks as he accompanied Khela into the building. Dorchester was racially diverse, but as Carter walked Khela through the packed auditorium to the stage, he saw few faces with his complexion.

Sitting between a bright-eyed young Latina, who flashed her braces at him in a dreamy smile every five minutes, and a scrawny Asian with tufts of purple hair and the X-Men character Wolverine tattooed on the back of his right hand, Carter felt completely out of place now that Khela's talk was over and she was fielding questions from her young audience.

He regretted his decision to sit in the center of the back row, a position he had wanted for its perfect view of Khela. His location made it impossible to make a smooth exit without having to squeeze past ten students in either direction. Hugging her huge Cape Cod leather handbag to his chest, he swallowed his discomfort and tried to enjoy the question-and-answer session. It was easy with Khela down on the stage in an elegant white silk blouse, a tan linen pencil skirt and tan heels.

That hundreds of students had given up a sunny August Saturday afternoon to listen to Khela impressed Carter. What impressed him even more was her ease in front of such a diverse crowd of young people. She had been so uncomfortable addressing her peers at the East Coast Writer's Association convention, but she radiated self-assurance while speaking to this audience.

A three-minute standing ovation followed Khela's remarks, after which the principal took the stage. In her smart brown pantsuit, she looked like a shorter, younger Ruby Dee.

"I would like to thank the senior class for coming out today," the principal said, "and for being so attentive and respectful of Miss Halliday. As you know, our budget for speakers is limited. I met Miss Halliday at one of her signings last year, and when I asked her to come to my school and speak to my children, she didn't have her people call my people. She accepted right there on the spot."

More applause interrupted the principal, who raised her hands to quiet the auditorium before continuing. "Not only did Miss Halliday forgo her usual speaking fee to talk to you today, she made a donation to our Library Improvement Fund. Miss Halliday has made it possible for us to purchase the new computer stations we need!"

A last round of applause drowned out the principal's final thanks to Khela. Even from the back row, Carter could see a blush tinting Khela's cheeks as the principal gave her a warm handshake. When the students and guests began to file out of the auditorium, Carter made his way down the center aisle to the stage, where quite a few students had hung back to speak further with Khela or to get books signed.

Taking his place in line behind them, Carter smiled and gave Khela a small wave. She responded with a quick wink without interrupting what she was saying to a student.

The young man immediately in front of Carter, his slight form drowning in baggy black jeans and a black hooded sweatshirt with CORTEZ in gold gothic-bold lettering across the front, turned to look at Carter. "Nice purse," he said, a smirk forming beneath the twenty black hairs forming what appeared to be a mustache.

"Thanks," Carter said brightly. "But it's not mine."

"Why you gonna go an' start makin' trouble, Cortez?" came the high-pitched, heavily-accented voice of the girl in front of Cortez, the color high in her caramel-colored cheeks. "You know that's Mr. Halliday, 'cause you saw him come in with her!" she chastised, punctuating it with a sharp smack to the young man's upper arm.

"I told you not to hit me, girl!" he said, his tone menacing but his body language meek and mild. "Dude is standing up here holdin' onto his woman's purse, so why you on me?"

The gold bamboo hoops in the girl's ears swung heavily when she spun to point a finger in Cortez's face. "Khela Halliday is my favorite writer and I'm not havin' you embarrassin' me! Act like you got some sense!"

Whether it was the fiery warning in her eyes, the tone of her voice, or the gold fingernail aimed perilously close to the tip of his nose, Cortez was cowed. When the girl turned back around, Cortez gave Carter a sheepish smile. "You know how it is," he snickered with a self-conscious tug at the diamond stud in his right ear. "You gotta let 'em feel like they're the boss once in a while."

Carter peered at the young man's neck, half expecting to see a collar.

The line moved forward slower than Carter would have liked as Khela signed books and autographs and patiently answered question after question. The principal moved people along when they tried to park at Khela's table, but she was no match for Cortez's girl.

Khela almost jumped off her chair when the girl dropped a heavy black backpack on her table. "Miss Halliday, I got all your books!" the girl said, rummaging through the backpack. "My favorite is *An Angel's Prayer*." She took it from the backpack and hugged it briefly before presenting it to Khela. "Would you sign this, 'To Luisa, my crazy, cool biggest fan?' You can sign all of them like that."

Luisa was pulling hardback copies of each of Khela's books from the backpack, stacking them neatly in front of her.

"Luisa, really," the principal began, "Miss Halliday doesn't have the time to—"

"I think I'm okay for time," Khela said, glancing at Carter.

He and Cortez were the last two in line, although several people continued to mill about in the auditorium. Carter gave Khela a subtle nod of assent.

Khela opened *An Angel's Prayer* and began writing the requested dedication. She was handing the book back to Luisa, who traded it for *Satin Whispers*, when Khela noticed Cortez. He had put on his hood, pulled the drawstring tight, and stood partially behind Luisa, who used her shoulder to impatiently push him back a step.

Khela stood and tapped Cortez on the shoulder. "I know you," she said.

Surprised, Carter and Luisa looked from Cortez to Khela.

"You were in one of my spring workshops at RoCoCo," Khela elaborated, referring to Roxbury Community College by one of its nicknames.

"What writing workshop?" Luisa asked, although it sounded more like an accusation. She thrust out a denim-clad hip and propped a fist on it.

"Man," Cortez whined under his breath. "I can't believe you ratted me out," he directed at Khela.

"Attending one of my workshops is a dirty secret?" Khela asked.

Cortez, his head down, scrubbed a spot on the stage with the toe of his Ecko sneaker.

"It must be," Luisa said testily, "because he didn't never tell me that he was writin' in workshops at Roxbury Community."

"He's a very talented writer," Khela said.

Luisa's eyes and mouth opened wide. With a flip of her wavy dark hair, she faced Cortez to really give it to him. "You let her read what you're always writin' in those composition books and you won't let me? I'm supposed to be your girl!"

Khela studied the sibilant movement of Luisa's elegant neck as she spoke, hoping to give the distinctive mannerism to one of her future characters.

"I don't let nobody read my notebooks," Cortez said, striking a defensive posture that made Luisa cross her arms over her chest. "It was professional between me and her."

"If by 'her' you mean me, it really was just for the workshop," Khela said. "Although you'll have to let someone read your work at some point, Cortez, if you hope to get it published."

"You think he's good enough to get published?" Luisa asked, now more proud than perturbed.

"Cortez knows what I think," Khela said.

Luisa, and Carter, too, waited for someone to elaborate. Khela returned to signing Luisa's books while Cortez renewed his efforts to scuff a hole in the floor of the stage. Her head bowed to a copy of *A Proper Princess*, Khela smiled when Cortez finally said, "I have a lot of raw talent." He spoke so softly with his face aimed at the floor that Carter had to step closer to hear him. "I should apply to colleges with good writing programs."

"Boo-Boo!" Luisa squealed, wrapping her arms around his neck. "You're gonna be a writer, just like Khela Halliday!"

"Cortez and I have a lot in common, but our writing styles are very different," Khela said, looking up from the book she had finished signing.

Luisa released Cortez and asked the question that Carter would have asked. "You and Miss Halliday have something in common?" she laughed.

"Her father's doing time," he retorted. "Same as mine. She was adopted, too."

Luisa's merriment faded, and she looked at Cortez and Khela with renewed admiration.

"I think Miss Halliday proves that talent and hard work is the recipe for success," the principal said. "You have the same pedigree as Miss Halliday, Cortez. Do you have her same drive to succeed?"

"Yes, ma'am," he answered, standing taller before she could order him to straighten his spine.

"Then I'll be expecting to one day invite you back to Crispus Attucks to deliver a lecture to another senior class," the principal said.

Blushing around a tiny smile, Cortez said, "Yes, ma'am."

Khela finished signing Luisa's books—and a few belonging to her mother and sisters—just as the principal told her that her cab had arrived. Khela spent another moment thanking the principal and saying goodbye before she joined Carter.

"I'm sorry that took so long," she apologized, juggling her briefcase and the leftover handouts she tried to stuff into it as she walked up the aisle with Carter.

Oblivious to her struggle, he held her handbag out to her.

"Could you hang on a second?" she asked.

A short jet of air from Carter's nostrils prefaced his response. "Sure. Take your time."

"Are you mad at me or something?" Khela asked, balancing her briefcase on the back of a seat.

"Nope. You warned me that the meet and greet after the lecture could take a while."

She put her papers away, snapped shut the briefcase, and then took her handbag from Carter. He stuck his

269

hands in his pockets as they continued toward the exit at the rear of the auditorium.

Carter kept his silence until they were settled in the back of the cab, and Khela asked, "Are you okay? You seem funny."

He sank deeper into the bench seat, draping his arm along the back of it. Khela turned slightly to face him, her big handbag sitting on her knees. "I'm fine," Carter said. His eyes darted to her lap. "That's a real nice purse you got there."

CHAPTER 13

"Jealousy, not hate, is Love's true foe."
—from Captured By a Captain *by Khela Halliday*

Lying on his stomach in the middle of his bed Sunday morning, Carter leafed through the catalog Khela had brought back from the Aphrodite's Feather party Friday night. Khela sat on his back, reading over his shoulder.

"Maybe I should have bought the Prixy Dust," she said. "We could have had it for dessert last night."

"*You* could have had it for dessert if we used it the way it's shown in the picture." His forehead furrowed, Carter spun the catalog upside down. "What's she doin' to him there?"

Khela lightly bit his shoulder. "The same thing I did to you a little while ago. Only hers was grape, strawberry or green-apple flavored."

"Hmm," he grunted. "Should I circle it?"

"Sure."

Carter plucked the party favor pencil from behind his left ear and circled the Prixy Dust. So far, he had circled every item in the first five pages of the Aphrodite's Feather fall catalog.

"I already bought the feather," Khela told him. "I think I left it in Daphne's car, though."

"I can't believe some of this stuff." He turned the page and whistled as he eyeballed a B.O.B. named, appropriately enough, Big Bob. "What the—?" He peered closer at the page. "Is that thing in the shape of a man?"

"Yep," Khela laughed. "See that? Around his waist?" She pointed to the midsection of the purple silicon figure. "That's his tool belt. Get it? A tool wearing a tool belt?"

"That thing is the perfect little Mr. Fix-It, ain't he?" Carter snickered.

"He's got a lot of power, too. He takes eight AA batteries."

"You go, boy!" Carter cheered.

"Carter?"

"Mmm?"

"How did you come into all your real estate?"

Using the pencil as a bookmark, Carter closed the catalog and tossed it onto his nightstand. He carefully rolled onto his back so as not to pitch Khela onto the floor, leaving her sitting on his hard abdomen. He caressed her knees and thighs as he pondered his response.

"Well, the short version of the story is that I won it," he said.

"Then tell me the long version," she said.

"I graduated BU with a degree in finance and business management, and I got my first job at Babcock Management Corporation in Mobile. A recruiter came to campus one day right before graduation. She took a shine to me, and next thing I knew, she had offered me a full-time, paid training gig."

"*She*, huh," Khela said woodenly. "It's always a she."

"I was a natural," Carter continued. "I seemed to recruit new clients everywhere I went. I'd go to Turner Field to catch the Braves from the Henry Aaron seats, and I'd leave Atlanta with ten new clients. I would go to my ex-fiancée's tennis club and come back to the firm with six or seven new accounts. It was amazing. I didn't think I was all that good a pitchman."

"How many of your clients were women?"

A lazy grin prefaced his response. "About eighty-nine percent. What can I say? I had a way with ladies with money to invest."

"What you have is a symmetrical caveman face," Khela said.

"Is that good?"

"It's fortunate. People with more symmetrical faces are seen as more attractive, and that can translate into seeming more trustworthy. In the animal kingdom, asymmetry, even the most minute differences in the eyes or mouth, can indicate genetic flaws. Symmetrical creatures get more sex."

"How do you know all this stuff?"

"Romance novelists are like sponges," Khela said. "We absorb everything because we can build a romance around anything."

"So you think that I was a successful broker because I'm symmetrical? Four years of college and two years of training didn't have anything to do with it?"

"Your symmetry gave the other stuff a big boost," Khela said. "You have great overall symmetry. Your arms, legs, feet, ankles, hands, ears, eyes are all equal. Your symmetry benefits me, too, you know."

"This should be interesting," Carter laughed.

"Women with symmetrical partners report having more orgasms than women with average-looking men," Khela said.

"I guess I'm symmetrical down there, too," Carter gloated, gyrating his hips and giving Khela a little ride.

"Your schlong has nothing to do with it," Khela said.

"My what?"

"Your Johnson. Your schvance. Your doodle. Your . . . you don't know what I mean?"

"I know what you mean." His pretty eyes twinkled. "I just like hearing all the nicknames you have for it."

"Your *ding-a-ling* doesn't have anything to do with why you please a woman," Khela said. "It's the total package. Symmetrical men typically have taller, more fit bodies. Women like a total package, not just a big ol' ding-dong."

"But a big ol' ding-dong is nothin' to complain about, right?"

"It is if its owner doesn't know how to use it," Khela said.

"What about women? Does it apply to them?"

"Women know exactly how to use a big ol' ding-dong. That's how places like Aphrodite's Feather stay in business, and why women don't go around shooting up malls and office buildings. We know how to channel our need for release in more pleasurable, private ways, whether it's gorging ourselves on HoHos once in a while or hibernating under the covers with a B.O.B."

"I don't mean that," Carter said, rolling his eyes. "Does symmetry help women?"

"Of course. The really neat thing is that a woman's symmetry changes through her menstrual cycle."

Carter's lip curled. "Ew."

"Stop, I'm trying to teach you something." Khela gave him a light thump on his chest.

"I'm listening," he said. "I just don't go for all that girlie talk."

"During that time of the month," she said pointedly, "a woman's fingers, ears, breasts—"

"Breasts are good," Carter cut in.

"—all become more symmetrical when she ovulates. She becomes more attractive when she's most likely to conceive. Nature is amazing, isn't she?"

Carter's eyes were glued to the open front of Khela's shirt. "Your breasts are symmetrical."

"Doesn't matter," she said. "I'm on the pill. Chemistry trumps symmetry when it comes to conception in my case."

"Are your breasts so beautiful because they're symmetrical?" He framed them in his hands.

"Why are you so fascinated with my breasts?"

"Because I'm just a caveman. You said so yourself."

"I said you had a caveman *face*," she clarified. "So does Will Smith. And Brad Pitt. Men with 'bulldog' faces have gotten the most girls through evolutionary history.

There's a paleontologist at the Natural History Museum in London, who—"

"What's her name? Maybe I know her."

Khela swatted at Carter. Laughing, he caught her hands and laced her fingers through his.

"She proposed that the distance between the lip and brow line was crucial to what we perceive as attractive. Researchers found that male chimps with shorter, broader faces get more play than other male chimps. You're in good company."

"You think I'm a caveman who looks like a chimp," he scoffed.

"Justin Timberlake, Thierry Henry, Johnny Depp, David Beckham and Kanye West are some of the most attractive men in the world, and they have 'bulldog' faces," Khela said. "That's the company I meant." She stretched out on top of him, resting her chin on her hands on top of his chest. "You don't look like a chimp. You act like one sometimes, but you definitely don't look like one."

"Thanks." He stared down his nose to gaze at her. "I think."

"So finish telling me how you got not one, but two, big ol' brownstones on Comm Ave."

"That tale isn't as good as your symmetrical caveman bulldog story."

"Tell me anyway," she said.

"As I said, I was a natural. I played the market as if it were my favorite baby toy. I had good instincts, and I could sniff out trends. I couldn't pick winners in college football games for crap, but I knew when to buy and sell stocks for other folks. I wasn't into the job the way some of the other kids were, but I definitely threw myself a little more into it after my bust-up with Savannah."

"Your pageant girl," Khela teased.

"Ex-pageant girl," Carter corrected.

"I think a lot of people devote their lives to their work after a bad break-up."

"It was a livelihood, not my life. Thinking that way made it easier for me to take big risks. One of my biggest paid off."

"What, you bought into Microsoft on the ground floor?"

"Yeah, something like that," he chuckled, which made Khela's head bob up and down with the movement of his torso. "Basically, I specialized in long-term holding of focused portfolios of between five and ten solid stocks chosen based on two criteria: high-earning yield and high return on asset. You follow me?"

"Yes," Khela lied.

"A couple of my portfolios hit the jackpot," he said. "I retired at twenty-six."

Khela rose on her elbows. Her mouth fell open. "How much did you make?"

"Are you asking me how much I'm worth?"

"I already know how much you're worth," she said. "You're priceless. I wanna know how much you retired on."

He shifted his gaze to the window, and he watched the sun's showy descent into the west as he said, "A few million."

"Merry Christmas," Khela gasped.

"It was about like that," Carter sighed. "Like winning the lottery twice."

"So what made you decide to go into real estate?"

"It was more like whom than what. Detrick convinced me to invest in the two Comm Ave properties. They were on the market, and they were good buys because they needed some work. I got my loans, got the work done, and started renting to chumps like you who pay three times more in rent than what most folks pay for a mortgage."

"I'm not a chump just because I'm crazy about my apartment," Khela said. "I seriously fell in love with the moldings and the fixtures and the deep, wide, tall windows. And I love living in the Back Bay. I've got the mall in front of me, the Charles River and MIT behind me, and I'm within walking distance of the Boston Public Library, the Public Gardens, the Common, the State House, Newbury Street—"

"With all those attractions and conveniences, maybe I should raise your rent," Carter chuckled.

She lowered her head to bring her mouth closer to the tawny disk of sensitive flesh capping his left pectoral muscle. "Actually, I was wondering if I could negotiate a decrease in my rent."

"Oh, yeah?" Carter intently watched her lips part and tracked the tip of her tongue as it moved toward his nipple. "What did you have in mind?"

"What do you want?" she asked, the heat of her breath sending tingles through him.

"Page six, nine and fifteen of that Aphrodite's catalog," he smiled. "And that's just for starters."

———∞∞∞———

At least a dozen brides-to-be and their attendant maids of honor crowded the sales floor of I/Deux, one of Boston's premier bridal shops. The chic boutique, located on Newbury Street near Exeter, was Daphne's top choice for wedding gown shopping. Competing with Jessica McClintock, Bella, Flair, Aria and Priscilla of Boston, I/Deux featured one-of-a-kind designer originals that ordinarily could be acquired only in Paris or Milan.

Daphne's fondness for edgy, contemporary designers and Llewellyn's robust bank account guaranteed that she and Khela would end up no place other than I/Deux to purchase dresses for the wedding.

"I love this!" Daphne gasped, clutching the sleeve of a pale pink strapless silk chiffon. She lifted the skirt and draped it over her chest. "Does it bring out the rose undertones in my skin, or the yellow?"

"The rose," Khela said, studying Daphne from several angles. "It makes your face glow."

Under the shop's cool white lighting, Daphne's eyes began to shine like freshly polished emeralds.

"Oh, for crying out loud," Khela whined. "You're not going to start crying again, are you?"

"I can't help it!" Daphne said, dropping the filmy skirt and pressing her face into Khela's shoulder. "Everything is happening so fast now. In two weeks, I'm going to be Mrs. Llewellyn Davies! I've finally got my dress, but I still have to find something old, something new—"

"I've got your something old," Khela said, leaning back to keep Daphne's tears from water-staining her silk tank top. "I can loan you Grandma Belle's pearls."

Daphne bobbed up. "Khela, no. You should save them for your own wedding." The freckles dotting Daphne's nose seemed to brighten when she smiled and said, "You and Carter will be dodging rice before you know it."

"Maybe." Khela smiled shyly. "I try not to think about it. In some ways, we've moved just as fast as you and Llewellyn, but in other ways . . . Well, I think it's best if we go slower. Thinking about marriage falls in the latter category."

Daphne's eyes began to water, and she touched two fingers to her lips. "When I saw him kiss you goodbye this morning . . ." Overcome, she stopped and fanned herself with her hand. "It was just the most romantic thing."

Khela stared at Daphne, her face severe. "Are you pregnant?"

A few other shoppers turned around, wide-eyed with anticipation.

"What?" Khela snapped at a particularly persistent rubbernecker. "Like pregnant women don't buy wedding gowns?"

The woman quickly scurried to the other side of the store.

"Well, are you?" Khela asked, cornering Daphne between two mannequins dressed in heavily beaded gowns.

"How could you tell?" Daphne whispered. "I only just found out myself a little while ago."

"How little a while?"

"This is nice," Daphne said, moving past Khela to feel the capped sleeve of a silk gown with a ruched Empire bodice.

Khela grabbed her arm and swung her in a circle that landed her back in her original spot. "That dress is horrible, and answer my question."

"Yesterday." Daphne's eyes swam again. She struck the tears away with the heel of her hand. "I took a stick test and it came up knocked up."

"Does Llewellyn know?"

"He was right there with me, until he fainted."

Khela giggled. "I'm sorry," she said, quickly choking back any show of further amusement.

"It's okay," Daphne said. "I thought he was faking, until I couldn't wake him up."

"Is he okay with it?"

"He's really excited." Daphne's footsteps became heavier as she moved to a less populated section of the store.

"Why aren't you?" Khela sat on a padded bench, patting the space beside her to encourage Daphne to sit.

Opting to stand, Daphne paced in front of the bench. "I'm scared, Khela."

"It's natural to be—"

"No, I'm really terrified!" Daphne clapped her hands to her abdomen. "There's a person in here! And it's a tough person. Lew and I used protection every time, but somehow this baby got itself made. A little tough person is going to come out of me and expect me to do all kinds of stuff I've never done before. I have *never* changed a diaper. I've *never* stuck my breast in someone's mouth!"

"Um," Khela mused, "so Llewellyn's not big on foreplay, is he?"

"You know what I mean! I've never had milk shoot outta my tits!"

A tall, thin sales associate in a butter-yellow sleeveless dress skittered into view, wringing her hands fretfully. "Ladies, I don't suppose I could ask you to take your conversation outside? We try to maintain a happy atmosphere in I/Deux, and I'm afraid the substance of your conversation is upsetting some of our other customers."

Daphne, her hormones swinging in yet another direction, turned on the saleslady.

"You want to get me outta here, lady?" she raged. "Bag that size four Junko Yoshioka, and I'll be out of your store and out of your life forever!"

"Will that be cash or charge?" the saleslady asked with a big, bright smile.

Daphne got her credit card from her purse and handed it to the saleslady, who took it and vanished.

"I guess we can continue our tit talk now that Big Bird can count on a four-figure commission," Khela said. "Are you sure you want that dress? You barely looked at it."

"I've had my eye on that dress ever since Llewellyn proposed," Daphne admitted.

"Then why the hell did you beg me to come dress shopping with you today?"

"It wasn't about the dress," Daphne said. "I wanted to tell you about the baby." She slapped her hands to her face. "I can't believe I'm having a baby."

Daphne plopped down on the bench, sitting close to Khela. "I thought Lew and I would have a few years to spend together before we had children."

Khela grinned. "In nine months, you'll be welcoming a bouncing baby antiques expert into the world."

"What will you be doing, Khela?" Daphne asked, her tone somber.

"I don't understand."

"What will you be doing? Will you still be having marathon sex with Carter? Or will you have built something more meaningful?"

"What is this?" Khela bristled. "It's all very new between me and Carter. We've gone from three years of polite passes in the hallway to tickling and tumbling between the sheets. We put the whole two-week thing to rest, but—"

"You deserve more than a friend with bene—"

"Here you go, Miss Carr," Big Bird interrupted, appearing with a credit slip for Daphne to sign and a freshly bagged wedding gown.

Daphne scrawled her signature, took the customer copy and the dress, and gave Big Bird the merchant copy and her silver I/Deux pen.

"Enjoy the dress, my dear, and have a lovely, lovely wedding day!" Big Bird called after Daphne as she and Khela exited the store.

"Carter and I aren't just friends with benefits," Khela said. "We genuinely care for each other. Everything we do together, we do out of—"

"Love?"

"Yes," Khela said defiantly, yet knowing in every part of her brain and heart that her answer was true. On her end, at any rate.

"Have you told him?" Daphne stepped closer to the curb to hail a taxi.

"Told who what?" Khela asked evasively.

"Have you told Carter that you love him?"

"Yes." Khela stared at her feet as she answered. "Not so much in words, but in other ways."

"Oh, yeah? Words are your specialty. If you haven't told him in words, how did you do it?"

"Liberal amounts of Prixy Dust," Khela answered as a Yellow Cab eased to a stop in front of Daphne.

———✦———

The same Yellow Cab that delivered Daphne and her new wedding gown to her near-empty apartment in Cambridge then took Khela to her brownstone, where Carter was waiting for her in the lobby.

Dressed in pleated khaki trousers, a crisp white shirt and black Hugo Boss wing tips, Carter looked dashing yet casual—exactly as he should to accompany Khela to her reading and signing at the Dorian S. Fielder House in Brookline.

"You don't need to change or anything, do you?" he asked, hurrying down the stairs in front of the building to meet Khela at the curb. "We're cutting it awfully close."

"No, I'm wearing what I have on." Charmed by his concern for her schedule, Khela executed a quick pirouette to give him a full view of her white sundress and Espadrilles.

Carter's approving smile earned him a kiss on the cheek.

"Calm down," she told him. "I've done this hundreds of times."

"Well, this is my first time, and I don't want to be late." He opened the door of the cab for her and helped her into it. He scooted in beside her and gave the driver the address in Brookline.

Khela found herself enjoying the luxury of having someone manage things for her. She settled back in what seemed to be the cleanest cab in Boston, resting her head on Carter's shoulder. Preoccupied with making sure the driver took the most expeditious route rather than a more time-consuming scenic route, Carter wasn't the best travel companion. Khela was glad when they finally arrived at the Fielder House.

"You don't have to stay," she offered as they walked the long stone path leading to the house. The tree-lined driveway leading up to the burnt yellow Federal-era home was filled with cars, a clear indication that Khela's publicist had done a good job in getting the word out about Khela's appearance. "This probably won't be much fun. It's not like the convention. This is an event for readers, not industry folk. It's a very different crowd."

"Do you want me to go?"

"No, of course not. It's just . . . It won't be like the convention."

"I Googled this place," he told her. "Dorian Fielder was one of the first women in America to publish a book under her own name. Of course, it helped that her name was also a man's name."

"You're quite the researcher," Khela said.

At the door, Carter offered his arm. "Ready, darlin'?"

Smiling, she looped her arm through his and let him ring the doorbell.

A short, stout woman in a sky-blue twinset, a white twill skirt that matched her white hair and white Keds opened the door. She had eyes only for Khela, and her bright-red painted lips pulled into a huge smile.

"Khela Halliday, we're so excited to have you here this afternoon!" the woman said, taking Khela's free arm. Snatching her free of Carter, she pulled her into the entrance hall. "We've got a full house, standing room only. Your publisher sent us twice as many books as we requested, and doggone if we didn't go and sell them all!"

"It's all for a good cause," Khela said, "so it works out well for everyone."

"We can begin whenever you're ready," the woman said. "Can I get you a beverage, or something to snack on, or—"

"If you could just show me where I can put my handbag, that would be great," Khela said.

"I can hold that for you," Carter offered, taking her purse and her hand.

The older woman flinched, as if seeing him for the first time. "Oh, are you Mr. Halliday?" she greeted. "I'm sorry; I didn't greet you properly at the door. I was too caught up in the excitement of meeting Khela."

"He's not Mr. Halliday," Khela said. "We're not married."

"Oh." The woman looked from Khela to Carter, then offered another wide smile. "Well, you sure look as if you should be. Your adoring fans await, Miss Halliday. Let's not disappoint them."

Khela gave Carter an apologetic smile, which he didn't have time to acknowledge, before Khela's guide opened a pair of heavy wooden doors. Exuberant applause welcomed Khela to her reading. Her guide once more pulled her free of Carter and dragged her into the center of the noise.

———

This event wasn't a thing like the convention or the lecture at Crispus Attucks High.

The Fielder House was on a street lined with big, Federal-era homes situated at the end of long driveways or behind enormous, well-tended lawns. While Carter took a tour of the historic house, admiring its post-and-beam construction, the decorative mantels and woodwork, and the Sheraton and Hepplewhite furnishings,

Khela held court as though she had been recently coronated. In a manner of speaking, she had. In winning the Torchbearer Award, she had become a hot commodity in romance reading circles.

She read a lengthy passage from her upcoming release, *A Runaway Romance*, and then signed copies of her books for two hours.

Carter had "heard" all of her books in her voice as he'd read them, but this was the first time he'd actually listened to her read her work. Her words, wrapped in the seductive rasp of her voice, captivated the audience. Her listeners had fallen so far into her tale that they remained still for a long moment at the end of her reading. Then applause erupted and shook the rafters.

Carter, perhaps, clapped loudest of all. He kept his distance, nursing a tall iced tea while Khela signed books and chatted with readers. Her female fans generally opened with a compliment, telling her their names or the name of the person to whom they wanted the book signed. They made small talk while Khela personalized the signing, and upon receiving the book, they thanked her and moved on.

As the afternoon wore on and Khela began mingling with her readers, Carter noticed that her male fans had a very different approach. They stalked her, waiting to catch her alone, at which point they would move in to offer a drink, a morsel to eat, or a business card. Khela was polite and charming, but in a way that left Carter wondering how she had managed to turn off the full force of her personality.

He was thankful that she didn't have it on full force when he entered the formal parlor, where Khela stood near the floor-to-ceiling windows talking to a man in a suit. Recognizing him as Fielder House executive director Bradford Sullivan from the photo prominently displayed opposite Khela's in the program, Carter detested him on sight.

His hair was so dark and neat, Carter was convinced that it probably snapped on and off like that of a Ken doll. His suit was tailored better than those Detrick owned, and Detrick never bought less than the best. Sullivan was very tan, and Carter guessed that it was from hours spent on a golf course or tennis court, perhaps even a yacht.

The worst thing about him, though, was his laugh. His booming guffaw carried through the house, and Carter seethed as he watched him laugh outrageously at everything Khela said.

"I believe in honesty," Sullivan said, his enunciation slick with the polish of his overpriced Ivy League education, "and I'm going to tell you right now that I've never read one of your books."

"Neither has Mahatma Ghandi," Khela retorted, clutching a glass of iced tea close to her chest. The gesture served to keep more distance between herself and the executive director, who was doing his best to press in on her personal space.

Sullivan laughed, and his amplitude blew Khela back a foot or so. "You're quite an intriguing young lady, Miss Halliday," he announced. "It is Miss, isn't it?"

"Miss," Khela confirmed, stepping back as he took a half step forward. "Or Ms., I'm not picky."

"As executive director of the Fielder House, I'm rather well connected in Boston's more elite literary circles," he said. "I've boosted the careers of many a New England pen friend. Lark Johannes, Peggy Cannondale, Selena Juarez and Orinda Kolo have all placed themselves in my capable hands."

"They're all good writers," Khela said. "I actually read Orinda's biography. It was quite moving. She put a human face on the situation so many thousands of children face in war-torn African nations."

"Orinda is really quite special to me," Sullivan said. "She came to this country having suffered brutalities in her homeland that I know I couldn't have survived." He moved closer to Khela, brushing her bare arm with the sleeve of his pricey sports jacket. "Orinda's strength and heart blew me away. She's the reason I started the Children's Relief Agency."

Khela stood a bit taller. "You're behind CRA?"

"I don't publicize it, but yes." Bradford took a step closer to her. "The proceeds from today's book sales will fund travel, healthcare and educational expenses for some of the child soldiers we've relocated from Uganda. *A Runaway Romance* will help a dozen children reclaim their lives."

"That's one of the advantages to writing," Khela said. She caught Carter's eye around Bradford's shoulder and waved him over. "My work on its own can't change the world, but the revenues it generates can."

"Hey," Carter said, standing beside Khela and slipping his arm around her waist.

"Mr. Sullivan," Khela said, "this is Carter Radcliffe."

Bradford spent another moment gazing at Khela before his eyes shifted to Carter's shoulder. Where Khela's handbag dangled at his side.

"Pleasure," Bradford said, giving Carter's hand a polite shake. "Are you an author, too?"

"No, I actually own a couple of properties in Boston," Carter said.

"That's how we met," Khela told Bradford. "I moved into one of Carter's buildings on Comm Ave."

"Commonwealth Avenue?" Bradford said, his interest in Carter now piqued. "Fine real estate in that part of Boston."

"It's not so bad around here, either," Carter said. "I imagine half the homes on this block are in the National Register of Historic Places. My brownstone was nominated for the register last year."

"It's a beautiful building, and Carter takes very good care of it." Khela placed her hand over his, which was on her right hip.

"We organize a house tour every fall to raise money for the Children's Relief Agency," Bradford said, speaking more to Khela than Carter. "We're scouting locations now. Would you be interested in having strangers parade through your building at a hundred dollars a head? The proceeds go to a very good cause."

"I don't see why not," Carter said.

"Give me your card and I'll have my assistant call yours to set up a time for us to meet to discuss the dates and details." Bradford lazily held out a hand to receive the business card, his eyes still fixed on Khela. "I think I might raise ticket prices since Miss Halliday would be an added attraction on the tour."

Khela smiled at the compliment. "Please, call me Khela."

"I don't have a card," Carter said flatly, his hand tightening at Khela's waist.

Bradford finally swung his gaze from Khela's face. "I'm sorry?"

"I don't have a business card," Carter said.

"That's no problem," Bradford said amiably. "Your assistant can call me first thing Monday morning." He fished two of his business cards from his inner breast pocket. Handing the first one to Khela, he said. "You're welcome to contact me if you'd care to learn more about the work I do with CRA." He offered the second one to Carter, who made no move to take it.

"I don't have an assistant," Carter said. "I don't work in an office. I don't do much of anything but polish banisters and hold onto my lady's purse." He turned to Khela, who was shocked by the sudden change in him, and pushed her purse into her arms. "Have your people call my management team if you want to use my house for your tour, Mr. Sullivan." With a grim nod, Carter turned and started for the front door.

"Please excuse me, Mr. Sullivan," Khela said before setting her tea on a music table and rushing after Carter. Politely nodding to the guests as they cut through them, she caught Carter by the arm and steered him into the rear garden. If she hadn't been so concerned about his behavior, she might have spent a moment appreciating the bountiful color and variety of the garden.

"I don't even know what to say to you right now," she said once they were well out of earshot of the house.

"Then don't say anything," Carter replied. "Just let me call a cab and we can get out of here."

Dismayed, Khela backed a few feet away from him. The angles of his beautifully symmetrical face were hard, and the sparkle that ordinarily lived in his pretty eyes was gone. His brow seemed to have lowered to hood his eyes, making him look that much more fearsome.

"I can't leave." Her voice broke over the hard lump that had formed in her throat. "I agreed to stay until five." She took his wrist to look at his watch. "Can you wait another twenty minutes?"

"Can't you leave twenty minutes early?"

"Are you sick?" she asked.

"I'm fine." He wouldn't meet her eyes. "I just need to leave."

"I made a commitment to these people, to this event," Khela insisted. "I can't just go for no reason."

A tiny muscle in his jaw jumped. Then he said, "I'm tired of holding your purse."

She tried to swallow the lump lodged in her throat, but it wouldn't budge. "I never asked you to do that."

"But I did it, and now it looks like that's all I'm good for." He laughed bitterly. "Well, that and being your man candy."

"I never—"

"Yes, you did," he said over her. "At the convention. I didn't mind so much because things were different then."

"Different?" She shook her head in confusion. "How? That event was business, same as this one."

"The difference is that I was only a prop at the convention," he said. "I'm not a prop anymore. If you need to stay, then stay." He cupped her face briefly, then turned to walk away. "But I'm goin' home."

"Carter, wait!"

Her shout stopped him, but he didn't turn around.

"You're leaving because of my purse?"

The emotion in her voice tugged at his heart, reeling him back to her. He embraced her, pressing his lips to her crown. "I love you, Miss Halliday. I really do."

Tears seeped from her eyes and wet his shirtfront. "I love you, too, you country-fried dumbass," she laughed.

"I want to be a part of your life," he said into her hair, kissing her temple. "I read your books so I could learn to love what you love."

She held him closer. "Did it work?"

"Yep." He kissed her then, tenderly touching his lips to hers. "That's why I have to go."

"Carter," she gasped, drawing away from him. "What is going on with you?"

"When I figure it out, darlin', you'll be the first to know."

"Miss Halliday?" a woman called from the glass doors. "We need you for photos."

"Not now," Khela responded sternly without looking at the woman. "Please," she added, softening her tone.

"Go on," Carter said. "I'll be okay."

She stepped closer to him and whispered, "I won't be! I need to know why you're walking out on me. *Again.*"

"Miss Halliday," the woman persisted, a touch of anxiousness in her voice now. "Everyone is waiting on you. The photographer, the volunteers, your fans—"

"You've got all these people in your life, Khela," Carter said, his voice cracking. "I don't just want to be someone you love. I want to be someone you respect. I want to be your hero."

"You are." Her eyes searched his, her tears striping her face.

"I'm a super, not a superhero," he said.

"I'm so sorry, Miss Halliday," the woman said, scurrying toward them, "but I really must insist—"

Carter took Khela by her shoulders and pulled her in for a quick, hard kiss. "Go," he said, giving her a little push toward the woman, who took her hand and started dragging her back into the house.

"Will you wait for me?" she called over her shoulder to Carter.

He gave no answer other than a somber wave as Khela disappeared into the recesses of the Dorian S. Fielder House.

CHAPTER 14

"How far past an ending can you claim a new beginning?"
—from A Runaway Romance *by Khela Halliday*

One of Llewellyn's colleagues volunteered the use of his home in Wakefield for the wedding ceremony and reception and, from her position on the dais facing a wall of French doors, Khela truly appreciated the beauty of the Colonial Revival home and its view of Lake Quannapowit.

Twenty-five guests sat in the solarium, an addition to the original blueprint of the 130-year-old home. Sunlight warmed the deep-mustard walls and bright white moldings, but a trio of white ceiling fans gently circulated the air coming through the open windows. The September breeze off the lake cooled the room more effectively than air conditioning would have, and Khela found it very comfortable in the ivory satin, knee-length Watters & Watters dress Daphne had chosen for the sunset ceremony. The A-line style of the garment and its simple tie at the Empire waist complemented the shape and style of Daphne's gown.

Khela's gaze went to Daphne, who sat beside the nattily dressed Llewellyn in seats of honor, just to the right of the dais. Daphne wanted no gift from Khela other than words, a reading penned by her best friend, maid of honor and favorite queen of romance.

Khela had kept the news of her bust-up with Carter to herself, so as not to distract or upset Daphne so close to the wedding. Daphne, Llewellyn and their guests had no idea that Khela Halliday, the reigning Torchbearer for romance, had failed yet again when her love was tested.

The reading had been one of the hardest pieces of writing Khela had ever attempted. It had been so difficult to put to paper words celebrating love when her own had crumbled around her. Two weeks ago, she had stood in the garden of a house every bit as beautiful as the one she was in now. Carter had explored the Fielder House, studying its details with an appreciation she respected but could never truly understand. She knew that, had he come to the wedding with her, Carter would have admired the architectural details of the Wakefield house as well. She entertained the sad possibility that Carter cared more for buildings than he did for people.

He certainly hadn't cared as much for her. By the time she had finished the photo shoot at the Fielder House, Carter was gone. He had left her for the second time, and this time Khela refused to be the one to initiate contact.

She gave her head a little shake, clearing it of her thoughts of Carter, and gazed at Daphne. The Yoshioka dress exquisitely complemented Daphne's skin tone and her hair, which had been intricately arranged in an upswept do styled around a gift from her new husband, a delicate, Cartier-produced replica of an emerald and diamond tiara designed by Prince Albert for Queen Victoria in 1845.

The jewels matched Daphne's eyes perfectly yet were no match for their beauty and sparkle as she gazed at Khela, Llewellyn's hand in both of hers and her heart in her lovely eyes.

Khela cleared her throat, but the lump of emotion plugging it refused to budge. She mustered a weak smile, one meant to put herself and her patient audience at ease, but all it did was make her feel as though her face was cracking. It had been fifteen days since Carter had stood sadly waving to her at the Fielder House. He hadn't just vanished from the garden. With no calls or e-mails from him, he seemed to have disappeared from her life entirely. The worst blow came a few days ago; she'd come home from Calareso's and found some overweight stranger in a Dickie's jumpsuit polishing the marble tile of the foyer.

She knew that it was unreasonable and immature to think that Carter had given up the care of his beloved brownstone just to avoid running into her . . . but that was exactly what she thought.

She cleared her throat again a bit louder, and then she smiled a bit wider. Taking a quick deep breath, she looked down at her note cards.

"I don't know what pornography is, but I know it when I see it," Khela began.

Daphne and Llewellyn, their guests, the officiate and the four members of the hired quartet all looked a bit taken aback. Some sat up straighter, Daphne's grand-mother's mouth dropped open, her grandfather—who hadn't changed the batteries in his hearing aids—bellowed, "Did she say something about pornography?" and Daphne's cheeks went five shades darker than her angel's blush gown.

"Even though I've made something of a name for myself as a purveyor of the stuff, I don't know what love is," Khela continued. "But I know it when I see it, and I see it there before me, between Daphne and Llewellyn."

A loving chuckle escaped Daphne, and with tears in her eyes, she blew Khela a kiss from her fingertips.

"Theirs is a true romance because it proves everything I know, in my professional opinion, to be true about love. It comes out of nowhere, like a force of nature. It won't be ignored, no matter how much you might want to. And it isn't static. It grows, day by day, and love changes as the people sharing it change. True love, real love, doesn't just wither and vanish in the face of adversity. On the contrary, adversity is the soil in which love thrives, growing stronger and more beautiful with each challenge it overcomes."

She paused, blinking moisture from her eyes. She looked up and beyond the guests seated on their fancy rented chairs, hoping a glimpse of the placid lake would ease the tightness growing in her chest.

Instead of the lake, Khela spotted Carter.

Dressed in a classically tailored ecru suit with a white shirt and tie, he stood outside the wall of French doors, hardly concealed by the narrow frames between the pairs of doors. His hands shoved in his pockets, he stood in profile, staring at his wingtips with one ear tipped to the door.

Khela wanted to call out to him, or even better, run to him. But with Daphne, Llewellyn and an assortment of their friends and relatives staring at her, Khela finished her remarks.

"Love is the most powerful and enduring commodity in the world. It is the currency that buys the only things we truly need in this life: companionship, respect, devotion and faith. True love, real love, is not the love I write about. It's what two people share, moving through each day as he rinses out the half-filled coffee cup she leaves in the sink, and she picks up the socks he puts on top of the hamper instead of lifting the lid and putting them inside."

Light chuckling from her audience accompanied Khela's wrap-up.

"Love isn't easy." She glanced up once more, and Carter was staring at her. "But it isn't hard, either, not if the people involved really mean it." She raised the flute of champagne at her right hand. "To Daphne and Llewellyn, and their once upon an ever after."

To warm applause, Khela left the dais and accepted kisses from Daphne and Llewellyn and handshakes from the guests seated nearest them. Her remarks had closed the wedding ceremony, so all the guests were now queuing up to congratulate the newlyweds.

Fighting her way through them, Khela crossed the big room to get to the French doors. She tossed open the middle pair and dashed onto the rear deck. The purple and magenta candy-colored light of the sunset bounced off the surface of the lake. The sight was so beautiful it almost erased Khela's pain at discovering that Carter had disappeared. Again.

⚬⚬⚬⚬⚬

Detrick shouldered his way between two patrons at the crowded bar and slid a twenty-dollar bill across its damp surface. "A roll of quarters, please," he told the bartender, speaking loudly to be heard over the din of pulsating music, conversations, video games and pool cues striking multicolored balls. "You can keep the change."

Spurred by Detrick's generosity, the bartender hastily traded the twenty for a $10-roll of quarters. Detrick thanked the black-clad woman, and inwardly cursed Carter for his bad timing as he left the bar and passed a group of young women stuffing themselves into an instant photo booth.

"Hey, you!" one of them called, a Latina with sparkling black eyes and a smile that could have seduced Detrick into burning down an orphanage. "Wanna take a photo with us?"

Wincing at the sight of the young woman's tiny waist and massive bosom, which was barely contained by her form-fitting, scoop-necked top, Detrick kept walking toward the rear exit. "I'm so sorry, baby, but I've got to go help my friend out."

"You know where to find me, okay, *papi*?" She turned, and gave him a saucy thrust of a hip that made the very most of what Detrick determined to be her best asset.

"I'm gonna kill you for this, Carter," Detrick swore under his breath as he hurried down a narrow flight of stairs, opened the service door and emerged into the loading area behind the club.

Carter was only vaguely aware of Detrick's arrival. The last punch he'd taken had left him on one knee, his head spinning crazily. He'd scraped a hole in the knee of his suit, and blood oozed from a cut underneath it. The cut on his knee was the little pain that distracted him from the bigger one in his face. The gorilla-sized Boston University football player who had invited him outside had dropped him with a right cross to his mouth. Carter's lower lip had blown up to twice its normal size.

The big blonde Terrier grabbed a handful of Carter's hair and pulled his head back, to better position Carter's face for another blow. "It's always the pretty ones that start fights they can't finish," the oaf said to his two friends, who laughed and sipped their beers.

The blond drew back his fist.

"I wouldn't do that if I were you." Detrick peeled off his jacket, an Italian wool cut on the bias for an exceptional fit. He handed it to one of the Terrier's friends. "Don't let this touch the ground," he commanded with a stern point of his finger.

"Gimme a minute," the Terrier grinned, looking every bit like a prize-winning hog at the Topsfield fair. "Let me finish with him and I'll deal with you."

Detrick shrugged his shoulders in wide circles and gave both sides of his neck loud cracks. "You gon' deal with me *now*, boy," he said, reverting to the 'Bama tongue of his youth. "Let 'im go."

The football player released Carter's hair, and Carter slumped forward on his hands and knees. The Terrier took three hard stomps toward Detrick, prepared to do the same thing to him that he'd done to Carter. He threw a hard right, which Detrick dodged. His left hand wrapped around the roll of quarters, Detrick launched his hammer hand in an uppercut that caught the big line-backer directly under the chin.

The Terrier's jaw snapped close, clipping the tip of his tongue. He squealed in pain and Detrick just managed to avoid the accompanying spray of blood before landing his second blow, a right hook to the Terrier's jaw that sent him spiraling to the greasy, grimy cement.

"Give me that," Detrick directed the friend who'd been holding his jacket. He gave the boy the roll of quarters as a tip, then spent a moment carefully turning the jacket inside out before he went to Carter and helped him to his feet. The Terrier's friends stood over his groaning, dazed form on the ground. Giggling, one of them poured beer on his face. Roused, the big Terrier growled and lunged for his friends, who ran off laughing. Wiping beer from his face, he stumbled after them.

Detrick spent a longing glance at the rear door of the club, somewhere behind which was a gorgeous young girl who had wanted to take a photo with him. Instead, he was half carried, half dragged Carter to his car.

"You know," Detrick grunted as he tumbled Carter into the front seat of his Jag, "I thought I'd like it if you started getting dolled up when we go out, but actually, I don't. We looked like Charlie Babbitt and Rainman when we got here." He buckled Carter's seatbelt around him. "Now we look like Charlie Babbitt and Crazyman."

Detrick got into the driver's seat and started the car, but he didn't pull away from the curb. "You were a Terrier," he said quietly. "You had to know what would happen after you told that big BU boy that Northeastern had a better defensive line this season than the Terriers."

Blood trickled from one of Carter's nostrils and his swollen lip impaired his speech as he said, "I was stating my opinion. No harm in that. I wasn't gonna back down from that kid."

Detrick snatched the handkerchief from his breast pocket and angrily thrust it at Carter. "No, you just stood there and let him get his licks in."

"I promised you I wouldn't fight anymore," Carter said. "I didn't."

"I get it, you can't beat yourself up, so you got some dumb kid to do it," Detrick said. He leaned back in the driver's seat, still too angry to trust himself in traffic behind the wheel of his car. "I don't care how upset you are about Khela. If you'd just manned up and taken your silly ass to that wedding, you could have made up with her instead of ruinin' my night."

"What happens after that?" Carter asked, his voice oddly nasal because of the blood clotting in his sinus cavities. "She'll still be the best-selling author, and I'll be Mr. Halliday, holding her purse."

Detrick's bald head whipped around so fast, the glint of the streetlight off his dome stabbed Carter's eyes. "Is that . . . You started a fight over . . . Man, have you lost your ever-lovin' mind?" shouted Detrick. He grabbed the steering wheel and stared upward. "Please, Jesus, tell me this dumb cracker boy is not really this stupid!"

"You wanna go a round?" Carter turned in his seat to face Detrick. "I didn't have it in me to beat that Terrier's ass, but I'll give you a run if you call me 'cracker' one more time."

"I read one of her books," Detrick confessed, changing the subject. "*Teacher's Pet.*"

"I was wondering where that one went," Carter said. "I haven't seen it since your last visit."

"Yeah, well, I needed something to read on the plane back to Mobile," Detrick said. "And once I started it at your place, I couldn't put it down. The girl can spin a tale."

"Don't I know it," Carter said. "She doesn't think that's enough, though."

"What do you mean?"

" 'From what we get, we can make a living; what we give, however, makes a life.' "

"Beg your pardon?" Detrick said.

"Khela's got that quote framed in her condo," Carter explained. "Arthur Ashe said it. Khela's got her own version of it. She believes you get what you give. She uses her writing to help other people because she's gotten so much from writing."

"She's a good person," Detrick said. He was calm enough to start driving, so he pulled into traffic.

"Too good for me," Carter said. "That's the problem."

"She donates a meat cake to an auction, and you think she's Mother Theresa?" Detrick asked incredulously.

"She's one of the most generous people I've ever met, and it's genuine," Carter said in defense of Khela. "She gives her time, her money, her talent—all without hesitation. What do I give? Nothing."

"She holds that against you?"

"Of course not. This isn't about her, it's about me. I want to be the kind of man she deserves, someone she can be proud of."

"Do you think she would have been proud of you tonight?"

Carter pressed the handkerchief a bit more snugly to his nose. "I don't know what to do, man. After I left her reading, I went home and called up some of my old contacts at my old firm."

"You're looking for a job?"

"I have a job, Trick," Carter said indignantly.

"I didn't mean it like that. I'm just surprised you're interested in going back into investing."

"That's just it," Carter sighed. "I'm not. I like taking care of my buildings. I'm good at it."

"Then if that's good enough for Khela, it should be good enough for you, too."

"But it's not good enough for me! Not anymore. I don't know how to fix this."

"Well, you better figure it out. And soon. That woman with her exploding, spiky genitalia and her meatloaf cakes is the best thing that's ever happened to you, cracker, and you truly are a dumbass if you let her get away. You like fighting so much. Fight for *her*."

———❧———

"What's the matter with you? We run out of that balsamic vinegar from Modena that you like so much?"

Khela looked her least favorite cashier right in the eyes and said, "Not today, Angela. I'm not in the mood. And I'd really appreciate it if you wouldn't put my eggs in the bottom of the bag this time."

Muttering under her breath, Angela continued to ring up Khela's groceries. "Excuse me," she mumbled. "Seems like everybody who comes in here today has to show me some attitude. First I get it from Mr. Alabama, now I gotta take it from—"

"You saw Carter today?" Khela interrupted.

Angela's eyes glittered. "He had a meeting with the manager." Her lips curled into a feline grin. "You didn't know about it?"

"I'm not his keeper," Khela snapped. "He doesn't have to report to me. We're not married, you know."

With deliberate slowness, Angela struck the TOTAL key. "Eighty-six dollars and nineteen cents. Would you like this on your account?" she asked.

"Please," Khela said.

"Plastic or paper?" Angela asked, turning to bag the items.

"It doesn't matter."

"Paper, it is," Angela said.

Angela kept glancing at Khela as she packed Khela's purchases into two bags. "Are you all right?" she asked.

Khela looked over her shoulder, convinced that Angela's kind inquiry was meant for someone else.

"He seemed a little funny when he was here," Angela went on, tearing off Khela's receipt and sticking it into one of her bags. "I thought for sure that you two were good to go."

"What does that mean?" Khela asked.

Another customer came up behind her and started emptying her basket onto Angela's conveyor belt. Khela took her bags by their handles and lifted them off the packing counter. She was pleased to see that Angela had voluntarily double-bagged them.

"It means that I thought you two were the real thing," Angela said as she began ringing out her next customer. "Look here," she said with a low whistle, taking a second to examine the customer's package of panko. "Japanese bread crumbs. American bread crumbs not good enough for you?"

Her bags in hand, Khela started walking toward the exit, Angela's words ringing in her head.

I thought we were the real thing, too, she thought as she made her way home.

Halloween was almost three weeks away, and all the storefronts were decorated in orange and black with witches and ghosts, jack-o-lanterns and black cats. The bakery on Boylston Street that had made Daphne's wedding cake featured a Halloween-themed wedding cake in its front window display. The five-tiered cake had a flawless covering of bile green fondant with royal icing spiders, ghosts and goblins applied all over it. A tiny witch and warlock, wands crossed, stood atop the cake.

"That's the ugliest cake I've ever seen," Khela muttered before moving on.

Her meatloaf cake might not have been traditional, but at least it had been pretty. And tasty, judging by Carter's reaction to it. Almost six weeks had passed since she'd last seen him. Daphne, who had spent two weeks in Spain and Portugal on her honeymoon with Llewellyn before settling in the UK, had threatened to come back to Boston specifically to confront Carter since Khela refused to do it.

Khela had hoped that, as more time passed, she would miss Carter less. The opposite had occurred. She spent her days writing to meet her next deadline, and her weekends were spent doing signings and other appearances. She had an event at a bookstore in Dorchester the next day, and as she walked home, she thought about the last time she had been in that part of Boston. Carter had been with her. Signings had been so much more fun with him there.

She turned the corner onto Commonwealth Avenue and found herself looking toward his building. She had long given up the hope of seeing him entering or leaving, but the last thing she expected to see was a big moving van parked in front of it.

A retractable ramp formed a bridge from the side loading deck to the front walkway. Eight uniformed men moved with the efficiency of worker ants as they loaded furniture into the van and marched out empty-handed, presumably to get more. Khela's stomach sank when she saw two men carrying the darkly-stained teak headboard of a sleigh bed. She recognized that bed. She was intimately familiar with that bed.

Dropping her groceries, she ran to Carter's building, scaling the steep, stamp-sized front lawn to bypass the movers. Another pair of movers was wrestling the footboard of the sleigh bed out of the elevator and, rather than wait for them to finish, Khela took to the stairs. Running faster than she ever knew she could, she flew up to the top floor, where she found Carter's front door standing wide open.

"Carter?" she called, fighting to catch her breath as she entered the apartment. "Car—"

The place was deserted and nearly empty. The only objects left in the living room were a neutral area rug and the sheers hanging from the windows. The unit seemed so much larger bereft of furniture.

"Can I help you with something, miss?" came a voice at Khela's right shoulder. She spun to find a mover holding a clipboard.

"No, I . . ." She stopped until she could speak through the lump plugging her throat. "I know the man who lives here."

The man gave her a good-natured chuckle. "He doesn't live here anymore. We've packed him up and we're taking everything to a storage facility."

"Can you tell me where he is?"

"Don't know," the man said. "All I know is that we're to have this apartment emptied by five so the new owner can take a walk-through and take possession by—"

"New owner?" Khela gasped. "This building's been sold?"

"All I know is what's on my packing form," the man said. "I'm to have this place emptied for an inspection by the new owner. I don't know if it's the whole building, just this unit, or—"

Khela took off again, digging her cell phone out of her purse as she hurried down the stairs. Once she had it, she dialed Carter's number. It picked up on the third ring: *"We're sorry, you have reached a number that has been disconnected or is no longer in service. If you feel you have reached this recording in error—"*

She closed her phone and shoved it into the back pocket of her shorts. While waiting for two movers to maneuver Carter's shrink-wrapped king-size mattress through the front doors, Khela caught sight of a notice posted above the five narrow mailboxes in the opposite wall.

It was addressed personally to the tenants of the townhouse, and Khela had to read it twice before she fully absorbed what it said:

As much as I have enjoyed owning and residing in this building, I must inform you that I have sold the property and will vacate the premises on October 15. There will be no changes to the rental agreements currently on file for each tenant. CR Management will continue to maintain the building and handle its leasing and rentals; however, I will no longer have a day-to-day hand in the operations and tenancy of this building.

Very sincerely yours,
Carter M. Radcliffe

The notice was dated October 1. Turning away, Khela's heart sank into her gut. Two weeks . . . for two weeks, his tenants had known that he'd sold the townhouse and was moving out, and he hadn't bothered to call, e-mail, or walk across the street to tell her. Panic exploded in her as she exited the building, nearly colliding with one of the movers. She dashed around the moving van and into Commonwealth Avenue, where two cars had to slam on their brakes to avoid hitting her. They leaned on their horns, the ugly blaring following Khela as she sprinted to her brownstone, up the stairs and into the lobby.

Breathing hard, she went to the mailboxes and scanned the wall. Had Carter posted a notice there, too, and she just hadn't seen it? She searched all the walls, and seeing nothing out of the ordinary, she calmed somewhat. But her heart continued to throb painfully.

He's leaving, she told herself. *He sold his building and he's leaving.*

Her heart heavy, Khela bypassed the elevator and went to the stairs. She was accustomed to being alone, but as she climbed to the top floor of the brownstone, she had never felt lonelier.

~∿~

Caravan Books was situated between Fa-Shoe-Nista and Bixby's Olde Style Good Eatin' Buffet in a strip mall in Dorchester. This particular Caravan store was new, and the manager had requested a signing by Khela as part of an effort to increase customer traffic to the entire mall, which had been completely renovated as part of an effort to revitalize the economically depressed neighborhood.

Cameo and Khela's publicist had wanted her to decline the invitation, but the minority-owned bookstore, the largest bookstore in the area, was less than a block from Crispus Attucks High School. Even though she was in no mood for a signing the day after finding out about Carter's sale of his townhouse, Khela had no intention of turning her back on the community that had so embraced her and her work. She showed up at Caravan with a smile, eager to do what she could to draw customers to the store.

Cortez and Luisa were among the first in line to receive signed copies of *A Runaway Romance*, Khela's latest. Customers, some toting copies of Khela's previous books, were lined up at her signing table before her arrival even though her driver had delivered her to the location a half hour early. Her handlers and the store representatives were experienced and patient, the magical combination for a successful signing.

Khela graciously thanked them for all the hard work they had already invested in displaying her books, positioning signage and keeping the waiting readers happy and amused. Calareso's Market had provided coffee, tea, soft drinks and fresh bakery goods, giving the independent store the café atmosphere of a Borders or a Barnes & Noble.

Khela always provided her own signing favors—promotional materials designed to stand out from the usual bookmarks and ballpoint pens other writers typically offered their readers. Taking her time so as not to forget anything, Khela positioned stacks of oversized refrigerator magnets, Post-It pads, boxes of wooden matches, miniature chocolate bars and tea bags adorned with the images of her book covers. One of her handlers questioned her choices of promotional schwag, noting that the items didn't seem to go together.

Khela's explanation had been simple. "I want people to think of my books at times when they aren't typically thinking of books. If my book cover is on the fridge, the reader will see it every time she opens the door to take out milk or eggs. The next time she's at the bookstore, hopefully she'll have my name, if not my book cover, in her head.

"As for the other stuff, I like to give people things that are useful. It's always nice to have matches in the house, and Post-It pads are handy in your purse, on your desk, or by the phone. And I'd love it if someone relaxed with a hot cup of tea brewed with one of my custom tea bags and munched a few chocolates while reading one of my books. Everything actually does go together because it all has something to do with my books."

Now, with what looked to be the entire female reading population of Dorchester lining up before her,

Khela was glad that the bookstore had provided *A Runaway Romance* tote bags for her readers. Determined not to have to lug all of her promotional items back to her hotel, she knew that she would be handing over schwag by the handfuls.

"Are you ready, Ms. Halliday?" her petite brunette handler asked.

"Send 'em on," Khela responded. "And please, call me Khela."

The first hour of the signing passed quickly, with customers familiar with her books taking *A Runaway Romance* from one of the tall, spiraling stacks, bringing it to her for a signature and then moving on to do the rest of their shopping.

Khela rose to greet and kiss the cheek of a reader named Mary, who always turned up at her signings no matter where she appeared in New England. Khela signed Mary's book after writing a long personalized message, and then placed a gold star on the book. Gold stars signified a complimentary copy of the book for which the customer was not to be charged.

Midway through the second hour of her signing, Khela found herself meeting a number of what she called "newbies," readers who had never heard of her or her work, but who showed an interest because she was live and in person in the store. At every signing, at least one person made a point to approach her, study her book cover, flip it over and read the back blurb, ask her questions about herself and her publishing history, and then slap the book down, telling her that romance wasn't real literature and that she—or sometimes he—wouldn't waste money on it.

Khela, her attention on a customer, caught a flicker of movement at the end of her signing table. The person had taken a book from the dwindling stack, and was standing there reading the back cover while Khela spoke to the woman in front of her.

"I have loved you ever since your first book came out," the woman said, her eyes as shiny and gray as her hair. "I only buy Cameo romances, and I'm so glad that you write so many books for them."

"Thank you," Khela said. "I think my publisher would be very happy to hear that."

"I introduced my sister Gustine to your books, and now she can't wait for your stuff to come out," the older woman continued. "She won't buy them, though. No, she waits for me to finish them, then she borrows 'em from me and won't give 'em back. It's been like that between us for some forty years."

"It's nice that you have a sister that you're so close to." Khela slid the signed book to the woman, whose name was Justine.

"You know," Justine said, lowering her voice. "I wrote a book."

Khela's face stiffened behind her smile. If she'd had a panic button, she would have slammed her hand on it.

One of her handlers noticed her panicked expression and swooped in to move Justine along before the inevitable request—to read or forward a manuscript— was spoken.

The lurker to Khela's right beat the handler to it, as a copy of *A Runaway Romance* was laid before Khela. She opened the book as the handler politely escorted Justine away, luring her with a pastel pink tote bag emblazoned with *A Runaway Romance* in glossy black letters.

"To whom shall I make this out?" Khela asked, flipping to the title page.

" 'Dumbass' will do."

Khela looked up, her eyes wide and her jaw falling.

"Carter," she sighed, slowly standing.

"Ooh, he looks just like Cale from *A Warrior's Secret*," one of the women in line gushed, clasping her hands under her chin.

"I think he looks like Ken, from *An Angel's Prayer*," offered another woman.

"Look at him," said a thin man in tight, skinny leg jeans and a bubble-gum pink Polo that stretched tight across his overdeveloped chest, biceps and shoulders. "That pretty little thing has to be the model for Lincoln Drake, from *Practically Perfect*." He crossed his arms and thrust out a hip. "It has to be a crime for a man to be so fine."

Oblivious to the speculation going on behind him, Carter touched Khela's face, near her chin. She leaned forward over the table, drawn to him by his whispery touch.

"Her boyfriend is white?" came a faint voice further down the line.

"I'll understand if you don't want to talk to me," he whispered against her lips, his fingers moving to hold her chin in place. "But I hope you'll do me the courtesy of just listening."

"I saw you at the wedding last month." Tears blurred her vision, and his handsome face swam before her. "Why didn't you come in? The ceremony was beautiful."

"I know. The best part was the ending."

"I know how much you like endings."

He cupped her face, tenderly, wiping away her tears with his thumbs. "Adversity is the soil in which love thrives," he said earnestly.

A tiny laugh escaped her. "Are you seriously going to throw my words back at me at a time like this?"

"None of my own are better. I'm sorry, Khela. I was jealous and pig-headed. When I saw you talking to Bradford Sullivan at the Fielder House, I thought he looked just like the men in your books. Like the kind of man you should be with. Someone smart and good-lookin', but someone who is a real hero. Someone who does what you do."

"I make up stories," Khela chuckled around a sob. "I don't fight fires or arrest criminals."

"You're here, aren't you?" Carter said. "You came down here today because you wanted to make a difference in this neighborhood. That's why I've been down here, too."

"I don't understand," Khela said, accepting a tissue from the woman in line behind Carter.

"I asked the manager here to invite you to sign at this store," he said. "I got Calareso's to cater the signing. I knew folks would come down to see you, and they'll patronize the other stores, too."

"If you wanted to see me, all you had to do was call," she said. "Or write. Or cross the street."

"I wanted to see you, Khela, but I wanted you down here today because there's something I need you to see."

"Why didn't you tell me that you sold your townhouse and moved out?" She pulled back a bit to dry her eyes and mop her nose.

"You found out about that." He dropped his hands.

"The hard way."

"I needed a lot of money quickly," he said. "A lot of folks have been interested in buying that townhouse for years. Detrick brokered a good price for it."

"You did an excellent job restoring it," Khela said. "Your work probably doubled its value."

"Just about," Carter smiled. "I got much more for it than Detrick imagined I would. I was able to do a lot with the proceeds."

"Like what?" Khela asked.

Carter showed her. He handed her a business card.

"Put Your Heart In A Home," Khela read from the card. "Carter Radcliffe, Founder and President." She looked at him. "What is this?"

"It's my new company," he said. "We go into depressed neighborhoods and buy up the existing housing structures. We demolish and rebuild from the ground up, if we have to, or make whatever repairs and improvements the buildings need. Once the homes are habitable, we'll open them up to low-income families in need of housing on a rent-to-own basis." He took her hand and guided her around the table. "You folks don't mind if Khela takes a little walk with me, do you?"

No one complained. In fact, the line of waiting readers decided to follow Carter as he led Khela to the front door of the store.

"See those rowhouses down the street a ways there?" he asked, pointing in the direction of Crispus Attucks High. "My company bought all of 'em. Got 'em for a good price, too. The foundations are solid, and you should see the moldings and fixtures in some of them. All those buildings need is some TLC and elbow grease, and they'll be tiptop. We should have them ready for folks to move in by March. We've already got eligible applicants who are interested in them, and we're starting a waiting list."

"This is what you've been doing in the past six weeks?" Khela said, her voice constricted by tears.

"This and getting a new place of my own." He took her hands and held them to his heart. "I think I'm ready for a house, too. Something with four or five bedrooms and a big ol' backyard. And a smart, beautiful, loving lady to share it with." Khela dropped her face and Carter had to take her chin to steer her gaze back to his. "Will you forgive me?"

"Of course, I'll forgive you," she said. "It's not like you were off carousing with other women. But . . ." She turned and retreated to her signing table.

"But you're not sure about taking me back," Carter finished, following close behind her.

"How do I know you won't leave again?" she asked, her tears starting anew. "What happens the next time someone calls you Mr. Halliday? And they will, you know. Or the next time some other man comes along and makes you feel like you're not doing enough to impress the world?"

"I don't need to impress the world," he insisted. "Just you. I don't care what anyone else thinks of me."

"I loved you just the way you were," Khela said. "I love what you've done. I think it's amazing and wonderful. But you didn't have to do it for me."

"Hold on, now, missy," Carter said. "I started this company for *me*." He emphasized his words with a poke to his chest. "I needed to feel that I deserved a woman like you. You're my hero. I wanted to be yours. I'm sorry I didn't handle the situation better, but I'm not as good with words as you are. I'm better with actions."

"Forgive him, honey!" came the urgent whisper of a little old lady clutching copies of *Captured By a Captain* and *A Proper Princess*.

"If you don't take him, I will," said the man in pink, patting his shellacked hair in place.

"I hope she says no," came another soft, female voice. "I'd love to be his rebound."

A flash of empathy smoothed Khela's way to forgiveness. "I love you," she said. "I wished for you. I didn't know it when I was doing it, but every hero I've ever written has been you."

"I think I fell in love with you that first day I saw you walk into the brownstone," Carter said with a big smile. "I don't know if it was that ponytail swingin', or this delicious dark skin, or that slammin' ass, but I haven't been the same since you moved into my heart."

"You mean your brownstone," she corrected.

He shook his head. "Nope. I mean my heart. I love you, Khela. Always have."

She wrapped her arms around him, and with the strength and style of an old-time movie hero, she spun Carter onto the table, cradling him in her arms and smothering him in a joyous, messy kiss of forgiveness.

Customers gathered around the table, some applauding, some recording the event on their cell phones, and others staring hard as though they could learn a thing or two about kissing by watching a romance novelist do it.

"Howdy," Carter exhaled once Khela allowed him to break for air. "You missed me, too, didn't you, baby?"

"Excuse me, Ms. Halliday," one of the handlers fearfully interrupted. "We've only got fifteen minutes left here. I hate to disturb this, but I've got to ask Mr. Halliday to let you get back to—"

"He's not Mr. Halliday," Khela corrected. "His name is Carter Radcliffe. He's not my husband yet. But he's going to be."

"Is that right?" Carter laughed, sitting up and scooting off the table.

"It's the only way to get people to stop calling you Mr. Halliday," she explained.

"Then I s'pose we best get hitched," Carter agreed. "But right now, you have some books to sell." He gave her cheek a final caress that sent glorious tremors of anticipation through her. "I'm gonna go and rustle up some more business for you."

Grabbing a stack of books, Carter made his way through the store, talking up *A Runaway Romance* like a carnival barker.

Khela's handler, wide-mouthed, stood watching until Carter disappeared into the Fantasy and Detective Stories section.

"Where did you find *him?*" the handler asked, clearly awestruck.

"In a real-life romance," Khela laughed.

She resumed her seat. With renewed excitement, she signed book after book, thanking her readers for believing in the kind of love that, until now, she hadn't believed in herself.

The End

ABOUT THE AUTHOR

Crystal Hubbard is the author of five highly acclaimed Genesis Press romances and an award-winning children's book. The mother of four, Crystal resides in St. Louis, Mo., where she is currently undergoing treatment for adenocarcinoma.

Visit her online at *www.crystalhubbard.com* or e-mail her at *crystalhubbardbooks@yahoo.com*.

2008 Reprint Mass Market Titles

January

Cautious Heart
Cheris F. Hodges
ISBN-13: 978-1-58571-301-1
ISBN-10: 1-58571-301-5
$6.99

Suddenly You
Crystal Hubbard
ISBN-13: 978-1-58571-302-8
ISBN-10: 1-58571-302-3
$6.99

February

Passion
T. T. Henderson
ISBN-13: 978-1-58571-303-5
ISBN-10: 1-58571-303-1
$6.99

Whispers in the Sand
LaFlorya Gauthier
ISBN-13: 978-1-58571-304-2
ISBN-10: 1-58571-304-x
$6.99

March

Life Is Never As It Seems
J. J. Michael
ISBN-13: 978-1-58571-305-9
ISBN-10: 1-58571-305-8
$6.99

Beyond the Rapture
Beverly Clark
ISBN-13: 978-1-58571-306-6
ISBN-10: 1-58571-306-6
$6.99

April

A Heart's Awakening
Veronica Parker
ISBN-13: 978-1-58571-307-3
ISBN-10: 1-58571-307-4
$6.99

Breeze
Robin Lynette Hampton
ISBN-13: 978-1-58571-308-0
ISBN-10: 1-58571-308-2
$6.99

May

I'll Be Your Shelter
Giselle Carmichael
ISBN-13: 978-1-58571-309-7
ISBN-10: 1-58571-309-0
$6.99

Careless Whispers
Rochelle Alers
ISBN-13: 978-1-58571-310-3
ISBN-10: 1-58571-310-4
$6.99

June

Sin
Crystal Rhodes
ISBN-13: 978-1-58571-311-0
ISBN-10: 1-58571-311-2
$6.99

Dark Storm Rising
Chinelu Moore
ISBN-13: 978-1-58571-312-7
ISBN-10: 1-58571-312-0
$6.99

2008 Reprint Mass Market Titles (continued)

July

Object of His Desire
A.C. Arthur
ISBN-13: 978-1-58571-313-4
ISBN-10: 1-58571-313-9
$6.99

Angel's Paradise
Janice Angelique
ISBN-13: 978-1-58571-314-1
ISBN-10: 1-58571-314-7
$6.99

August

Unbreak My Heart
Dar Tomlinson
ISBN-13: 978-1-58571-315-8
ISBN-10: 1-58571-315-5
$6.99

All I Ask
Barbara Keaton
ISBN-13: 978-1-58571-316-5
ISBN-10: 1-58571-316-3
$6.99

September

Icie
Pamela Leigh Starr
ISBN-13: 978-1-58571-275-5
ISBN-10: 1-58571-275-2
$6.99

At Last
Lisa Riley
ISBN-13: 978-1-58571-276-2
ISBN-10: 1-58571-276-0
$6.99

October

Everlastin' Love
Gay G. Gunn
ISBN-13: 978-1-58571-277-9
ISBN-10: 1-58571-277-9
$6.99

Three Wishes
Seressia Glass
ISBN-13: 978-1-58571-278-6
ISBN-10: 1-58571-278-7
$6.99

November

Yesterday Is Gone
Beverly Clark
ISBN-13: 978-1-58571-279-3
ISBN-10: 1-58571-279-5
$6.99

Again My Love
Kayla Perrin
ISBN-13: 978-1-58571-280-9
ISBN-10: 1-58571-280-9
$6.99

December

Office Policy
A.C. Arthur
ISBN-13: 978-1-58571-281-6
ISBN-10: 1-58571-281-7
$6.99

Rendezvous With Fate
Jeanne Sumerix
ISBN-13: 978-1-58571-283-3
ISBN-10: 1-58571-283-3
$6.99

2008 New Mass Market Titles

January

Where I Want To Be
Maryam Diaab
ISBN-13: 978-1-58571-268-7
ISBN-10: 1-58571-268-X
$6.99

Never Say Never
Michele Cameron
ISBN-13: 978-1-58571-269-4
ISBN-10: 1-58571-269-8
$6.99

February

Stolen Memories
Michele Sudler
ISBN-13: 978-1-58571-270-0
ISBN-10: 1-58571-270-1
$6.99

Dawn's Harbor
Kymberly Hunt
ISBN-13: 978-1-58571-271-7
ISBN-10: 1-58571-271-X
$6.99

March

Undying Love
Renee Alexis
ISBN-13: 978-1-58571-272-4
ISBN-10: 1-58571-272-8
$6.99

Blame It On Paradise
Crystal Hubbard
ISBN-13: 978-1-58571-273-1
ISBN-10: 1-58571-273-6
$6.99

April

When A Man Loves A Woman
La Connie Taylor-Jones
ISBN-13: 978-1-58571-274-8
ISBN-10: 1-58571-274-4
$6.99

Choices
Tammy Williams
ISBN-13: 978-1-58571-300-4
ISBN-10: 1-58571-300-7
$6.99

May

Dream Runner
Gail McFarland
ISBN-13: 978-1-58571-317-2
ISBN-10: 1-58571-317-1
$6.99

Southern Fried Standards
S.R. Maddox
ISBN-13: 978-1-58571-318-9
ISBN-10: 1-58571-318-X
$6.99

June

Looking for Lily
Africa Fine
ISBN-13: 978-1-58571-319-6
ISBN-10: 1-58571-319-8
$6.99

Bliss, Inc.
Chamein Canton
ISBN-13: 978-1-58571-325-7
ISBN-10: 1-58571-325-2
$6.99

2008 New Mass Market Titles (continued)

July

Love's Secrets
Yolanda McVey
ISBN-13: 978-1-58571-321-9
ISBN-10: 1-58571-321-X
$6.99

Things Forbidden
Maryam Diaab
ISBN-13: 978-1-58571-327-1
ISBN-10: 1-58571-327-9
$6.99

August

Storm
Pamela Leigh Starr
ISBN-13: 978-1-58571-323-3
ISBN-10: 1-58571-323-6
$6.99

Passion's Furies
AlTonya Washington
ISBN-13: 978-1-58571-324-0
ISBN-10: 1-58571-324-4
$6.99

September

Three Doors Down
Michele Sudler
ISBN-13: 978-1-58571-332-5
ISBN-10: 1-58571-332-5
$6.99

Mr Fix-It
Crystal Hubbard
ISBN-13: 978-1-58571-326-4
ISBN-10: 1-58571-326-0
$6.99

October

Moments of Clarity
Michele Cameron
ISBN-13: 978-1-58571-330-1
ISBN-10: 1-58571-330-9
$6.99

Lady Preacher
K.T. Richey
ISBN-13: 978-1-58571-333-2
ISBN-10: 1-58571-333-3
$6.99

November

This Life Isn't Perfect Holla
Sandra Foy
ISBN: 978-1-58571-331-8
ISBN-10: 1-58571-331-7
$6.99

Promises Made
Bernice Layton
ISBN-13: 978-1-58571-334-9
ISBN-10: 1-58571-334-1
$6.99

December

A Voice Behind Thunder
Carrie Elizabeth Greene
ISBN-13: 978-1-58571-329-5
ISBN-10: 1-58571-329-5
$6.99

The More Things Change
Chamein Canton
ISBN-13: 978-1-58571-328-8
ISBN-10: 1-58571-328-7
$6.99

Other Genesis Press, Inc. Titles

A Dangerous Deception	J.M. Jeffries	$8.95
A Dangerous Love	J.M. Jeffries	$8.95
A Dangerous Obsession	J.M. Jeffries	$8.95
A Drummer's Beat to Mend	Kei Swanson	$9.95
A Happy Life	Charlotte Harris	$9.95
A Heart's Awakening	Veronica Parker	$9.95
A Lark on the Wing	Phyliss Hamilton	$9.95
A Love of Her Own	Cheris F. Hodges	$9.95
A Love to Cherish	Beverly Clark	$8.95
A Risk of Rain	Dar Tomlinson	$8.95
A Taste of Temptation	Reneé Alexis	$9.95
A Twist of Fate	Beverly Clark	$8.95
A Will to Love	Angie Daniels	$9.95
Acquisitions	Kimberley White	$8.95
Across	Carol Payne	$12.95
After the Vows	Leslie Esdaile	$10.95
(Summer Anthology)	T.T. Henderson	
	Jacqueline Thomas	
Again My Love	Kayla Perrin	$10.95
Against the Wind	Gwynne Forster	$8.95
All I Ask	Barbara Keaton	$8.95
Always You	Crystal Hubbard	$6.99
Ambrosia	T.T. Henderson	$8.95
An Unfinished Love Affair	Barbara Keaton	$8.95
And Then Came You	Dorothy Elizabeth Love	$8.95
Angel's Paradise	Janice Angelique	$9.95
At Last	Lisa G. Riley	$8.95
Best of Friends	Natalie Dunbar	$8.95
Beyond the Rapture	Beverly Clark	$9.95

Other Genesis Press, Inc. Titles (continued)

Blaze	Barbara Keaton	$9.95
Blood Lust	J. M. Jeffries	$9.95
Blood Seduction	J.M. Jeffries	$9.95
Bodyguard	Andrea Jackson	$9.95
Boss of Me	Diana Nyad	$8.95
Bound by Love	Beverly Clark	$8.95
Breeze	Robin Hampton Allen	$10.95
Broken	Dar Tomlinson	$24.95
By Design	Barbara Keaton	$8.95
Cajun Heat	Charlene Berry	$8.95
Careless Whispers	Rochelle Alers	$8.95
Cats & Other Tales	Marilyn Wagner	$8.95
Caught in a Trap	Andre Michelle	$8.95
Caught Up In the Rapture	Lisa G. Riley	$9.95
Cautious Heart	Cheris F Hodges	$8.95
Chances	Pamela Leigh Starr	$8.95
Cherish the Flame	Beverly Clark	$8.95
Class Reunion	Irma Jenkins/	
	John Brown	$12.95
Code Name: Diva	J.M. Jeffries	$9.95
Conquering Dr. Wexler's Heart	Kimberley White	$9.95
Corporate Seduction	A.C. Arthur	$9.95
Crossing Paths, Tempting Memories	Dorothy Elizabeth Love	$9.95
Crush	Crystal Hubbard	$9.95
Cypress Whisperings	Phyllis Hamilton	$8.95
Dark Embrace	Crystal Wilson Harris	$8.95
Dark Storm Rising	Chinelu Moore	$10.95

Other Genesis Press, Inc. Titles (continued)

Other Genesis Press, Inc. Titles (continued)

Other Genesis Press, Inc. Titles (continued)

Last Train to Memphis	Elsa Cook	$12.95
Lasting Valor	Ken Olsen	$24.95
Let Us Prey	Hunter Lundy	$25.95
Lies Too Long	Pamela Ridley	$13.95
Life Is Never As It Seems	J.J. Michael	$12.95
Lighter Shade of Brown	Vicki Andrews	$8.95
Love Always	Mildred E. Riley	$10.95
Love Doesn't Come Easy	Charlyne Dickerson	$8.95
Love Unveiled	Gloria Greene	$10.95
Love's Deception	Charlene Berry	$10.95
Love's Destiny	M. Loui Quezada	$8.95
Mae's Promise	Melody Walcott	$8.95
Magnolia Sunset	Giselle Carmichael	$8.95
Many Shades of Gray	Dyanne Davis	$6.99
Matters of Life and Death	Lesego Malepe, Ph.D.	$15.95
Meant to Be	Jeanne Sumerix	$8.95
Midnight Clear	Leslie Esdaile	$10.95
(Anthology)	Gwynne Forster	
	Carmen Green	
	Monica Jackson	
Midnight Magic	Gwynne Forster	$8.95
Midnight Peril	Vicki Andrews	$10.95
Misconceptions	Pamela Leigh Starr	$9.95
Montgomery's Children	Richard Perry	$14.95
My Buffalo Soldier	Barbara B. K. Reeves	$8.95
Naked Soul	Gwynne Forster	$8.95
Next to Last Chance	Louisa Dixon	$24.95
No Apologies	Seressia Glass	$8.95
No Commitment Required	Seressia Glass	$8.95

Other Genesis Press, Inc. Titles (continued)

No Regrets	Mildred E. Riley	$8.95
Not His Type	Chamein Canton	$6.99
Nowhere to Run	Gay G. Gunn	$10.95
O Bed! O Breakfast!	Rob Kuehnle	$14.95
Object of His Desire	A. C. Arthur	$8.95
Office Policy	A. C. Arthur	$9.95
Once in a Blue Moon	Dorianne Cole	$9.95
One Day at a Time	Bella McFarland	$8.95
One in A Million	Barbara Keaton	$6.99
One of These Days	Michele Sudler	$9.95
Outside Chance	Louisa Dixon	$24.95
Passion	T.T. Henderson	$10.95
Passion's Blood	Cherif Fortin	$22.95
Passion's Journey	Wanda Y. Thomas	$8.95
Past Promises	Jahmel West	$8.95
Path of Fire	T.T. Henderson	$8.95
Path of Thorns	Annetta P. Lee	$9.95
Peace Be Still	Colette Haywood	$12.95
Picture Perfect	Reon Carter	$8.95
Playing for Keeps	Stephanie Salinas	$8.95
Pride & Joi	Gay G. Gunn	$15.95
Pride & Joi	Gay G. Gunn	$8.95
Promises to Keep	Alicia Wiggins	$8.95
Quiet Storm	Donna Hill	$10.95
Reckless Surrender	Rochelle Alers	$6.95
Red Polka Dot in a World of Plaid	Varian Johnson	$12.95
Reluctant Captive	Joyce Jackson	$8.95
Rendezvous with Fate	Jeanne Sumerix	$8.95

Other Genesis Press, Inc. Titles (continued)

Other Genesis Press, Inc. Titles (continued)

Sweet Tomorrows	Kimberly White	$8.95
Taken by You	Dorothy Elizabeth Love	$9.95
Tattooed Tears	T. T. Henderson	$8.95
The Color Line	Lizzette Grayson Carter	$9.95
The Color of Trouble	Dyanne Davis	$8.95
The Disappearance of Allison Jones	Kayla Perrin	$5.95
The Fires Within	Beverly Clark	$9.95
The Foursome	Celya Bowers	$6.99
The Honey Dipper's Legacy	Pannell-Allen	$14.95
The Joker's Love Tune	Sidney Rickman	$15.95
The Little Pretender	Barbara Cartland	$10.95
The Love We Had	Natalie Dunbar	$8.95
The Man Who Could Fly	Bob & Milana Beamon	$18.95
The Missing Link	Charlyne Dickerson	$8.95
The Mission	Pamela Leigh Starr	$6.99
The Perfect Frame	Beverly Clark	$9.95
The Price of Love	Sinclair LeBeau	$8.95
The Smoking Life	Ilene Barth	$29.95
The Words of the Pitcher	Kei Swanson	$8.95
Three Wishes	Seressia Glass	$8.95
Ties That Bind	Kathleen Suzanne	$8.95
Tiger Woods	Libby Hughes	$5.95
Time is of the Essence	Angie Daniels	$9.95
Timeless Devotion	Bella McFarland	$9.95
Tomorrow's Promise	Leslie Esdaile	$8.95
Truly Inseparable	Wanda Y. Thomas	$8.95
Two Sides to Every Story	Dyanne Davis	$9.95
Unbreak My Heart	Dar Tomlinson	$8.95

Other Genesis Press, Inc. Titles (continued)

Uncommon Prayer	Kenneth Swanson	$9.95
Unconditional Love	Alicia Wiggins	$8.95
Unconditional	A.C. Arthur	$9.95
Until Death Do Us Part	Susan Paul	$8.95
Vows of Passion	Bella McFarland	$9.95
Wedding Gown	Dyanne Davis	$8.95
What's Under Benjamin's Bed	Sandra Schaffer	$8.95
When Dreams Float	Dorothy Elizabeth Love	$8.95
When I'm With You	LaConnie Taylor-Jones	$6.99
Whispers in the Night	Dorothy Elizabeth Love	$8.95
Whispers in the Sand	LaFlorya Gauthier	$10.95
Who's That Lady?	Andrea Jackson	$9.95
Wild Ravens	Altonya Washington	$9.95
Yesterday Is Gone	Beverly Clark	$10.95
Yesterday's Dreams, Tomorrow's Promises	Reon Laudat	$8.95
Your Precious Love	Sinclair LeBeau	$8.95

Order Form

Mail to: Genesis Press, Inc.
P.O. Box 101
Columbus, MS 39703

Name _____
Address _____
City/State _____ Zip _____
Telephone _____

Ship to (if different from above)
Name _____
Address _____
City/State _____ Zip _____
Telephone _____

Credit Card Information
Credit Card # _____ ☐ Visa ☐ Mastercard
Expiration Date (mm/yy) _____ ☐ AmEx ☐ Discover

Qty.	Author	Title	Price	Total

Use this order form, or call 1-888-INDIGO-1

Total for books _____
Shipping and handling:
  $5 first two books,
  $1 each additional book
Total S & H _____
Total amount enclosed _____
Mississippi residents add 7% sales tax

Visit www.genesis-press.com for latest releases and excerpts.